DESERT ENCHANTRESS

*L*ight played over the sharp planes of his face, the familiar Kaffiyeh, the patch over one eye, as he pulled her closer. Kate caught her breath, and her lips parted in anticipation, but he hesitated, needing to see her desire before he lowered his mouth over her responsive lips. He could feel her breath rise and fall against his chest as he caressed her thigh through the soft fabric of her skirt. He knew where this was bound to lead, where he wanted it to lead, but drew back.

"Why? Why have you come?" she stammered.

"My life is misery without you," he said.

"But I cannot come away with you, I've already explained—"

He was the only man about whom she'd ever given a second thought: She burned at his touch. . .

"Nothing is impossible, Kate, if you want it badly enough," he said, and she knew she would have him no matter what the cost.

DESERT ENCHANTRESS

LAUREL COLLINS

ST. MARTIN'S PRESS / New York

Copyright © 1988 by Linda Catherine Wiatr

Library of Congress Catalog Card Number: 87-063541

ISBN: 0-312-90864-4   Can. ISBN: 0-312-90865-2

Printed in the United States of America

First St. Martin's Press mass market edition/August 1988

10 9 8 7 6 5 4 3 2 1

For my mother
who taught me, by her example,
that intelligence is
as important
as feminine charms

CHAPTER I

1860

*I*t had been a brilliant sunset. Remnants of the rose and gold tapestry that had been woven in the sky still lingered, as ominous clouds scudded in across the Hudson River. Thunder claps bounced off the green hills of the Highlands and echoed through the valley. Despite the encroaching darkness and portent of foul weather, Katherine Wrightwood anxiously waited on the veranda, watching the road that wound up from the landing. After his ship docked in New York City, there was only a short trip upriver and then he'd be home again. It seemed as though he'd been gone forever. . . .

She vaguely heard the door open behind her. "Come in and have your supper, Miss Kate. You've waited long enough now."

The girl did not take her eyes away from the road

but said confidently, "He'll be here, Mrs. Davies. He's never missed my birthday."

The sturdy housekeeper sighed and pushed a stray lock of silver hair back up into her cap. The wooden porch groaned under her weight as she walked over to Kate and put her hand on the girl's shoulder. "Come along, Miss Kate. I've made a roast of beef and those little potatoes you like so well, and a chocolate cake."

"But is there enough for all of them? Papa is sure to have his students with him, and Ahmad as well."

"Yes, heaven help me, I've made more than enough and likely as not we'll be eating tonight's supper for days until it's finally gone."

"But Papa promised in his letter that he'd be home in time," Kate insisted.

"Egypt's a long way off, child. His ship could've come across foul weather in crossing. Why, even if they did reach New York on schedule, any number of things could delay them. You know how particular your papa is about those old relics; they must be unloaded in the city and then reloaded onto a river steamer."

She felt Kate's shoulder slacken. It was a shame to dampen the child's spirits like this, but Kate couldn't very well sit waiting out here all night. Mrs. Davies was very fond of the girl, having raised her almost single-handedly since Mrs. Wrightwood's death ten years ago. And she often worried for her, feeling that Kate was far too serious-minded for a thirteen year old. Rather than cultivating friendships with her classmates at Miss Frazer's Academy for Young Ladies, Kate passed the time with the Egyptian artifacts and archaeological volumes in her father's study. Mrs. Davies fondly remembered her own girlhood, all the giggling and sharing of confidences, of trying to catch a young man's eye, of parties and picnics. This was the type of life Kate should be enjoying now, yet it held no interest for her. Now when whe was not in her father's study, she was content to go down to the riverbank in a faded cotton dress, her beautiful golden curls tucked under a straw hat, and dig in the mud for Indian relics.

But tonight, Kate had traded faded cotton for a white cotton lawn dress with organdy ruching that Mrs. Davies had made her. The cobalt blue sash complemented the vivid color of Kate's eyes. Her hair, fastened with a ribbon that matched the sash, hung in heavy locks down her back. Yes, Mrs. Davies decided, Kate was a beautiful young woman when she wanted to be. If only she would have the desire to be that more often . . .

"Come in now, dear, before the rain starts."

Kate raised herself up from the wicker chair, but instead of following Mrs. Davies inside, she ran down the steps, into the drive. "Look there, Mrs. Davies. They're coming, do you see them? Two wagons and a carriage."

"Well, I'll be. . . . I do see them at that. I suppose I'd best set supper on the table."

Mrs. Davies hoped that those wagons did not carry another of those nasty Egyptian mummies. The last one had given her nightmares until it had been taken to the professor's workshop at the university. She sighed. Well, whatever surprises were in store, she thought, at least Miss Kate would have a very happy birthday.

In Professor Elias Wrightwood's study that evening, Kate sat at her father's feet, as he regaled her with stories of his latest expedition. He looked hearty. The Egyptian sun had provided him with a healthy glow, and he had added some weight to his normally wiry frame. The students who had accompanied him— Stephen Perry, Eric Latham, and Nicholas Hammonton—also looked well. Throughout the evening, each of them pondered what their efforts this past winter might mean for future expeditions—as well as for their own future.

Ahmad, the professor's personal servant, made his way effortlessly around the room with a silver tray, offering glasses of brandy to the professor and to the three young gentlemen. "Ahmad, please pour a little for Miss Kate." When she had been served, her father said, "Gentlemen, today is my daughter's thirteenth birthday, as you know. Let us toast to her youth—and to the years to come, full of promise."

"Yes, happy birthday, Kate," Eric Latham said, as he held up his glass.

"Here, here," said Stephen Perry.

Nick Hammonton held up his glass and, similing, nodded his head at her.

Kate blushed and was only able to manage a soft "Thank you."

"As I was saying, dear," the professor explained to her, "we've unearthed portions of a village and what we take to be an artist's workshop. It was not a rich find, but important just the same, as I have been trying to impress upon these young men."

"You can't fault us, sir," interjected Stephen Perry, "for hoping to find some fabulous treasure in a pharaoh's tomb."

"No, Mr. Perry, but if that is your sole motivation, then I would suggest you turn your attentions westward: California, Colorado, Nevada. There's plenty of gold and silver to be mined there. We, as archaeologists, must be primarily men of science in search of knowledge."

Kate beamed. Her father never failed to express himself forthrightly or eloquently.

"I think," said Nick Hammonton, as he casually leaned against the mantel, "that what Professor Wrightwood is endeavoring to impress upon us is that we are not likely to wander about the Egyptian landscape, only to stumble upon a plaque that says something like 'Here lies the tomb of the great pharaoh. Priceless treasures are enclosed within.'"

Everyone laughed heartily at this, and Kate looked more closely at him as he continued.

"Perhaps the work we have done this past winter is of a very vital nature. Perhaps the first step—the groundwork, if you will—to a most important discovery. Think of it, gentlemen. The artisan's workshop alone yielded hundreds of artifacts, each with its own story to tell. When we have catalogued our finds, all of the statues and tablets and papyri, when we have translated their hieroglyphs and they have given up to us their secrets, how many other treasures will they lead us to?"

The room was silent as each person considered the young man's words. Nick Hammonton had the ability to project his ideas and enthusiasms well. His dark good looks and elegant bearing were equally impressive. He was tall and lanky, with intense gray eyes and a mass of unruly curls. As he stood there in full evening dress, his elbow resting casually on the

5

mantel, a long cheroot hooked in his index finger and the rest of his hand curved easily around his brandy glass, he looked like a man fully confident of himself and his powers. And Kate was finding it difficult to take her eyes off of him.

Outside the storm began in earnest, the windows shuddering as the rain closed in about them. There by the blazing fire in her father's study, Kate took in all she had heard, wishing she too could have gone on the expedition. Her greatest wish was to be able to take her place among her father's prized students, as a future archaeologist. But that night, she also was becoming aware of certain feelings, feelings that were growing stronger as the evening progressed. The feelings centered on Nicholas Hammonton, and they nearly took Kate's breath away.

Professor Wrightwood was the first to break the silence. "Bravo, Mr Hammonton! I am relieved to know that I have not been wasting my time. However, I must now watch my back at every turn, lest you be after my chair at the university, or perhaps it is my post as director of the Society for the Preservation of Antiquities you aim for."

Nick found this amusing and flashed a smile over his dark moustache. "Rest easy, sir," he said. "I've still have far too much to learn."

━━━━━━━

It was late when Professor Wrightwood came to his daughter's room, yet he found her awake. Though she had kept her eyes shut against the lightning, sleep had eluded her. She had been too busy speculating about Nicholas Hammonton.

"I'll wager you thought I'd forgotten about your birthday gift," he said as he lit the lamp beside her bed.

Kate propped herself up on one elbow and smiled. "You never forget, Papa."

He smiled too and left the room momentarily, returning with a small wooden crate in his arms. Kate threw on her dressing gown and joined him at her desk near the window, where he had lay the crate. "This is, perhaps, the most promising of our finds this winter," he told her, as he lifted the lid. "The workmanship is superb."

Professor Wrightwood gently pushed aside the straw packing and unwound the gauze that had protected an oval-shaped painted plaster mask of an Egyptian woman. At the sight of it, Kate drew an astonished breath.

"Oh! It's magnificent, Papa!"

"I believe that this is a sculptor's model, made from a clay mask," he said excitedly. "You see how well defined the features are? This piece would enable the sculptor to more accurately portray his subject."

"She must have been a very important woman for the sculptor to take such pains," Kate said.

"Very perceptive. Now look at these markings on the back. The paint is flaked off in some vital areas, but this one is the symbol for the goddess Isis, the protectress of the dead and wife of Osiris, god of the dead. My instincts tell me that if we delve further, we shall find more evidence of this woman."

"Another expedition, Papa?"

He nodded. "In time. I've work to finish here before any definite plans can be made."

7

He gently placed the mask in her hands. "I want you to keep this mask safe and study it. Perhaps when the time comes, you and I shall seek out the answer to its mysteries."

Kate gingerly placed it on its bed of straw and threw her arms around her father's neck. "Oh, Papa! This is the most wonderful gift I've ever received. I should like nothing more than to help you in your work."

His eyes widened momentarily as he realized he may have gone too far in his effort to please her, but Kate was not aware of it. "I wanted to write to you," she said, "to tell you about my plans, but I thought it might be best to explain when you returned—"

The professor looked puzzled. "What is it, dear?"

"I don't plan to return to Miss Frazer's in the fall."

"Kate, whyever not? The woman comes highly recommended. The school has a faultless reputation."

Kate sighed deeply and walked to the desk to study the mask once again. "I'm tired of luncheons and finger sandwiches, and I'm sick to death of painting flowers on china teacups, Papa. I want to go to the university and study with you."

"The university does not accept female students, Kate. You must be aware·of that."

"I thought that perhaps with your influence—"

He shook his head and put his hands on her shoulders. "I'm afraid that I could do nothing for you."

"But how shall I ever learn all that I need to know to help you in your work?"

"If you are serious about continuing your education, you could apply to a teacher's college."

"I don't want to teach, Papa. I want to study archaeology, and I want to go with you on your expeditions for the Society. I want to uncover pieces of history that have lain undisturbed for thousands of years."

She sat down on the bed, feeling dejected. After a moment, the professor came over and sat beside her. "You move too quickly, child. There is so much to learn and the work is usually not very exciting."

He paused and looked deeply into her eyes, hoping to read her thoughts. He then spoke cautiously. "If this is what you want, Kate, truly, then you know I will do all that I can to help you."

"What is there to do, Papa? You've painted such a bleak picture."

Her chin dropped onto her chest, but her father gently propped it up between his fingers. His eyes twinkled.

"Not hopeless, never hopeless, my dear, if you want a thing badly enough. We shall make a bargain, you and I. If you will spend one more year at Miss Frazer's, I will recommend the books to give you a start in the field. At the end of the school term, I shall take you on as my secretary. Your duties will include assisting me as I need it, handling correspondence and taking notes. You understand that this means you shall have to attend all of my classes and lectures?"

"Is it possible? Will they allow it?" Kate asked excitedly.

"How can the board object to my secretary sitting in on my classes to make notes?"

Kate threw her arms around his neck. "Papa, thank you! I shall study hard and be your very best pupil ever."

"It's an honor you shall have to share," he replied, referring to Nick Hammonton.

She shrugged her shoulders. "Mr. Hammonton will be graduated by the time I begin sitting in on your classes, though I should have given him some worthy competition in any case. I intend to learn all there is to know about archaeology."

Professor Wrightwood let out a short laugh, but then turned serious. "A formidable task, indeed. Mrs. Davies has told me that you have already begun, by trying to digest all the books in my library."

"You don't mind, do you? I was especially careful with them."

"How could I mind when my child takes such an interest in my work?" he said, patting her arm.

Kate went to her desk and removed from the center drawer something wrapped in a scarf. "Do you remember once telling me about the Indians who lived here long ago?"

He nodded slowly.

"Well, I've been digging down by the river, and I think I've found evidence of a village."

She unwrapped the scarf and held out some items for his inspection.

"This comb is made of bone, and this is a clay pipe, I think. Part of the bowl has cracked away."

Professor Wrightwood examined the items closely. "Do you mean to tell me that you found these all on your own?"

"It took several tries before I came upon a likely site," she admitted.

"I am most pleasantly surprised," her father said as she rewrapped her finds and put them away. "It may just be that you shall provide some competition for Mr. Hammonton after all."

"Is he such a good archaeologist, Papa?"

"He will be someday. He is entirely devoted to the work. I've never seen a young man assimilate so much in one season. He will be a great scientist one day, Kate. I only fear that it will be through the exclusion of all else in his life."

"Perhaps it isn't such a bad trade," Kate thought out loud.

She assumed that her father, of all people, would understand such a statement but apparently he did not, for as he drew her closely into his arms, she saw the concern in his eyes. "You must never believe that," he said.

───────────

Around noon the next day, he was sitting in the garden, propped against a tree trunk diligently checking the figures in his notebook.

Kate was painfully aware of her appearance as she came up the path from the river and saw him. The clean apron she had put on this morning was now grimy, and the hem of her dress was caked with mud. Last night's rain had turned her excavation into a mire. She had worked in the mud all morning and had only been able to claim a handful of pottery shards. When she saw him sitting in the garden, she considered crossing the lawns and entering the house by the front door, but then quickly chastised herself for being foolish. What did it matter whether

Nick Hammonton saw her in her muddy apron or not?

She drew a long breath and swiped at a wisp of hair that had fallen across her cheek. "Taking the air, Mr. Hammonton?" she said lightly as she paused before him.

He looked up, his dark brow furrowed in thought. "Just going over my notes. We've been cataloguing our finds all morning for our report."

"I see," she replied. She stared at him for a moment, longing to say something relevant, but found her tongue strangely numb.

"Have you been gardening, Miss Wrightwood?" Kate was puzzled.

"You've mud on your cheek," he explained and drew a handkerchief from the pocket of his linen coat and handed it to her.

She laughed uneasily while she cleaned her cheek. "I've been excavating. There's a spot by the river that's proved promising. Papa says there was an Indian settlement hereabouts, you know."

Mr. Hammonton raised an eyebrow. "Following in your father's footsteps?"

"I'd like nothing more," she admitted.

He chuckled and turned a page of his notebook. "You'll change your mind when you've grown. Women aren't suited to archaeology. I've not yet met a woman who liked getting dirt under her fingernails."

Kate looked at her hands and at the dark crescents beneath each nail. Even though she didn't mind the dirt, his words still stung, and she quickly hid her hands in the folds of her skirt.

"I—I found some bits of pottery today," she stammered and drew them out from her pocket.

He gave them a cursory glance and nodded. Of course he wouldn't be impressed with such a meager find. He'd spent the past winter exploring the glorious monuments of ancient Egypt. Suddenly, Kate felt very young and insignificant. She shuffled her feet and prepared to retreat into the house.

"You'd do well to avoid Mrs. Davies," he told her in a parting shot. "If she sees how you've spoiled your dress, she's liable to tan your hide."

Kate threw his handkerchief to the ground and ran into the house, not stopping until she had reached the safety of her own room. She slipped out of her apron and dress and tossed them angrily in the corner. How she hated Nick Hammonton! She went to the washstand and filled the basin. The face staring back at her in the mirror was blotchy and tear-stained and still streaked with mud. She splashed water over it and then scrubbed her fingers with the nailbrush until they were raw. She then dried off and finally threw herself across her bed.

Thirteen was, by far, the worst age in the world to be, and Kate was very impatient for those around her to take her seriously. As the day wore on, she consoled herself with the thought that the time would come when she would prove herself Nick Hammonton's equal. Even perhaps, she dared to think, his better.

CHAPTER II

1886

"**I** am the resurrection and the life; whosoever believeth in me, even if he die, shall live; and whosoever lives and believeth in me, shall never die."

As the pastor's voice died away, Nick Hammonton said a silent prayer for his grandfather and tossed a damp handful of earth onto the coffin. Jacob Mallory had led a long and fruitful life, and none gathered here on this gray and dismal day could say but that he had been a generous, God-fearing man. Nick knew firsthand of his grandfather's goodness. He had taken in Nick and his mother when she could no longer tolerate life with her philandering British husband. Nick was but an infant at the time. When Nick's mother died, old Jacob had raised him like his own son, saw to his schooling and advised him when the occasion arose. Jacob had been a stern man, which had caused a number of disagreements between him and the boy, but these never became too serious. As Nick stood here now, he found it difficult to say his final goodbye to the old man.

Friends and relations had gathered here to offer Nick their condolences, but he felt strangely distant from the scene; everything seemed to blur around him. Yet the sudden presence of a young woman, clad in a dark cape, its hood raised against the gentle rain, remained strongly in focus. She moved up to the grave and let the single white rose she held gently slip down.

Nick did not recognize her, but she made such a vivid impression on him that he longed to meet her. She had a strong, attractive face, but regarded him with such an absence of feeling, such an utterly blank expression, that he shivered in his Inverness coat.

Just then, the bell in the church tower rang out and startled her. Pulling the cape closer around her, she turned and hurried out of the cemetery. Nick almost cursed the fact that following her was simply out of the question now. After a few minutes' reflection, Nick realized that he could not recall the shade of her hair, nor the color of her eyes. Yet he was totally confident that he would see her again—and that he would recognize her.

———

Nick made his way on horseback to the Wrightwood home, which lay nestled in the green Hudson Highlands, only a few miles north of the hilly town of Creighton and Creighton University. Nick's grandfather's estate was also in the area, a pleasant ride away. As he came up the drive, Nick admired the mellow red brick veranda, overgrown with ivy, and the pair of white elm that arched gracefully on either side of the house. He noted that it had changed little in the six years since his last visit, and that it still seemed quite comfortable.

It had been some time since he'd seen Professor Wrightwood, though they had corresponded often. Nick had been fortunate enough to spend the last five years in Egypt, on various surveys and expeditions.

Recently Nick had heard rumors that the professor was ill, dying in fact, but Nick chose not to give them credence, even when he had received the professor's last letter, asking to see him as soon as possible.

Nick dismounted from his horse and walked up the porch steps to the front door.

Before he could knock, Ahmad opened it.

"This way, *effendi*," Ahmad said, emphasizing the Arabic word for sir, and led Nick into the professor's study.

Nick refused any refreshment. He quickly noted, some of the professor's Egyptian artifacts—first, on the mantel, a pair of ushabtis, tiny statues that were put in tombs with mummies to perform duties in the afterlife; then, on a corner shelf, a bust that exemplified the noble Egyptian profile; and finally, in a glass case by the window, a number of pieces of papyrus. These were but a few of the objects the professor had acquired over the years. Most of the others were in the adjoining room, the one the professor called his trophy room.

"Ahmed, how is he?" Nick asked.

"His heart grows weaker. He rests often and takes those potions his doctor brings. We pray he will be strong once more, *inshallah*."

"Yes, God willing," Nick echoed.

Ahmad, then left the room and soon returned, wheeling the old man into the room. He had lost a good deal of weight, and he had an unhealthy pallor, with a slight blue cast to it. But still managed to reach across the desk, and give Nick a firm handshake.

"My boy, it's good to see you."

"And you, sir. It's been too long."

The professor nodded in agreement. "So, you've kept yourself quite busy, have you? Exciting prospects?"

"Not terribly. The discovery. I've always dreamed of making has, of course, thus far eluded me. You heard the news of my grandfather?"

"Yes, I'm terribly sorry."

Professor Wrightwood leaned his head back on the chair and closed his eyes. The atmosphere here was becoming oppressive to Nick, and he longed to throw up the window sash so that the crisp spring air might revive him. It shocked and disturbed him to see the professor in such a state.

"Your grandfather never approved of your work, did he?" the professor finally asked.

"My grandfather was a businessman, full of practical notions," Nick said. "He saw the world in terms of red and black figures on a ledgerbook. Such a man has little appreciation for history or scientific pursuits."

"I only hope that he did not dissuade you from

your calling. You have much to contribute to the field, Nick."

"I'll admit that he'd have preferred to see me come into the family business, but I told him I had no head for management. He founded Mallory Glass-works, you know, started from nothing. I'd hate to be the one to bring it down. He was understanding enough when I told him. I think he held out hope right until the very end that I'd tire of digging in the desert and take over for him."

"You must pursue your own dreams in this life," the professor said, tapping a bony finger on the desk for emphasis, "no matter what the cost."

Nick resettled himself in the chair, wondering what the true purpose was for his visit.

"Fortunately, I've a cousin better suited to manage the company. I plan to sell him my interests."

The professor nodded in approval. "Good, good . . . Do you know that the Society has planned another expedition?"

This revelation caught Nick's attention. He leaned closer.

"As we expected, our last venture yielded some promising information, though it has taken all this time to assess it and to totally convince the Society of its possibilities. The members are now whole-heartedly endorsing my proposal, and plans are in the making."

"You will lead the expedition?" Nick guessed, though he doubted the professor would be fit to travel anytime soon.

The professor gave a short laugh, but the effort seemed to drain him, and he paused to draw a long breath. "No, my boy, I'm afraid that by the time the expedition leaves next spring, I shall be dead and buried."

"Surely not," Nick countered, though he was beginning to feel otherwise.

"My doctor tells me I must prepare for it, and there is much yet to do. The Society would like me to choose a sucessor, but I can give it no thought until I see Kate comfortably settled."

The professor paused. "She is such a pleasure to me and yet such a problem. I suppose I am to blame. When first I discovered her interest in my work, I was flattered. I encouraged her; she became my secretary and now knows much about the field and about my work. She has been of immeasurable help to me during my illness and totally neglects her social life, as she has always done. The child has no friends to speak of, and she discourages those young gentlemen who do show an interest."

The professor leaned back in his chair and closed his eyes again, searching for strength within himself.

"She is just a child, sir. These things work themselves out in time," Nick assured him.

Professor Wrightwood shook his head. "She is nineteen years old and as stubborn as her father. Partly because of my own selfish need for companionship, I let her further her interests in archaeology. I enjoyed having someone here who shared my passion, but I've spoiled her. She'll never do for the wife of anyone but an archaeologist, and such a union is not likely to come about on its own.

"In all my years of teaching, Nick, you were my

greatest student. You have the capacity for greatness that will not be denied. Had I a son, I could ask for no better than you."

"You flatter me, sir."

"No, indeed. I want to help you, Nick, to achieve all that you deserve."

"You have helped me," Nick insisted, "in more ways than I can number."

"And yet, my boy, in order to get on with your work, in order to distinguish yourself as a first-rate Egyptologist, you will need money. Your own assets are not limitless, so you are in need of assistance, perhaps in the form of an organization . . . perhaps one such as the Society for the Preservation of Antiquities."

Nick searched the old man's face for a hint of what this could mean. He dared not hope—

"I have a proposal for you, Nick, one which may prove most beneficial to you if you stop to see the logic in it. And if it means anything to you at all, your acceptance will mean that I shall die without worries to weigh on my soul."

"What is it you are asking of me, sir?"

The professor leaned over the desk, grasping it with both hands to support himself. There was still enormous strength and fierce determination in him, and he met Nick head-on.

"Marry my Kate," he said, "and I shall recommend you to the Society as my successor. You shall direct the forthcoming Egyptian expedition."

Nick fought to keep his composure. Whatever disjointed thoughts had come to him in the past minutes, he could not have predicted such a proposition. "But Professor Wrightwood, Katherine is only a child," he protested.

"My daughter is many things, Nick, but certainly no child."

Nick shook his muddled head to clear the fog in his brain. "Even so, would she agree to such a scheme? You've said she discourages those gentlemen—"

The professor knitted his brows as if he were pained or irritated. Nick could not say which. "Damn it, man, you shall have to win her! If Kate caught wind of what I was about, she'd likely pack her things and leave me here to die on my own."

Nick was perplexed. He left his chair and strode to the window, kneading his brow. He pretended to study the papyri in the glass case to give himself time to think.

"I never said this proposal would be easy to carry out," the professor said. "Things that are worth having seldom are easy to be had. You are eminently qualified, though, my dear Mr. Hammonton, to be my daughter's suitor: firstly, you are an archaeologist, but more important, to my knowledge you are the only gentleman in whom she has ever shown the slightest interest."

Nick thought this odd. He could remember only the most cursory meeting with Katherine Wrightwood six years ago. "But, sir, surely you are wrong," he said.

The professor merely smiled. "Kate will have," he continued, "a considerable inheritance—this house, and my entire collection of artifacts, as well as all of my papers. I'm sure that you can appreciate their value."

Each second that passed was dangerous for Nick, for it allowed him to imagine himself as director of the Society and contemplate what he could achieve in that position.

"Can't you see what an ideal arrangement this is?" the professor cried. "You need a home and family to round out your life, and I need to know that Kate will be cared for."

Nick gripped the back of his chair to steady himself. Such an "arrangement" went against his well-ordered view of the world, and yet its logic was faultless. He was being offered a chance at all that he had hoped for. Yet suddenly he was overcome by the memory of the young woman at his grandfather's funeral, as if to remind himself that it was she and others like her who would be lost to him by such an arrangement.

Nick cleared his throat, hoping his voice could convey a firmness of purpose that he did not yet possess. "You will understand if I tell you that I must think on this, sir."

There was a contented look about the old man that said that, despite Nick's hesitancy, there was a victory to be had.

"Yes, of course, but time is all important, Nick, as I have no idea how much is left to me. If my hand is forced, I shall not hesitate to approach one of your less suitable colleagues, so long as I am sure of his sincerity."

Nick nodded, running a hand through his dark curls.

"But know this, young man. It is you I want for my Kate and you who, by rights, should succeed me to direct the Society. Now the choice is yours."

———

Nick headed straightaway for the house of his closest friend, Doctor Eric Latham. Eric lived in a two-story townhouse in Creighton with his sister, Daphne. He had decided to become a doctor, opting for a more secure life than one as an archaeologist. Yet he still dreamed of joining another expedition someday and making an important discovery.

Nick left his horse in the mews, and walked quickly to Eric's house. He rapped impatiently on the front door. Eric appeared almost at once and took him into the parlor.

"My friend, you look as though you are in sore need of a glass of whiskey."

"An astute diagnosis, Dr. Latham." Nick replied.

Although Eric had a boyish look about him, fair haired and clean shaven, he was the picture of a prosperous young gentleman in his dark frock coat and trousers, and gold chain hanging from his waist-coat pocket.

Nick sank into a comfortable chair near the fire-place and stared into the empty grate while Eric poured them each an ample shot.

"Still thinking about old Jacob?" Eric asked, handing his friend a glass.

Nick shook his head and took the liquid in one gulp, then swirled the residue around the bottom of the glass. "At the cemetery yesterday," he began, "after the service, there was a woman—"

"There were several as I recall," Eric said and took the chair opposite Nick.

"Yes, but this was one I'd never seen before. She stood away from the rest. She was wearing a hooded opera cloak. Did you see her?"

Eric pondered for a moment, then shrugged. "I couldn't say. Why does she interest you?"

"I can't think who she might be. I was introduced to most of my grandfather's acquaintances, business or otherwise."

One corner of Eric's mouth turned up in a wry smile. "Then perhaps it was one of your many conquests come back to haunt you. You never seem able to remember their names."

Nick ignored this as he saw the woman once again in his mind's eye. "It was a most unusual experience, Eric. I felt as though she had physically touched me, though we were yards apart. The look in her eyes was so cold, and then she just ran off."

"Is that why you've come here today, to enlist my aid in searching for your mystery woman?"

"Hardly. I've just come from Professor Wrightwood's," Nick replied, propping one foot on the cherrywood table in front of him.

"Mr. Hammonton, kindly remove your riding boot from my table, else I shall come after you with my broom."

Daphne Latham stood in the doorway, in starched apron and sprigged cotton dress, arms akimbo. She was a slip of a woman with sharp tongue, but not so formidable as first seemed, for her cheeks would dimple when she laughed and her chestnut curls still bounced in a girlish manner whenever she tilted her head.

"Leave him be, Daphne, he's bewitched."

"What, again?"

"Fortunately, it's never a lasting ailment for our Nick."

Nick shook his head and sat upright, inspecting the table with his hand. "No harm done. I'm sorry, Daphne, but I'm still rather in a shock. I've just come from Professor Wrightwood's."

"He must be doing very poorly then," Eric guessed. "I've discussed the case with Dr. Iverson. It's only a matter of time."

"Poor man," Daphne said, and her words hung in the air for a while.

"Is old Iverson still encouraging you to hang out your shingle and open a practice here in town?" Nick wanted to know.

"The subject has been broached—"

"And?"

"It smacks of permanence, and I'm not ready for that yet, even though I've been living in New York these past years. I've worked hard and I'm due a sabbatical. The trip we made with Professor Wrightwood whetted my appetite for travel and adventure. And you know how Egyptology fascinates me. I'd like to make one more trip, perhaps help in some small way on another expedition before I settle here in Creighton."

"You'll not get an argument from me," Nick told him.

Daphne went over to Eric and put her hands on his shoulders. "You mustn't settle here on my account, if travel is what you want. I've my church work to keep me busy."

"Nonsense. I can't roam forever. But I would like

to go on one more expedition," Eric said. He patted Daphne's hand.

Nick went to the whiskey decanter and filled his glass. "The Society's planned another expedition," he said with his back to them.

"What luck!" Eric exclaimed. "But who do you suppose will direct their efforts? Surely not Professor Wrightwood—"

Nick turned to face his friend. "The professor feels certain that the Society will accede to his wish that I succeed him as director."

Eric jumped to his feet in surprise, and Daphne clapped her hands together. "How wonderful for you!" she said.

"Yes, yes, congratulations," Eric added, setting aside his glass to shake Nick's hand.

"Let's not launch our celebration just yet," Nick said quickly. "There are conditions to this appointment."

"Conditions?" Eric echoed.

Returning to his chair, Nick stared into his glass.

"I can't presume to understand what goes through the mind of a dying man, but there must be a good deal of fear. Professor Wrightwood is deeply concerned for the welfare of his daughter, so much so that he has offered to endorse my appointment to the directorship if I agree to marry her."

Eric studied his shoes for a minute before responding. "There's no doubt but that you're qualified for the position, but bartering your freedom for it seems a bit archaic. What did you tell him?"

"What would you do in my place? I'd never hoped to be considered for such a position. I'm thirty-two years old, my friend, and under ordinary circumstances I could spend another ten, perhaps fifteen years teaching or assisting on expeditions before a position like this was open to me."

"So you didn't turn him down, then," Eric assumed. He took his seat again and, with a thoughtful expression, pulled at his chin.

"I told him I'd consider it," Nick said. "I can't recall anything about the girl, you know. Her father describes her as the bookish type, and I imagine she's rather plain now.

"I haven't seen her in years either, though she seemed a lively enough child," Eric said.

Nick closed his eyes as he swallowed his whiskey. "I shouldn't even consider the proposal, but if you'd seen the determination in the old man's face— The least I can do is to meet his daughter again. I owe him that much."

He turned to Daphne. Although she was only two years their senior, she had always been like a mother figure to them. Now she had a look of disapproval about her.

"Well, Daphne, you've been silent through all of this. What do you think?" Nick asked.

"I think it's positively medieval the way you both discuss this girl's fate, and your own, too, for that matter, Nick Hammonton, as though it were of no great consequence. Marriage is an important business, at least as important as poking around in some dusty Egyptian ruins, and one day you and my brother will realize it."

With that, she turned on her heel and left them.

"Dear sister," Eric called out after her, laughing

27

heartily at Daphne's sober demeanor, "don't spare our feelings. Tell us what you really think."

Nick tried to share his friend's amusement, but all he could manage was a thin, uneasy laugh that died away quickly, leaving them both to consider Daphne's words in silence.

CHAPTER III

One week later, on a warm spring evening, the Creighton University Hall was the center of activity on the campus. Nick and Eric, looking elegant in their evening clothes, followed a few paces behind Daphne, who was wearing a dress of salmon-colored silk. They made their way up the marble steps to the hall, a substantial edifice built in the Federal style, and walked inside, through the massive double doors. The musicians had begun tuning up on the corner platform that had been built for the occasion, amidst the many clusters of people who were chatting animatedly.

In the entry hall, several glass cases had been set up, containing some of the artifacts that had been collected on previous expeditions funded by the Society. These included a black granite likeness of the lion-headed goddess Sekhmet, some well-preserved papyri, a silver jug with a gold handle in the form of a bird, and some colorful amulets. These objects were mainly on loan from the museums that had purchased them, but Nick recognized several pieces belonging to Professor Wrightwood, including a bronze statue of Osiris that formed the centerpiece of the exhibit.

"An impressive turnout," Eric commented. "The Society has made this tribute to Professor Wrightwood quite an event."

"He has turned quite a profit for them over the years," Nick retorted. "Backing archaeological treasure hunts is pure speculation, at best. I wonder how the professor has been able to keep them satisfied all these years, following his own scientific pursuits yet still providing the Society with a sufficient supply of salable antiquities."

"I see that you have been considering the professor's proposition. Have you decided that you don't envy him his job?"

"I haven't reached any decision as yet," Nick said thoughtfully.

He was no less confused than he had been a week ago, when the professor had proposed his idea. But tonight Nick's course might be more easily decided upon, for tonight he would meet Katherine Wrightwood again. Because the professor's health had further deteriorated, forcing him to stay in his bed, Katherine would attend in his place, accepting a plaque from the Society on his behalf and reading a speech that he had written. Nick had decided that he would introduce himself to her at some point, and try to form an opinion on whether they were at all compatible. If they were ill-suited to one another, it would make his refusal of the professor's idea that much easier.

A few minutes before they were to be seated for dinner, Nick suddenly noticed the young woman he had seen at his grandfather's funeral being escorted into the hall by Simon D'Arcy, a professor of literature at Crieghton and, to Nick's way of thinking, a rather foppish character.

"Eric!" he said, poking his friend in the ribs with his elbow. "There by the door! It's the woman I told you about, the one I saw at my grandfather's funeral. Who is she?"

Eric looked every bit as startled as Nick. "Damned if I know, Hammonton, but this is the most interest you've shown in anything that hasn't been buried for two thousand years. Maybe that's a good sign, at least."

"Where's Daphne gotten off to? Perhaps she'd recognize her."

Eric laid a hand on Nick's shoulder. "Easy, man," he told him in quiet tones. "She's an intriguing woman, I'll grant you, but there's no need in drawing attention to yourself. I'm sure we can manage an introduction before the evening is out, even if it means I must listen to D'Arcy's drivel while you engage the lady."

As Nick watched, she took off her mantle and handed it to D'Arcy. She seemed nervous, clutching her reticule as she turned toward the crowded room. There was none of the cool detachment Nick had witnessed that day of the funeral. He wondered what she saw in D'Arcy. Granted the man was attentive to her and had a certain charm, but she did not strike

31

Nick as the frivolous type D'Arcy usually attracted. Her blond hair was wound in a neat, simple coil at the back of her head, not adorned with the flowers or frills most women wore on such occasions. Except for its luminous blue color, her gown was plain, severe almost, and the only ornamentation she wore was a silver necklace set with blue stones. His eyes lingered over her slender neck and round white shoulders.

As the evening progressed, she drove him to distraction from across the room. If she noticed him at all in the crowd, it was not apparent by her expression. Perhaps on another night he mightn't have allowed himself to be so preoccupied, but many thoughts were weighing on him now. He wanted just for a few moments to indulge himself in this attraction without any thought to the future. Yes, there was always tomorrow for Miss Katherine Wrightwood and the decision he must make.

When the final course had been cleared away, Mr. Samuel Thayer, who sat on the Society's board, went up to the podium.

"Ladies and gentlemen, ladies and gentlemen, may I have your attention please?"

He paused a moment and when the crowd had settled somewhat, he went on. "I'm sure you are all aware of why we are gathered here this evening. Professor Elias Wrightwood has served as director of the Society for the Preservation of Antiquities since its inception nearly fifteen years ago. His Egyptian expeditions over the years have salvaged for posterity hundreds of artifacts, such as those you see here tonight, and in gratitude we members of the Society, as well as his friends and colleagues, come here tonight to honor him and to present him with this brass and wooden plaque, expressing our thanks."

Mr. Thayer held up the plaque and the audience applauded heartily.

"Unfortunately," Mr. Thayer went on, "due to an illness, the professor is unable to be with us tonight. However, he has sent along his lovely daughter, Katherine, to accept the plaque and to read a speech drafted by him for this occasion. Miss Wrightwood?"

Mr. Thayer held out his hand, and Nick's interest peaked as he watched for the woman who would take it. Eric crossed his long arms over his chest and regarded his friend. Suddenly, the woman in blue rose from her chair and went to the podium, to the utter amazement of Eric and Nick.

Nick was overjoyed. So this was Katherine Wrightwood!

As he looked at her now, he saw that the necklace at her throat was, in fact, a winged scarab amulet of lapis lazuli, a piece that had been found by the professor on one of his earliest expeditions. Nick anxiously waited for her to speak.

"Mr. Thayer, Society members, ladies and gentlemen . . . My father did so want to be here to thank you all for this honor. It distressed him to miss this opportunity to thank the Society as a whole for the financial support which has allowed him to carry on his research into ancient Egyptian culture for these many years. It is a work he dearly loves, to that I can attest, and he has asked me to read this missive on his behalf:

First let me express my humble gratitude to the Society for the Preservation of Antiquities and Creighton University for according me this honor. I do not seek personal recognition in my endeavors, but if such recognition serves to enlighten even a few to the importance of the work we do as Egyptologists, then I am well pleased. It is my opinion that the Society has done mankind a great service by rescuing, yes, I stand by that word, rescuing the remnants of ancient Egypt from those who would exploit, deface, even destroy these priceless treasures. Each day that passes sees the khedive barter Egyptian antiquities to Europeans as it pleases him, and steamers unload tourists only too anxious to carve their initials into the great monuments. The Egyptians themselves little appreciate or understand their heritage, for they must concern themselves with daily survival in a harsh land. They build villages atop ruined temples or scavenge stone from these ancient relics, little realizing the importance of the hieroglyphic inscriptions upon them.

She hesitated only long enough to catch her breath before reading on, but it seemed to Nick that she was not merely reading from the paper before her. Her voice vibrated with emotion, almost as if the words were her own.

And so we must redouble our efforts and our commitment to the preservation of the past. It is my fondest hope that together we shall discover a significant number of those missing pages of mankind's history.

The applause was tremendous, and Kate found herself trembling as she took her seat. Her palms were damp inside her gloves, and a thin smile masked her tension.

"Well done, my dear," D'Arcy said as he held her chair for her. She sipped at her champagne to let its coolness run through her.

Kate wished she could now retire for the evening, but such a suggestion probably would not have been well received by Mr. D'Arcy. Though she would have preferred to come alone this evening, Papa had insisted that she have an escort, so when Mr. D'Arcy offered to take her she felt compelled to accept.

From the first she found him a disappointment, and he, no doubt, felt the same about her, for he was accustomed to fawning women, who were quite unlike Kate. There was no mistaking that he was a professor of literature, for his conversation was imbued with the poetic. And that he imagined himself a romantic in the style of Lord Byron was only too apparent.

"Shall we join the others in the ballroom?" he asked, drawing her out of her thoughts.

"As you wish," she replied.

She took his arm as he guided her into the ballroom, where she obliged him with a waltz. As he led her across the floor, she caught sight of many of her father's friends. She promised herself she would relate every detail to him and would remember every face she saw here tonight.

" 'Oh! Might I kiss those eyes of fire, a million scarce would quench desire,' " D'Arcy said to her in a low voice and squeezed her gloved hand.

His sudden ardor surprised her, and she drew back somewhat. Upon reflecting she decided that he probably took this sort of approach with all women, thinking that the poetry of Byron was as effective as any love potion.

She smiled at him as one might at a naive child, though he was several years her senior. "One might expect, Mr. D'Arcy, that a man of your literary experience would praise a woman's charms with his own words."

She bore him no malice but wanted it understood that she was not one of his simpering female admirers.

He was startled by her comment, but recovered well enough to say, "Alas, Miss Wrightwood, you leave me speechless."

When their dance had ended, D'Arcy escorted Kate to one of the chairs that had been set along the wall, where she was immediately besieged by half a dozen enthusiastic young gentlemen, each vying for her attention. Kate recognized most of them as her father's former students and did her best to be polite, but it was still unsettling for one so accustomed to solitude.

"A truly enlightened speech, Miss Wrightwood."

"Only a man of your father's genius could have expressed his views so eloquently."

"The Society is, indeed, fortunate to have had such a man as its director for all these years."

"Yes," Kate told them. "Well, thank you, gentlemen. I'm certain that he will be pleased—"

"I hope you will not think me forward if I tell you, Miss Wrightwood, that you look particularly lovely this evening."

"Why, how nice of you to say—"

"Would you care for a glass of punch, Miss Wrightwood?"

"No, but thank you for asking, Mister—I am sorry, I seem to have forgotten your name.

"Across the room, Nick drank yet another glass of champagne and studied the scene. They were clustered around her, thick as a damned swarm of bees and she the only flower in the field. Her full lips curved into an enticing smile for one of them, and then she turned her attention to the next, intent upon his every word. How many of his students had Professor Wrightwood approached with this insane scheme to find his daughter a husband? Nick wondered. And why on earth did he feel such a step necessary? They were drooling over her, for God's sake, the whole unworthy lot of them!

Katherine was wondering how to make her escape when a fair-haired gentleman at the center of the group said, "I wonder, Miss Wrightwood, if you might favor me with this dance?"

"I should like that very much," she said and held out her hand to him.

"Perhaps you don't remember me," he began as he led her onto the dance floor. "My name is Stephen Perry. We met once a number of years ago. I was a guest in your home after the Society's last expedition."

"Yes, yes, I do remember. I will be sure to mention to my father that you were here this evening."

Her partner was an accomplished dancer, and Kate found it a little difficult to follow his lead as he whirled her about.

37

"It is a shame that the professor was unable to attend the festivities," he said. "I would imagine that such a fashionable young lady as yourself must find all our talk of ancient relics rather boring."

"Quite the contrary," Kate told him. "I have been fortunate enough to assist my father from time to time, and I find Egyptology fascinating."

He raised a brow in surprise but kept his thoughts to himself. Kate decided that Stephen Perry was a more intriguing figure when he was silent. He had an intelligent countenance, with sharp green eyes that missed nothing, and a thin mouth. She found that she could read very little of his character in those features, but the neatly trimmed beard he sported could not mask his florid complexion. From this she guessed that Stephen Perry was accustomed to an excess of the finer things in life.

"Have you returned to Egypt since the Society's last expedition?" she asked.

"Just last season," he replied. "I assisted a group of German antiquarians from the University of Berlin on a dig near Deir el-Bahri."

"And were you successful in your efforts?"

"Hardly. A whole season spent working a dusty passage on a hillside that was hotter than blazes and in the end all we had to show for our efforts were two chambers with some rather uninspired wall decoration and half a dozen funerary urns."

"I imagine there were wall texts," Kate ventured. "Have you attempted any translation? My father has always professed that there are no unimportant finds."

As the last strains of the waltz died away, Stephen took her arm, escorting her to a chair. He quickly dispensed with the scowl he had been wearing and smiled for her.

"My dear Miss Wrightwood, I do not wish you to distress yourself on account of my tribulations. I feel that I am destined for a truly spectacular find, and one day I will unearth a cache of pharaoh's treasure the likes of which the world has never seen."

Kate couldn't help but laugh at such a boast. She hoped that she hadn't hurt his pride, though it was apparent by his expression that he was wounded.

"I'm pleased to see that you've escaped the Egyptian desert with your confidence unscathed, sir," she said, "and I wish you all the luck in the world."

"Then I'm certain of success," he told her and kissed her gloved hand.

Kate did not know exactly what to think of Mr. Stephen Perry. His desire for fame and pharaoh's gold certainly far outweighed his interest in scientific pursuits, but she had to admit that he wasn't the only man in his field with such motives. Certainly his confidence would carry him far, and sometimes the key to achieving success was in wanting something more than the next fellow.

"I was hoping that I might call on you at your home, Miss Wrightwood," her companion said, "later in the week, perhaps, to inquire after your father's health . . . and to enjoy your pleasant company once more."

She met his eyes and read the determination there. Stephen Perry was nothing if not a man who knew what he wanted.

"I know that my father would be pleased to see you again," she told him.

"And you?"

"I think I'd like to hear more of your expedition to Deir el-Bahri."

He bowed as he left her, smiling as though he were very much pleased with himself. Kate opened her fan with a snap of the wrist and sighed, hoping to be alone, for a few moments at least. She'd decided that comporting one's self at this type of social function was far too much work. As her fan fluttered lazily, she studied the room. Mr. D'Arcy, had found himself a suitably attentive young woman clad in yards of lace, and the two of them whirled gaily about the dance floor. While Kate watched them, she felt as if she were being scrutinized by some unseen presence.

She scanned the crowd until her gaze was caught by a pair of gray eyes she had not seen since that day at the cemetery. As much as Kate told herself she despised him for his arrogance, she couldn't explain why her heart stopped now and every time she was in Nick Hammonton's presence. She barely managed to collect herself before he reached her.

"Good evening, Miss Wrightwood."

Kate waved her fan in a slow, deliberate manner, using its movement like a metronome to regulate her thoughts. "Good evening, Mr. Hammonton," she said, keeping her voice even.

"You remember me then. I was afraid after all these years—"

"I attended your grandfather's funeral in my father's place. You mightn't have seen me," she said, though she knew full well that he had, "as I had an appointment to keep and couldn't stay long enough to offer you my condolences."

"It was a mysterious exit," he admitted, "though I had no idea you were the lady with the rose. You've changed these past years."

"I'm glad. When last we spoke, you made some rather disparaging remarks on my appearance. Have I still dirt under my nails, Mr. Hammonton?"

He watched, confounded, as she snapped her fan shut and drew off her gloves, one at a time, to show him her well-manicured hands. "I've not lost my interest in archaeology; only discovered that the dirt washes off easily enough," she told him, a mischievous twinkle in her eye.

Too much time had passed for Kate to be truly angry with him for the offhanded way he had quashed her girlish infatuation. Still, she had never forgotten the pain it had caused her, and it pleased her now to see how uneasy this badinage made him.

He stood there in silence for a few moments and smoothed his moustache with his finger, laughing uneasily.

"You've a faultless memory, Miss Wrightwood. I only hope that you won't hold the words of impetuous youth against me for I, too, have changed these past years."

"I won't." She assured him. "It would be most unkind."

Kate appraised her companion. He looked quite elegant in his white tie and waistcoat, the upturned wing collar accentuating the sharp line of his jaw. A few threads of silver graced the dark curl of his forelock.

"Perhaps you would like to dance?" he asked.

"I've promised my father that I'd fetch some

papers from his office," she explained, rising from her chair. "I ought to go now."

He touched her arm to help her rise, but her body tensed. "If you will excuse me, Mr. Hammonton."

Before he could respond, Kate walked quickly away, toward the French doors that opened into the courtyard. How she would welcome the night air to clear her head! Even while she'd been trifling with Nick Hammonton, he had been having a strong effect on her, especially when he had touched her arm. Kate disliked the warm flush that spread over her when she saw him. It sapped her of her normal strength. What made him so different from other gentlemen? she wondered. Why did his touch disconcert her so? To her way of thinking, he was full of arrogance and pride, bent on greatness at any cost, and she needed none of that. She was determined to keep a distance between herself and Mr. Nick Hammonton!

As she reached the doors, a pleasant-looking man crossed her path. "Ah, there you are, Miss Wrightwood. I'm Eric Latham, if you recall—"

"Yes, Doctor Latham, isn't it? Doctor Iverson speaks so highly of you. It's a pleasure to see you here this evening. I haven't seen you in many years."

"Your—I mean your father's fine speech reignited my memories of the Society's last expedition. I must admit I haven't been able to get the Nile water out of my veins since."

Kate smiled. "Then perhaps you ought to speak with Mr. Thayer about the expedition the Society has planned for next spring."

"I might just do that, Miss Wrightwood, thank you."

Dr. Latham then hesitated. "I wonder," he said, "if I might have the honor of this dance."

"Why, thank you for asking. I'd like that very much," she replied, forgetting that she had been on her way out.

She gave him her hand and tried to follow his capable lead through a sprightly polka. He even managed to make her laugh at those few missteps she made.

"You are a remarkable young lady," he told her.

"What? Do you mean to say that not all your partners trample on your toes so unmercifully?"

He gave her a boyish grin. "I was referring to your eloquent speech on your father's behalf. Mr. Hammonton told me that you must be very familiar with your father's work in order to speak with such facility. He thought your address to the Society impressive indeed."

Kate's brows arched in surprise. What she might have replied was lost as she caught sight of Mr. Hammonton himself. He was watching them, with a most unpleasant look on his face. Almost in reply, Kate smiled sweetly at Dr. Latham. "It is my understanding that Mr. Hammonton is seldom impressed by anyone but himself."

This greatly amused the doctor, but after a moment he regarded her soberly. "You mustn't confuse dedication to his work as self-absorption. Nick is given totally to his archaeological pursuits. Surely, as your father's daughter, you can understand that."

"I hope that Mr. Hammonton appreciates your loyalty, Doctor Latham. But what of yourself? Are you so dedicated a man as your friend?"

"Hardly," he replied. "I must experience something more of life before I become such a serious-minded fellow."

———————

It was a quarter hour more before Kate was able to escape to her father's office and examine the jumble of papers on his desk. It occurred to her that she might just as well bring all of his things home, for it was not likely he would ever come here again.

He had tried to convince her that he had taken leave of his teaching post to recoup his strength and to put the notes from his expeditions into some semblance of order so they might be published, but Kate knew better. Though they both knew he was dying, neither of them knew what to say to the other. Kate's strength never waivered in his midst: She scowled and chided him like a naughty child when he would not take his medication or obey the doctor's strictures, and when he was at his worst, she would smile serenely and assure him that all would be well. Through it all, her father played the ornery patient, sick of all the fussing and anxious to be back at his work, yet knowing full well that he never would.

And so, Kate listened to the lilting strains of the orchestra from her father's office, after months of suppressing her feelings, she lay her head down on the desk and wept like a child. She wept for them both that they could not face the truth together.

Suddenly, Nick Hammonton said from the doorway, "D'Arcy isn't worthy of your tears. 'Tis he who

44

should be jealous of all the hearts you've collected tonight."

At this misunderstanding of what her tears meant, Kate sputtered a short laugh. Looking rather perplexed, Mr. Hammonton came and offered her his handkerchief, then sat down beside her.

"Honestly," Kate said as she wiped away the tears, "I don't care a whit for Mr. D'Arcy. Papa insisted, though, that I have an escort for the evening."

"Then why the tears?" he asked.

She fixed her gaze on a dark corner of the room. "My father is dying," she said hollowly.

"Yes, I know. He told me."

Kate gasped. She was surprised and hurt. Why could her father say to this man what he could not say to his own daughter?

"Perhaps you would have preferred that I not know," Nick said as he took her hand in his. He looked at her intensely. "Are you very frightened of losing him?"

She began to relax a little. "Perhaps," she answered, "but also angry and bitter that my father is slipping away from me and will never know me for who I truly am."

"You may expect too much of him. What parent can view his child objectively? Each of us sees something different in those around us."

"It's more than that," she explained. "My father will go to his grave regretting the son he never had, the son who could have followed in his footsteps, yet here I am all that he ever wanted, but in a woman's shell."

She leaned toward him, the lamplight softly illuminating her features. "I've been my father's secretary for four years now. I've copied his lecture notes, sat in on all his classes and read every volume on Egyptology I could acquire. When Papa became ill, I even wrote some of his lectures for him. If he had a particularly feverish night, I'd do the work and hand it to him the next morning as his own. I was never truly sure whether he knew or not."

"You wrote the speech for him this evening, didn't you?" he guessed.

She tensed at the thought that she may have made a grave error in giving herself away.

"It was a fine speech," he assured her, sensing her concern, "but the words were far too impassioned to have come from a dying man. It was a speech of beginnings, of plans for the future, and I must congratulate you on it."

He patted her hand. Though she was feeling more comfortable in his company, Kate was suddenly frightened. Why had she shared her most intimate thoughts with a man she barely knew? The tears had surely made her weak, and the strong shoulder he offered had been too tempting.

"Thank you for your kind words, Mr. Hammonton," she said as she drew her hand from his. She then began to gather up her father's things.

"Here, let me help you," he said. When they had finished, Nick said, "Now we shall return to the hall so that you might say your goodbyes, and then I shall escort you home."

"But Mr. D'Arcy—" Kate stammered.

"I must pass near your home on my way and rather than have poor Mr. D'Arcy go out of his, I have assured him that I would see you safely home. I hope it does not wound your vanity if I tell you that he was not unduly distressed at my proposal. Whatever did you say to make such an impression on the poor man?" he wondered.

"I'm afraid I may have wounded his vanity," she confessed. "So I must thank you again it seems, Mr. Hammonton."

"Nick—please—and I shall call you Kate. That is what your father calls you, isn't it? I would very much like for us to be friends, Kate. I can see that you need a friend."

During Kate's school years, friendship had meant nothing more than a pair of schoolgirls giggling together over trivial things. What Nick Hammonton offered her now was something quite different. With him she could quite possibly share her thoughts about ancient Egypt, and about the tombs and temples she was so desperate to visit, some of which he had already visited himself. For the moment she was content to put her other, more confusing feelings about him aside.

"I'd . . . I'd like that very much . . . Nick," she replied at last.

CHAPTER IV

Professor Wrightwood's notes on the island of Philae were engrossing, but not so much that Kate was unaware of a horse and buggy turning into the drive. She pushed her reading spectacles back up her nose and went to the window. There was Nick coming up to the house, a fine sight indeed in his buff-colored frock coat and trousers, and cravat of rich mulberry. She went out to meet him on the porch.

"Hello, Nick. Papa will be so pleased you're here. He's resting now, though."

"Actually, it's you I've come to see," he admitted. "Have you had your lunch? No, of course you haven't. A fine summer's day and you've shut yourself up with your father's papers. Well, we shall remedy that directly. I've brought a picnic lunch."

Kate was taken aback. She settled herself onto the bench below the parlor windows. "I've promised to organize Papa's notes—"

Nick sat down beside her. "Come now, Kate. You've shown me your Indian relics and excavations. Now I want to show you the very first discovery I ever made, when I was twelve years old."

"Where was that?" Kate asked.

Just south of here, down by the river, in some caves in the undercliff."

Kate blushed. She was unaccustomed to such attention. The summer's breeze felt cool against her cheek as she smoothed imaginary wrinkles from her skirt. Nick took her hands to still them.

"When we return, I'll help you with your father's notes," he promised. "Surely two can accomplish more than one."

Kate took a deep breath. She could not fathom why this man's proximity affected her so. In the past weeks Nick had become a good friend. He had come regularly to visit her father and had always found time to sit and talk with her about his experiences in Egypt, about the Indian relics she had found, and about so many other things. Together they would talk with her father about past expeditions, the Society's role in the future and what treasures might yet be discovered. And Nick made her laugh, with his fine sense of humor. It was, in fact, the perfect friendship except for this betrayal by her body each time he drew near.

"Very well," she decided. "Only allow me a minute so that I might tell Mrs. Davies that I'm going out. She does worry so. I think she imagines that I'll go for a walk by the river some day and fall in."

"Then by all means ease her worry. Tell her that I'll come in after you should you decide to go for a swim. And do take off those spectacles. You look quite the priggish school mistress, you know," he called after her.

After informing the housekeeper of her plans, Kate paused before the hall mirror for an uncharacteristic moment of primping. Her face was full of color, but she frowned at the severe upsweep of her hair as she adjusted her combs. Perhaps she might try a few curls one day. . . . She hadn't been much aware of the mauve cotton dress she had slipped on this morning, but it passed her inspection now, simple though it was. Finally, she tossed her spectacles onto the hall table and went out the door.

Nick was waiting on the porch and helped her into the buggy.

"I've told Mrs. Davies you'll be staying to supper this evening," she informed him, "unless you have other plans."

"Who could say no to one of Mrs. Davies' fine suppers?" Nick replied, climbing into the seat beside her.

The picnic hamper provided a welcome buffer between them, but Nick set it down at their feet and moved close enough to her that she could feel his hard thigh. Her heart fluttered in her breast.

"Daphne was gracious enough to pack this hamper for us," Nick said.

"You must thank her for her trouble."

"You can do so yourself, if you like. We've been invited to call on Sunday afternoon. Does that suit you?"

"Why—. . . of course. I'd like to meet her. You

speak so fondly of her that I feel as though I know her already."

Kate turned back to look at the house and for a moment thought she had seen her father watching them from his upstairs window, but perhaps it was a trick of the light, or the sun reflecting off the glass pane, for he had not been out of his bed in weeks.

Nick's special place was delightfully feral. They followed a narrow path down from the road, until they reached a grassy ledge that overlooked the bend of the river. While Nick spread out the blanket, Kate gazed at the boats in the water. There were perhaps half a dozen of them, including the steamer that had come round the bend, its sidewheel churning foam in the dark water. From this distance, she could just make out the passengers strolling the wide decks.

"Come along then." Nick's voice brought her back. He quickly began heading for the undercliff, anxious to share his first discovery. Kate ran after him, undergrowth tugging at her skirts. When she reached him, he took her hand, pulling her up the incline. The outcropping of jagged rock above their heads led Nick to warn her to stoop low as he led her into a wide-mouthed cave. Another opening somewhere above allowed in a small amount of daylight. Nick produced some candles from his pocket and pressed one into her hand. There was a snap and hiss as he struck a match. He grinned as he first lit her candle and then his, filling the cave with dancing yellow light. Its interior was larger than Kate had first imagined.

"However did you find this?" she asked, her voice only a whisper.

"I stumbled across it, literally, while I was fishing down by the river one day. And there's no need to whisper, Kate, we're the only ones about."

He hesitated. "You aren't afraid of close spaces? You can't be, you know, if you intend exploring Egyptian tombs someday."

"Oh, no," Kate replied quickly. "But you fairly dragged me up here. I only need to catch by breath, that's all."

"I'm sorry," Nick said. "I'm anxious for you to see what I've found. Come and have a look at this."

He took her hand and together they crossed the wide cave, their candles illuminating a section of the wall where a crude figure of a man and two stick-figure animals had been etched in. Kate decided the figures were elk and reached out to touch them.

Kate was fascinated. "I've never actually seen cave paintings before. Just imagine, some person recorded his day's hunt here thousands of years ago, and here we are, thousands of years later, connected to him through his recorded communication. How old do you suppose they are?"

Nick shrugged his broad shoulders. "Without closer inspection, I wouldn't venture to guess, but perhaps when this was being recorded, the Egyptians were laying stone for the pyramids."

"What were you thinking of when you discovered this?" Kate asked.

"I'll admit that, at twelve years old, I would have been happier with some arrowheads or pottery, something more portable. I couldn't very well drag everyone out here like this."

"I wouldn't have missed this," she said.

"Yes. I know." He smiled. "But I've promised

you a picnic lunch, and we'd best be at it before you wither away."

Kate laughed. "Hardly likely. Papa says I've far too healthy an appetite for a respectable young lady."

"You are a sensible young lady, Kate Wrightwood, and that's one of the things I like best about you."

Nick snuffed out his candle and bent down to go out. Kate did the same, following a step behind him. She paused a moment to stare after him and smiled. "Sensible" was, perhaps, not the most flattering compliment another young lady might have hoped for, but it meant a great deal to Kate, for it was one of the qualities she prided herself on.

The picnic lunch was delicious, seasoned by Nick's fascinating and humorous conversation. As she sipped the last of her wine, Kate thought that she had never been happier. Nick was describing for her, in intricate detail, the murals that graced the interior of the tomb he had helped to excavate on his last trip to Thebes.

"The banquet scene was particularly well preserved. The colors were so vivid that one would have thought they'd been painted only yesterday. When our lanterns shone on the mural, the entire chamber seemed to come alive. It was all there to see: the musicians, the guests in their finery, their expressions of mirth—and the abundance of food laid out before them."

"Oh, I do envy you your experiences, Nick," Kate told him as they cleared away the remnants of their meal. "I've always lived vicariously through my father's letters, but it's not enough—I want to know it all firsthand."

"Perhaps you shall someday," he replied thoughtfully.

─────────

Nick and Kate were so absorbed in conversation that they were not aware of the gray clouds that had rolled up in the valley. The large cold drops of rain startled them both, and they quickly clambered to their feet. Nick had the presence of mind to toss the carriage blanket over their heads and lead Kate toward his cave.

Before they could reach the shelter of the trees, Kate's skirts had become sodden, hampering her progress. Nick then lifted her up and began carrying her. As her head rested on his chest, she could smell sandalwood and the lingering aroma of his cheroot. When they reached the mouth of the cave, he moved to set her down, but stumbled, sending them both tumbling to the ground in the tangle of the blanket.

When Kate looked up, Nick's face was very close to hers. His eyes were opaque as he regarded her. He freed one hand and carefully wiped the damp strands of hair from her brow. Caressing her face, he traced her lips with his thumb before he bent over and kissed her, taking her breath away. Kate was startled at first, but found herself giving way and responding to him. Shamefully, she realized how little she knew of such things and how eager she was to learn. She rested a splayed hand on his damp linen shirt and could feel his heartbeat beneath the hard sheath of muscle, as his long fingers played lightly over her throat, trailing down to the soft swell of her breasts and leaving in their wake a delicious tingling. He hooked one arm around her waist and drew her full against him, and it seemed to Kate that every muscle in his lean frame was taut. Her stays dug into her soft flesh and she longed to be free of them, longed for Nick's practiced hands to continue their travels.

He kissed her again, and his breath was hot aginst her cheek as he whispered urgently, "Marry me, Kate!"

Those three words seemed to restore her sensibilities all at once. "I—I thought you wanted friendship," she replied, and thought afterward how absurd it must have sounded.

"Of course, that," he said, caressing her cheek with the back of his hand, "but so much more."

Together they eased into an upright position, and Kate sat there, hugging her knees, while Nick tucked the blanket around her and continued.

"I need you, Kate," he told her. "We're cut from the same cloth, you and I. There's not a woman alive who understands me as you do."

But Kate was not sure of that; she was not very sure of anything at this moment.

"We share the same passions and can converse for hours on end. We're never bored with each other. What better foundation for a marriage? And I've never told you, but when I saw you at my grandfather's funeral . . .

His manner suddenly became more lighthearted and he flashed a smile. "Well, what say you, Kate?"

"I'm . . . I'm overwhelmed."

Resting her chin on her knees, Kate contemplated his proposal, hoping to rely on that sensibility she so prided herself on. Was she in love with Nick? She had known there was something different about him since that evening in her father's study six years ago. He was the only man about whom she'd ever given a second thought; she could not deny it, nor could she deny that for some time now she had been dreaming of his touch. . . .

With a conscious effort, she quelled these giddy thoughts and returned to practical considerations. Papa was dying and she would soon be left on her own. Nick would be an ideal companion. He was right, they were cut from the same cloth. And then a thought came over her that cuased a rush of excitement: As Nick's wife, Kate might accompany him on his Egyptian expeditions. This thought would cause her many hours of guilt in the months to come and lead her to a painful questioning of her own motives, but it was enough to tip the balance now.

"Yes, Nick," she said at last. "I'll marry you."

———————

Kate had never seen her father so pleased as when she and Nick announced their engagement. In the weeks that followed, he seemed to regain some of his vigor, taking an active interest in the compilation of his notes for publication and meeting with the many friends and associates who came to call. Kate was surprised and pleased when he showed her the draft of a letter he had written to the Society, recommending Nick as his successor, and even more so when the recommendation was promptly approved by the Society board.

The days passed swiftly. With the advent of winter came the planning of the Egyptian expedition

Nick would lead the following spring. Kate could barely contain her excitement. After studying about it all these years, finally she would see Egypt with Nick as her guide. Surely the two brightest students of Professor Elias Wrightwood were destined for success.

———————

Alas, Nick had little faith in destiny. Experience had taught him otherwise. He had stood more than once in the pit of a desolate Egyptian valley, with walls of amber rock rising up on all sides, and wondered where to begin. Now as he sat across the desk from Professor Wrightwood, with a map that detailed Luxor, Thebes and the surrounding areas spread out before them, he felt suddenly overwhelmed by his responsibility.

"We could lodge at Qurna across the river," he suggested, "and center our work in this area near Deir el-Bahri."

"The choice is yours, of course," the professor told him and pointed a bony finger at the map. "These grids indicate what have been my own areas of concentration over the years, and marks such as these are the trial pits that were sunk. My work was centered more to the south and west, as you can see."

Nick hadn't heard Kate come in, but the gentle touch of her hand on his arm made him aware that she was peering over his shoulder.

"I think Deir el-Bahri would be a waste of time," she said. "Johannes Dümichen was there in '64—wasn't he Papa?—and just last year Mr. Perry and a group of archaeologists from Berlin spent a disappointing season there."

Nick wondered if he'd ever learn not to underestimate her.

"Is that right?" the professor asked, regarding his daughter with surprise. "Disappointing, you say? Well, it is up to Nick to decide."

"Yes," Nick replied, still nonplussed. "But I—"

There was a mischievous glint in the professor's dark eyes, and he chuckled. "Tell us, Kate. If the decision were yours, what would you do?"

"Truly?" she asked, trying to read his intent.

He nodded and looked to her for a reply.

"Well," she began, "Nick once compared all of this to an enormous jigsaw puzzle. He said that by putting together those pieces we already have and studying them carefully, we can perhaps discover a few of the missing ones. I think he was right. It makes more sense than digging holes willy-nilly, don't you think?"

Nick could see such pleasure in the old man's eyes. He remembered what Kate had said about her being all that her father had ever wanted in a child, but in a woman's shell. Perhaps the professor had finally realized this, and was now appreciating her for all that she was.

"Go on," he prompted her.

"Yes," Nick agreed. "If you're to be my wife and partner, you certainly have a right to voice your opinion about this venture."

Kate came around and leaned over the map. "If the decision were mine to make, I would concentrate efforts near the site of your last expedition, Papa. The catalogue of artifacts culled from that ruined village is intriguing, you must agree. I've studied the list myself several times, and I feel that there is more to be discovered there."

Nick had to admit that her enthusiasm was infectious. Kate seemed to have no qualms about how to proceed with the work, but he found such utter confidence on her part daunting in the face of his own indecision.

The professor pulled on his chin and nodded, then lowered his head as if intent upon the map, but not before Nick had seen the bright gleam of a tear in the old man's eye. "Indeed," he told his daughter, and his voice cracked with emotion. "You've learned your lessons well, my dear."

Kate turned to move closer to the hearth, pretending to study one of the ushabtis on the mantel. She was practically bursting with pride, for this was the first time she could ever recall that her father had asked her opinion about the work, and that he seemed pleased with her ideas.

Mrs. Davies knocked on the door and peered in. "There's a gentleman to see you, Miss Kate. It's Mr. Perry."

"Send him in please, Mrs. Davies."

The housekeeper wrung her hands in her apron. "Yes, well, he's asked if he might speak with you alone. I've put him in the parlor."

"What's this about?" Nick asked good-naturedly.

"Just paying a friendly call, I suppose," Kate said.

"Well, send our regards," the professor said.

Kate reluctantly left them to their planning, and walked down the hall to the parlor.

She'd not heard from Stephen Perry in more

than two months, since he'd gone home to see his family in Connecticut. Before that, though, he'd been a regular visitor, stopping by at least once a week to visit her and the professor.

Kate opened the parlor doors to find Stephen standing, hands thrust into his pockets, and staring out of the window at the bleak winter landscape. "Why, Stephen, it's good to see you! Your family is well, I trust?"

As he turned to face her, she noted the look of alarm on his face. This surprised her, as she'd come to think of Stephen as a man who was adept at hiding his thoughts and feelings.

"I've only just returned this afternoon, Kate, and I came as soon as I heard. I've promised myself, though, that I'd not believe it until you told me yourself. Is it true? Have you agreed to marry Hammonton?"

Kate breathed a long sigh. "Sit down, Stephen. Let me get you a drink."

She went to the small table beside the sofa and poured a generous amount of brandy into a glass. He seemed so distressed, but Kate could scarcely understand why. Their relationship thus far had been polite and friendly, but no more. Could she possibly have misread his intentions?

She turned to him and offered him the glass. "Answer me please, Kate."

"Yes, Nick and I are to be married in the spring."

Stephen sat down and stared into the glass for what seemed like a long while before he set it down.

"I can't say that I expected this," he told her. "We seemed to be getting on so well. I thought that—"

Kate sat beside him. "We've become friends, Stephen, good friends. My marriage won't change that."

He shook his head. "I'm a man accustomed to having exactly what I want. It comes from being a spoilt child, I suppose. When I realized that you were what I wanted more than anything else, I went home to Connecticut to sort out my feelings. I'd come back with the intention of proposing to you myself, only to find I'm too late."

He sought out her hands, resting in the folds of her gray merino skirt and covered them with his own. "Am I too late, Kate?"

"Yes," she said and dropped her eyes to avoid his fervent gaze. "I'm afraid so. You're a fine man, Stephen, and a good friend, but—"

"I'm a better man for you than Hammonton," he insisted. "I'll admit that I'm an adventurer and a treasure hunter, and perhaps I'm not as serious-minded as you when it comes to the work, but I'd have let you have your head. He'll never allow you that. With Hammonton, you'll always be relegated to a place in his shadow, and you'll come to hate him for it."

Kate slipped away from him and went to the window. She did not believe what Stephen was saying, though perhaps it was a nagging doubt that made her turn her back on him before replying.

"We shall be partners—no less. Nick respects my abilities and tells me that I shall be a great help to him in the work."

Stephen approached her and turned her around to face him. "I'll ask you once more and then I'll not ask again, Kate. Am I too late to change your mind?"

There was no turning back now. Nick Hammonton was what she wanted, what she needed. Stephen was striking out at Nick because he was hurt, and much as Kate did not wish to cause him more of that, he had to understand. She met his eyes straight on.

"Yes, Stephen, I intend to marry Nick in the spring and accompany him as his wife and partner on the expedition. I hope you can be happy for us."

Nick stood silent in the doorway, having listened to his villification at Perry's hands, and was surprised to find how little it affected him. Perhaps, though, this was due to the calm way in which Kate had defended him.

He hadn't meant to eavesdrop, but when he'd passed the open door and saw Stephen Perry making overtures to his financée as she sat beside him on the sofa, he obviously couldn't walk away. He watched Kate, mesmerized by each graceful gesture she made. As she listened to Perry's proposal, she turned her blue eyes on him, eyes with depths a man could drown in, and Nick barely could breathe waiting for her to reply. He spent a paralyzing moment considering what he would do were she to reject him in favor of the eloquent Mr. Perry. True, Nick had already been appointed director of the Society, but it no longer seemed the irresistible prize it had been when Professor Wrightwood had first offered it to him. Though he was certainly happy with the post, it wasn't enough; he wanted Kate, too.

He ought to have known that Kate was far too sensible to change her mind at this point. But it occurred to him that she might have accepted his proposal not out of true affection, but because it was such a sensible match. He suddenly remembered that he had used that very argument when he had proposed to her. The thought irritated him more than a little, and he determined that even if such were the case, he'd make her want him, as much as he wanted her.

———

Kate was a little ashamed of herself for being relieved when Stephen announced that he would be unable to stay for dinner. He'd been sullen since their conversation, and even after he'd bid them good evening, Kate found herself uneasy. She could feel Nick's eyes on her, and when at last she dared to meet them, it was to find his brow raised as if there were questions he wanted to ask but didn't quite know how to phrase them.

After dinner, Ahmad wheeled the professor back into his study, leaving Kate and Nick alone.

"What is it?" Kate found the courage to ask him at last. "There's something on your mind."

Nick only smiled as he came to pull out her chair for her. He whispered "Come into the parlor, Kate, and sit by the fire with me."

He took her arm and led her there, and she settled on the sofa while he stoked the fire. Its amber blaze was the only light in the room.

"I've a confession to make," he said and sat down beside her.

Kate felt her heart hammering hard against her breast, but proposed to remain calm until she'd heard him out.

"I overheard Perry's proposal to you this afternoon," he explained. "I didn't mean to but . . . the door was ajar, and he spoke quite plainly."

Kate sighed in relief. "Nick, honestly, I had no idea that he—"

"Yes, I know. It's only that, well . . ." His head was bent as he studied his hands. "I feel I must offer you the opportunity, if Perry's the man you truly want—"

"No!" Kate replied, too quickly.

He captured her eyes with his. "Are you sure?"

"Yes. Yes, of course."

Beneath his moustache, Nick's mouth twisted into a wry smile. "I'm glad to hear it."

He slowly turned her hand and pressed his lips against the soft inside of her wrist. "I'd not have given you up without a fight, you know. No matter what I might have said."

Firelight played over the sharp planes of his face as he pulled her into the circle of his arms. Kate caught her breath, and her lips parted in anticipation of his kiss, but he hesitated a long moment, needing to see her desire for him before he lowered his mouth over hers.

Her lips were soft and responsive beneath his, and Nick pulled her slim form closer still, until he could feel the soft swell of her breasts rise and fall against his chest. A pulse throbbed in his temples, keeping a staccato beat, urging him onward as he caressed her thigh through the soft fabric of her skirt. He knew where this was bound to lead, where he wanted it to lead, but drew back when he sensed her reticence.

He studied her face for an explanation and could not help but smile. Despite her youth, Kate was the strongest, most capable woman he'd ever met, but now as she peered up at him through the dark fan of her lashes, her blue eyes wide, she looked quite the frightened child.

"I'm sorry, Nick," she told him and rested her head upon his strong shoulder. "I've no experience—"

He toyed with a lock of jasmine-scented hair that had slipped from her chignon. "No man wants to believe his wife is experienced in such matters," he assured her. "It's something he'd prefer to teach her himself."

She pressed her palms against his chest and edged back a bit that she might meet his gray eyes.

"Teach me, Nick," she said.

He took up her hands and kissed them, one at a time. "There'll be plenty of time for that, my love," he said, and Kate could see that he was struggling for control of his senses as he exhaled, long and low. "But it's late, and you remember that I promised Eric I'd come by this evening to discuss the expedition."

"So he's decided to come along, then?"

"I think that he has. Such an opportunity may not present itself again . . . for any of us."

Kate had never before heard Nick express doubts about the success of their venture, and though his words startled her, she chose to ignore them. But she could not ignore the surge of pleasure that had coursed through her veins at his touch. She was glad that she'd sent Perry away. Nick Hammonton was the only man who could make her forget all else but her desire for him, and she knew she would marry him, no matter what the risk.

———

After Nick had chastely kissed her goodnight, Kate went to find her father. He was not in his room, though. She was surprised to find him still in his study, poring over his notes.

"It's late, Papa," she said. "I'll ring for Ahmad to come to take you up to bed."

"I'm not tired," he protested. "There's so much to do, and I don't know how much time is left me."

"Oh, Papa," Kate said, her voice ending on a wistful note.

It was the first time he'd ever so much as alluded to his fate, and Kate had to struggle to keep her composure. Finally, she said, "I'll make some tea, then."

"Don't fuss, Kate," the professor ordered. "Come here and sit by me."

She did as he wished, and he took her hand. His grip was still firm, which somehow reassured her.

"If I've not told you before," he began, "I am proud of all you've accomplished. When you first told me that you wanted to study archaeology, I never expected that you should be such a dedicated student."

He pointed to a stack of composition books piled on the desk. "These are your notebooks, are they not?"

"Yes, but how—?"

"Nick came across them in my study a few weeks back and insisted that I read through them. When I'd done so, I discovered why he'd been so amazed. These notebooks were a compilation of research notes, summaries of lectures I'd given, critiques of books on Egyptology, hieroglyphic transcription and the like, along with personal observations pertaining to the field, and these incredible notebooks, each and every one, had been penned in my own daughter's hand."

The conversation had left him winded. He closed his eyes, and his chest heaved as he tried to draw breath. He sputtered a cough, and his grip on Kate's hand tightened.

"You're tired, Papa," she said, trying to hide her distress. "Please let me ring for Ahmad. We can talk in the morning, after you've rested."

"No!" he insisted, his dark eyes glittering fiercely.

He would not release her hand. "Listen to me, Kate," he said, his voice only a harsh whisper now. "Nick is a good man. He'll care for you, and more than that, he'll understand you if you give him the chance. I fear you've been alone for too much of your life, and for that I am to blame."

"That's not so!"

He drew a long, uneven breath before he calmly replied. "It is, and it's made you stubborn and intolerant . . . but also determined. That's one thing to be thankful for at least."

His mouth turned up at the corners, but even his attempt at a charming smile could not coax Kate out of the uneasy state in which she found herself. She realized he was slipping away from her.

"Don't ever lose your determination, Kate. Go to Egypt if it's what you want, and show them all what you're made of, and remember—nothing is impossible if you want it badly enough."

CHAPTER V

A scant two weeks after the coming of the new year, Professor Elias Wrightwood died in his sleep, his weakened heart finally giving out. Although Kate had been prepared for it, it was a shock nonetheless, especially considering the energy he had exhibited in his last months.

The wedding was planned for early spring. Although Kate and Nick would have preferred a more intimate ceremony, circumstances dictated that the nuptials be turned into a social event, especially following the notice that ran in the newspapers a week before the wedding:

Local Couple to Wed:
    Miss Katherine Wrightwood, daughter of the late Professor Elias Wrightwood of our own

Creighton University, and Mr. Nicholas Hammonton, a graduate of the University and recently appointed director of the Society for the Preservation of Antiquities, will be wed this coming Saturday in the Creighton University chapel. The ceremony is to take place at half past ten in the morning, with a luncheon reception to be held immediately thereafter in the University Hall.

And so, awash in the customary lace and orange blossom, Kate Wrightwood and Nick Hammonton were married. They were greeted by a sea of wellwishers at the chapel door and fêted by yet another crowd in the University Hall. For two such solitary people, it was a trying day, but they found comfort in one another. As Nick quite accurately pointed out, they must now be in the business of public relations, ready with a smile and a few kind words for the Society's members, upon whose donations their livelihood depended. He did not realize, though, just how quickly his new bride would take such advice to heart.

"A honeymoon in Egypt, spent searching for ancient artifacts? Oh, I do envy you that, Mrs. Hammonton," the portly old gentleman said to Kate in the receiving line. "I've a copy of a delightful narrative by the Italian adventurer Giovanni Belzoni, which recounts his own Egyptian exploits, and I've read it over more than once. Exciting business, I can tell you. Has your husband decided where he'll begin?"

"Of course the Valley of the Kings is a likely

spot," she told him. "But you mustn't be disappointed if we don't live up to Belzoni's record. Four new tombs in twelve days is an amazing feat and not one likely to be duplicated."

"You've read the *Narrative*?" He sounded surprised. "But then I've nearly forgotten who your father was. Certainly he'd have read you such a tale in lieu of a bedtime story. Rest assured, Mrs. Hammonton, if you come away with no more than a good adventure story, I for one will consider the money well spent."

Kate took his hand and favored him with a smile. "I can promise you that much at least."

"What's this, Matthews?" the next gentleman piped up. "Extracting promises from the pride on her wedding day?"

" 'Twas only for a story," the first man retorted. "As I'm too old and gouty to have my own Egyptian adventure, Mrs. Hammonton has kindly offered to relate to me the tale of this latest expedition when she returns. It will, I'm sure, be replete with Arabs, plundered tombs, fabulous treasures and desert sands."

"Why, you old pirate!"

"Have you no interest in adventure, Mr. Gilliam?" Kate asked the second gentleman, hoping she'd remembered his name correctly.

"Actually, I joined the Society because of an interest in ancient cultures. It is my hope that our efforts will add to the meager body of knowledge that now exists about the Egyptian people themselves."

"You, sir, are a man ahead of his time," Kate commented, "much like my father was."

Mr. Gilliam flushed behind his spectacles. "Why thank you for saying so, Mrs. Hammonton."

"I know that you would find my father's notes fascinating reading, especially with regard to the 1860 excavation of an ancient settlement south of Thebes. Perhaps you would allow me to send you a copy when they're published?"

"I would be honored."

Though Nick had been involved in a conversation with the loquacious Mrs. Matthews, he'd not missed Kate's adroit handling of the two gentlemen. He put out his hand out to them now. "Gentlemen, we are so pleased that you could be here with us this afternoon."

Mr. Gilliam spoke first. "Congratulations to you, my boy. Your bride is quite a remarkable young woman."

"Yes," Mr. Matthews agreed as he shook Nick's hand. "You are fortunate to have garnered such a gem for yourself."

As he watched her weaving her spell over the Society members, Nick had to agree. "She is a rare find."

"And possessed of more knowledge of Egyptology than I've seen in any woman," Mr. Matthews put in. "I wouldn't be surprised if she could show us all a thing or two."

A twinge of jealousy came over Nick, but he dismissed it at once. There was no competition between them, he thought. But as Kate flashed a bewitching smile to win over yet another of their guests, he had to admit that her uncanny knack left him feeling uneasy . . . and inadequate.

When the newlyweds were finally ushered into a carriage for the drive back to the Wrightwood home, where they would be taking up residence, neither of them spoke, preferring to enjoy the stillness after their hectic day.

Kate unpinned her veil and folded it on the seat beside her, then rested her upswept coif of golden curls against her husband's shoulder and laid a hand on his arm. From this perspective, she admired his strong profile, etched in shadow. More than one young lady today had eyed her with envy as she stood at Nick's side. He was an impressive figure of a man, she mused, perhaps not what one might picture a scholar to be. He was never less than impeccably tailored and today had been no exception. He had worn a frock coat of dove gray with waistcoat and trousers to match, and a striped silk cravat held in place with a diamond stickpin. Perhaps, she decided as she studied him, it was the moustache that gave him his rougish air and set the ladies' hearts aflutter.

Nick appeared to be staring most intently out of the carriage window, but Kate could tell by the tilt of his dark head that he was absorbed in thought. At her touch, though, he was brought back and leaned over to kiss her brow.

There was only a sliver of a moon to light the way as they turned into the drive at last, and Kate could see the yellow lamplight spilling out of the front upstairs bedroom that had not been used since her mother's death. Apparently Mrs. Davies had everything prepared. When the carriage rocked to a halt, Nick promptly opened the door and stepped into the drive, tossing a gold coin up to the driver.

"Thank you!" Nick called as he leaned back into the carriage and lifted Kate off of the seat.

"Aye, sir! Best wishes to you and your lady!"

As the carriage turned out of the drive, Nick ceremoniously carried Kate and her yards of lace train up the porch stairs and over the threshold. There was one chamberstick on the hall table, and another on the landing, to light their way upstairs.

"The fairies are tending to us this evening, it seems," Nick commented.

"Yes, orchestrated by Mrs. Davies," Kate replied as they reached the bedroom, and Nick set her back down on her satin-slippered feet.

The room was warm and inviting, bathed in lamplight and the orange glow of the fire. A small table and matching chairs stood before the hearth; on the table had been placed a light supper of beef in wine sauce and greens, and a bottle of champagne.

Nick let go a low whistle. "Whatever her stipened, remind me to see that it's doubled."

Kate smiled at him, and they sat down to their supper. With all the day's excitement neither had eaten very much. Kate felt sure that her senses were heightened this evening, as each morsel tasted better than the last.

"I fear I've eaten more than my share," Kate said, as she finished her meal, pushing herself away from the table.

A smile twisted on Nick's lips. "You've warned me of your 'healthy appetite,' Mrs. Hammonton, and as I've told you, I approve. It wouldn't do to have my wife fainting away at the drop of a hat from a lack of food."

"Small chance of that," Kate retorted as she went

into the adjacent dressing room to divest herself of her bridal raiment. She stopped to view the moon through the small window over the vanity table.

Kate twisted the wide gold band on her third finger and realized her heart was beating fast. As she began to unfasten the long row of satin-covered buttons, she realized that her hands were shaking. She was anticipating what was to come, hoping that her husband did not find her inexperience tiresome. She wished that her mother were alive to offer her the comfort and advice she so desperately needed. Here in her mother's old dressing room, Kate was suddenly filled with very early memories of her. She was still toying with the buttons at the nape of her neck when a hand closed over hers. A sharp breath caught in her throat as she wondered if her mother had come back to her.

"Here now, I'll do that," Mrs. Davies said, as she set down her lamp. She unfastened the tiny buttons, then helped Kate undo her lacing.

" 'Twas a lovely wedding," Mrs. Davies whispered. "Even Ahmad had a tear in his eye."

Kate was silent but smiled to herself.

Mrs. Davies saw to each article of clothing as Kate shrugged it off, and helped her into a batiste nightgown with a corsage of Brussels lace. Next she deftly pulled the pins from Kate's hair and brushed it out in long strokes. Kate closed her eyes, enjoying this pampering.

"You'll have a good life together," Mrs. Davies assured her. "I'm not the one to be givin' advice, child, but you've naught to fear. Mister Nick is a good man, and he'll do right by you."

She laid down the hairbrush on the table and reached in her apron pocket, drawing out a heart-shaped locket on a gold chain.

"Before he died, your papa said I was to give this to you on your wedding day. It belonged to your mama."

"Yes, I know," Kate replied. "Thank you, Mrs. Davies . . . for everything."

The housekeeper reached over and fastened the chain about Kate's neck, then patted her shoulder and reached for her lamp. Kate hugged her.

"Goodnight, Miss Kate. Best not keep your man waiting."

Kate returned to the bedroom, clutching the locket at her throat as if it were some magical amulet. Nick had put out the lamp, but by the soft light of the fire, Kate could see the two tall stemmed glasses full of champagne he had poured. He, too, had shed his formal attire, in favor of a dark silk dressing gown. Kate noted again how striking he was, how the sight of him took her breath away. And he was totally bewitched by her, as she faced him with her hair unbound and her shapely form silhouetted beneath her nightdress.

"Champagne?" he asked, offering her a glass. "A toast, to my wife."

"To my husband," Kate replied. The liquid cooled and relaxed her.

As they chatted and laughed for a few minutes, Kate felt they would have a very comfortable relationship. But suddenly she was caught in Nick's gaze. He put down his glass and threaded his hands through her pale tresses, intoxicated by her jasmine-scented skin. He touched her lips gently with his own, a controlled effort, as he was already eager for her.

Nick approached the tiny pearl buttons on her nightdress and unfastened them, one at a time, until the soft fabric fell away. Firelight gleamed on the bared curves of her body. All the while Kate's eyes, which were forever reminding him of lapis lazuli, did not leave his face, as if she were gauging his reaction. In a single move she slipped off the night-dress, and it slid to the floor at her feet. Nick admired his wife's body, amber in the fire light and free now of stays and hoops, petticoats and endless yards of fabric. Hers was a form to rival the classical statues, full-breasted and flat-bellied. The pressure in his loins was quickly growing unbearable, and his lips were hard as they moved on hers. "Shall we retire then, Mrs. Hammonton?" he whispered in her ear.

She nodded, and he lifted her up easily and carried her to the bed. Kate watched in curious silence as Nick stripped off his dressing gown and came to her. While his lips caressed her temple, her cheek and hollow of her throat, his hands skimmed over her satin skin, memorizing each curve and leaving her feeling lightheaded, as though she'd had much more than one glass of champagne. Following his lead, Kate let her hands travel the planes of his back to his narrow hips, sensing some of the power in that lean frame.

"My sweet Kate!" Nick cried.

His breathing was ragged against her ear. He rained kisses on her perfumed skin, down the valley of her breasts. Her breath was caught at the back of her throat as his mouth sought one nipple, teasing it until it was taut, and then moved on to the other. His practiced hands kneaded the soft flesh of her thighs and throwing out one long leg, he rolled over her, trapping her beneath him.

Kate was not aware of his weight on her, only the heat of his hard body and the hair matting his chest as it brushed over her sensitive breasts. There was only a slight resistance when he lowered his hips between her thighs and then a feeling of utter completeness.

A low moan vibrated through his chest, and as instinct took over, Kate matched his thrusts. Her mouth lagged open, her breathing shallow and uneven, until Nick stilled the sound with his lips. The shudder of his release drew her to the edge as well, and then waves of pleasure washed over her.

———

When Kate opened her eyes, the room was aflood with sunlight. Boldly she reached for Nick, only to find him gone. She gathered her nightdress and robe and quickly put them on before going downstairs in search of her husband.

She was momentarily distracted as she walked past the parlor, which now resembled one of the fancier emporiums in New York City. Wedding gifts had been placed on two long tables and on every other available space. There were embroidered linens, silver trays, an ornate tea service, crystal bowls and vases, and porcelain in every form imaginable. The sheer quantity was enough to take one's breath away. Kate's interest, though, was captured by

77

a single goblet, translucent in a warm ivory color, in the shape of a lotus flower. She lifted it carefully out of its packing case, feeling its weight and examining the workmanship.

"Exquisite!" she said, her voice a soft whisper.

Kate thought that the cup was not a reproduction, but a valuable Egyptian artifact. She wondered who might have sent such a gift, and setting it back on its bed of straw, snatched up the card. It contained an elaborate crest and only a short note: "Best wishes for a long and happy life together. Peter Hammonton."

Who was this Hammonton? As Nick had never spoken of his father's family, Kate had assumed that he was the last of the line. Tucking the case under her arm, Kate went into the hall, where she saw Ahmad carrying a coffee service into her father's study. She followed him in and found that Nick, still in his dressing gown, had installed himself at her father's desk and was perusing her father's notebooks. She was immediately angry with him. He had certainly wasted no time. It seemed that Nick would take up where her father had left off: directing the Society, carrying on his work and running the household. How convenient! Even Ahmad seemed to be attaching himself quite easily to Nick. She began to fear that through her marriage, she might have lost control over her life, and that all her dreams and aspirations would be swept aside in favor of Nick's.

But her fears evaporated immediately when he looked up at her, his lips curved into a crooked smile that tilted his moustache awry.

"Good morning, my dear."

His eyes took stock of her in a most intimate

manner, and there was no doubt but that his thoughts had turned to what had passed between them during the night. Kate blushed, and found herself studying the pattern on the carpet as he rose to kiss her lightly on the cheek.

Ahmad had set the tray on the desk and now looked to Kate as Nick settled himself back in his chair.

"You would like coffee, Miss Kate?" he asked and then corrected himself. "I mean Missus Kate?"

"No, thank you," she said and left him to pour for her husband.

"It was . . . unsettling," she said to Nick, after searching for the right word, "to wake and find you gone."

"I'm a restless soul, my love, but I'm sorry if I distressed you. I woke with the expedition on my mind. I've only a few short months to decide on a definite site, you know."

He reached for the coffee, blew away the steam that hovered over the cup and sipped at it.

"I thought your father's notes might provide me with some possibilities. All this winter, while we made our plans, he would just tell me to trust my instincts, yet I had the feeling that he had some very definite ideas of his own that he might have told me, but he never did."

Kate could see just how unsure of himself Nick was in his new position. It was vital that this expedition be successful, so that he might prove himself worthy of being the professor's successor and that the Society might continue with its work. Such matters obviously weighed heavily on him.

"Papa had such confidence in your abilities,

79

Nick, as do I. This is what you've wanted. You mustn't let the responsibilities distract you from the work you love."

Nick regarded her with surprise, amazed that she often sounded much older than her nineteen years.

"Now, let's get you interested in something else for a while," Kate began.

She sat down the packing case on the edge of the desk. "Have a look at this."

Nick reached in and held the goblet up to the light. "A lotus cup," he commented. "Superb workmanship. It's a fine piece. Where did it come from?"

"A wedding gift," Kate explained and handed him the card.

When he read the notation, his expression suddenly turned sour. He laid the goblet back in its case and pushed it toward her as if it had offended him.

"Send it back."

Kate's mouth hung open. "But it's a wedding gift," she protested. "I couldn't do such a thing."

Nick's face was a study in hard lines. "Don't cross me on this, Kate. Send it back!"

Even though his words stung, she immediately replied, "Who is this Peter Hammonton that you should hate him so?"

With his back to her, Nick pretended not to hear and stared out of the window. Kate turned on her heel and walked out, leaving Ahmad to retrieve the goblet. He followed her into the hall, his black eyes full of compassion. "I will return the gift," he told her.

Kate was even more distressed to realize that Ahmad felt sorry for her. He was not a tall man, not a particularly imposing one, yet for as long as she could remember, Kate had been somewhat frightened by him. It could have been his gaunt features and dark eyes, or the silent grace with which he moved, like a cat. Now, however, she was aware of his desire to protect her, a young bride, from the wrath of her husband. Her voice was firm but kind.

"Thank you, Ahmad, but no. Put the goblet in the trophy room. I'll not return it until I know the reason why."

He looked askance. "Hammonton-*effendi* is now *Sidi-el-Kebir*."

Kate could translate the phrase: Hammonton-sir is now the great, respected master. She was furious. "I have a partner, Ahmad, but no master, and I will have an explanation before this matter is concluded!"

CHAPTER VI

*"D*amn the man!"

Nick paced before the window, sorry now that he had let his hatred of Peter Hammonton spill over and hurt Kate. He thought he'd exorcized the man years ago, yet now here he was again, trying to inveigle himself into Nick's life.

Nick knew that he ought to go to Kate now and try to explain, but where the man who had destroyed his mother's life was concerned, he feared he could not maintain his composure long enough even for the explanation.

Nick actually remembered very little of his mother, but what he did recall had been augumented over the years by his grandfather, and colored by her portrait which hung in his grandfather's parlor. Within that gilt frame was the image of a slight young innocent girl, with soft dark curls and a complexion that rivaled the pale luster of Dresden china. But it was her dark, trusting eyes that haunted him even now, and the memory of them fuelled Nick's hatred of the vile and debauched drunkard whose cruelty had been too much for her to bear.

No, he could not explain, not even to Kate, for it shamed him to admit that such a man was his father.

———————

Despite her anger, Kate decided to be tolerant of her husband's moods, especially in light of his anxiety over the expedition. It seemed that he was just beginning to come to terms with the responsibilities of the post. Kate, by contrast, was very much aware of such responsibilities. Had she not watched her father struggle with them for years?

Moreover, the Egyptian sands were no longer freely open to plunder, due to the presence of Auguste Mariette, the noted French archaeologist who was now director of government excavations for Ishmael Pasha, khedive of Egypt. Mariette now oversaw all excavations and made certain that all important antiquities were turned over to the pasha for the museum at Bulak. Archaeologists now had to be content with only the most insignificant artifacts or else try to smuggle their finds out of the country. It was little wonder that tomb robbers were doing a brisk business.

The task that fell to Nick was, therefore, a nearly impossible one. He not only had to concern himself with his scientific pursuits, but also had to hope for a discovery of significant wealth so that he might be amply rewarded for his efforts by the pasha. Kate intended to do everything in her power to help him accomplish that task.

In the beginning, Nick welcomed Kate's enthusiasm as they huddled together over maps and conversed for hours about the coming expedition. Kate inquired about the places that intrigued her, and Nick would try to make sketches of them for her. She characteristically kept meticulous notes on their discussions and showed remarkable insight. Nick was impressed by her aptitude. It was only after the visit of the Society's board members to their home that his feelings began to change.

He had gone to New York early that morning to finalize the arrangements for the trip. He'd intended to return in plenty of time for his meeting with the board members, but had been delayed and had been forced to catch the late afternoon steamer. Pacing the wide deck of the river boat in utter frustration, he hoped that Kate could somehow entertain the four stodgy gentlemen until his return. He needn't have worried.

The sun was setting when he finally returned home, and Mrs. Davies was at the door to meet him.

"Are they—?"

Before he could finish, she pointed to the closed parlor doors.

Nick expelled a long sigh, shaking his head. "How's Kate holding up?" he asked. "Have any of them fallen asleep on her yet?"

Mrs. Davies took his coat. "Not to worry, sir," she told him. "You'd be proud of her."

"Have I time to change for dinner?"

"Just enough. Shall I tell Miss Kate that you've returned?"

"No, thank you," he said. "I'll just peek in before I go up."

Nick quietly drew open the doors and was more than a little surprised to find Kate at the center of the group, in animated conversation, holding up a map.

"You can see from this facsimile, which I have copied from one of my father's more detailed maps, exactly how rich an area western Thebes has proven to be, gentlemen. Those areas I have shaded in indicate sites we know to have been excavated in recent years. Those bordered in red denote successful operations."

"Might I ask, Mrs. Hammonton, who compiled this information?" Mr. Gilliam inquired. "And how? It seems an exhaustive task."

"I put it together myself in order to aid my husband in choosing a definite site. When he decided to center his work within the Valley of the Kings, I thought it wise to create such a map as a visual aid. It was time-consuming, but not particularly difficult. I scoured my father's journals and his extensive collection of writings by early excavators and travellers for information and interpreted, as well, what observations my husband was able to provide from the years he himself spent in Egypt. Some inaccuracies are unavoidable, but the more information we begin with, the better prepared we will be."

Mr. Thayer crossed his arms over his chest and pulled on his long chin. "I, for one, am quite frankly amazed."

"Perhaps," Mr. Matthews suggested, "we have appointed the wrong member of this family to direct our Society's expedition."

It was a polite bit of flattery, nothing more, really. Surely Kate recognized it for what it was, and yet Nick could see just how much she was enjoying the attention.

As he stood unnoticed in the doorway, Nick tried to deny that it was jealousy that was creeping over him like a sickness.

"Good evening, gentlemen," he said at last, drawing attention to himself. "I must apologize for my late return. I was detained in the city on business. I hope, though, that my wife has managed to keep you entertained in my absence."

Nick looked across the room to meet Kate's eyes, but he didn't see the beautiful woman who'd become such an important part of his life. He saw only another archaeologist, poised and confident of her abilities, who'd garnered the respect of each of the astute businessmen grouped around her.

Mr. Schuyler, the eldest of the board members, had been silent thus far, but now cleared his throat. "Entertained? Hammonton, all I can say is you're damned fortunate—beg pardon, ma'am—to have found so brilliant a wife."

"So I've been told," Nick replied, a smile frozen upon his face. "If you will excuse me, gentlemen, I shall go and dress for dinner. Kate, may I have a word with you, please?"

He walked out, and Kate followed him into the hall, shutting the doors behind her. He turned on her suddenly.

"What was all of that about?" he demanded, keeping his voice low.

"Mr. Matthews inquired about the expedition. I was merely explaining—"

"You might have waited for me," he cut in, "seeing as how this is my project."

Kate's anger was on the rise, as evidenced by her whitened fists, clenching at the taffeta skirts of her peach evening gown. "I thought we were to work as partners in this, Nick. What's come over you?"

He paced on a small section of the hall carpet, trying to put his thoughts into reasonable form. "What is it, exactly, that you are trying to prove, Kate? That you are a better archaeologist than your husband? Or is it your intention to humiliate me? If so, then you've succeeded. You've convinced every one of those men that you are the genius behind our 'partnership.' And me? I'm the bumbling figurehead, a man of mediocre abilities, who married you only for—"

Kate was restrained. "Go on. . . ."

He had nearly told her of his bargain with her father. Nick's guilt over it weighed heavy on him, even though in the end the bargain wasn't the real reason he'd married Kate, as he had fallen completely in love with her. Perhaps it was partly due to this guilt that he was so determined to prove himself, to prove that he would have been worthy of the directorship even without the professor's recommendation. But as he thought about it all, Kate's feelings were uppermost in his mind. She must never find out about the bargain because if she did, she would probably think she had been just her father's pawn in a game that had decided her future for her.

Nick shook his head, suddenly feeling very tired. He forced himself to look at Kate, who no longer looked angry, only disappointed. "Why must whatever I achieve come at your expense?" she wondered. "If I am more, why must that make you less? Can we not succeed . . . together?"

It struck Nick then, after considering Mr. Matthews' offhand remark, that perhaps the professor had recognized his daughter's potential all along, and realizing that, as a woman, she could not easily achieve success on her own, he'd decided to provide her with a partner through whom she could gain her success. Perhaps it was Nick who had been the professor's pawn all along.

———

Although Kate was prepared to overlook Nick's recent harsh temper and accusations, she was not prepared for what happened in his study just a few weeks before the expedition was about to depart.

"I've been thinking, Kate," he said, shuffling his papers around so that he might escape her eyes. "Perhaps it would be best if you did not accompany me on the expedition."

Her jaw dropped, but she quickly recovered and strode to the desk. "How can you suggest such a thing when you know how badly I want to see Egypt?"

Nick rose up out of his chair, standing over her. "I have only your best interests at heart," he said. "Egypt is no paradise. It is a harsh place, devoid of so many of the creature comforts we take for granted. I have, in my experience, camped in a tent like a Bedouin and even slept on the floor of an excavated tomb when occasion called for it, but I shall not subject my wife to such rustic conditions."

"I see," Kate replied, pressing her lips so tightly

together that they drained of blood. "And have I nothing to say on the matter?"

"You'd have no companionship," he went on, ignoring her question. "I will be occupied elsewhere much of the time. You'd be left to your own devices. Oh, you would probably find the sightseeing exhilarating for a few weeks, but then the boredom would set in. Month after month of stagnation. The heat is unbearable much of the time and the dust gets into everything. It's not half the glorious picture that your father has painted for you with all of his stories. It's hard and dirty work, with scant reward for the time you devote to it."

"If your hope was to dissuade me from my purpose, then you've failed. I've heard nothing from you that I didn't learn years ago from my father, despite what you think. I'm no hothouse orchid, Nick. I thrive on neglect, a fact you seem to have learned quickly enough."

Nick was stung by her words. "That's unfair, Kate. I thought you understood how much time must be devoted to these preparations."

"All that I understand at this moment is that I'm to be left behind . . . for my own good, no less."

They stood staring at each other, both stubbornly clinging to their own views. Kate's eyes were bright with tears she would not allow to fall. She looked so wounded that Nick wanted to fold his arms around her. If only she would believe that staying at home was better for her . . . but even he did not believe it. But it would be simpler for him, if she did for it would end this competition between them.

"I could help with your notes," Kate protested.

"Make sketches, catalogue items, all of the tedious chores—"

"This expedition is vital to the survival of the Society. There will be no amateurs involved."

Nick realized, too late, that he had spoken without fully considering what effect such words might have. Kate reacted as though he'd struck her. Her face paled, and her composure crumbled. For one awful second he saw utter disillusionment in her eyes. Fear welled in him and knotted his stomach. If she'd harbored any affection for him at all, then surely he'd snuffed it out with his careless words.

She turned away, and he heard her draw a ragged breath. He stepped cautiously toward her, and she turned on him. "Damn your arrogance!" she spat. "I've as much education in this field as you have. I was weaned on stories of the pyramids and Cairo, Philae and Thebes. The temple statues in Papa's trophy room were my first playmates: Anubis, Horus, Isis, Osiris. All that I lack is practical experience, dear husband, and you seem determined to deprive me of that."

Before he could reply, she had stormed out of the room.

———————

Kate retreated in a blind rage to the bedroom she had occupied until her marriage. She felt safe there, behind the closed door, as she paced back and forth across the wood floor, hoping to release some of her anger.

The man she had called her friend seemed to have disappeared on the day she was wed, and in his place was an irritatingly paternal figure. She hoped that this change was not permanent, but was only due to his recent pressures.

Kate suddenly noticed the wooden box on her bureau containing the Isis mask. With all the confusion of the past few weeks she had quite forgotten about it.

As she took the mask out of its case, she felt the plaster cool her hands. Perhaps it should be displayed in the trophy room, she thought, instead of hidden away here. She carried it to her desk that she might examine it better. Yes, there was a quality that set it apart from traditional Egyptian statuary and had told her father that it was a molded mask. Could it have figured prominently in his plans for the expedition? She felt certain that it must have.

Kate knew that she should show it to Nick and let him decide on its importance. But if Papa had meant for Nick to know about it, surely he would have told him about it, yet he had not. This seemed to justify Kate's decided course of action. The Isis mask would be her secret, but to what purpose she would use the information gleaned from it, she could not yet say.

Kate stayed absorbed in thought as she examined the mask. She sketched its front and back, faithfully reproducing the sensuous slant of the eyes, the angular cheekbones and the full lips. She penned in the broken hieroglyphic characters that were painted across the back, intending to translate them later. Papa had translated only one of them, the Isis symbol.

She was just finishing checking over her work when she heard a knock at the door.

"Yes?" she called. "Who's there?"

"It's me, Kate," Nick said. "I'd like to talk to you."

A long silence ensued.

"Please, Kate, let me in."

"All right," she agreed. "Yes, just a minute."

She quickly put the mask back into its case and shoved her sketchbook in the desk drawer.

She opened the door and he entered the room, taking in all that was around him: the bed with its floral stitched counterpane, a doll's house set in the corner, the child's rocking chair. It seemed to him that Kate had run from him into the security of her childhood, and he was sorry to have hurt her by being so insensitive.

"Our guests are waiting, and I wish to apologize," he began. "I suppose I have been preoccupied of late, too preoccupied to sense your feelings, and for that I am truly sorry."

The words had come out so stiff and formal that he might have laughed at himself, but the knot that had been in his stomach earlier returned to plague him.

"I shall rent a house in Luxor for you, if it can be done, and as her brother will be accompanying us, perhaps Daphne will agree to come along and offer you some companionship."

Kate wished that it did not seem so much like he were humoring a petulant child. "I shan't be a bother to anyone," she promised, but there was a hard edge to her voice.

"I know that you won't, Kate, and I'll be glad of your company. You must believe that, from the first, my primary concern has been your well-being."

His words struck her as pretty, not indicative of his true feelings, but she remained silent about her feeling.

Nick met her eyes. He had expected them to be red from crying, but they were not. They were cold and clear, like deep water, and in them was nothing but reproach.

After their guests left, she did not return to him that night, nor the night after.

———————

As he studied the map and focused on one of the obscure gorges that stretched out like so many fingers in the Valley of the Kings, Nick decided to concentrate his efforts in the western valley. To have reached a decision relieved him somewhat. He slid the professor's maps back into their leather portfolio and went to the window for a breath of air.

The scent of spring flowers hung on the breeze. Just across the lawn, Kate was tending her roses. With her shears, she cut a single white rose, of the same type she had tossed on his grandfather's grave. Could a year have passed so quickly? In spite of their current troubles, she still had the power to bewitch him. He watched her delicately add the rose to the bouquet in her basket, her lavender gown frothing around her in the grass where she knelt. He followed the line of one bared white arm to the graceful arch of her neck, where fluttered the ribbons of her straw bonnet. She looked so deceptively feminine, so unlike the little hellion he was becoming accustomed to. Why, he asked himself, did she feel compelled to make herself over into the son her father had always wanted, even now after his death?

Nick closed his eyes and tried to deny the ache in his loins. It had been an insufferable week. Kate had made excuses and avoided him most of that time, her eyes silently accusing him. Somehow she'd managed to rise very early each morning, even before the servants, and to retire well after they had gone to bed so that no one would guess she'd been sleeping apart from her husband. Nick, though, was very much aware of her absence. He missed her perfumed body, her velvet embrace. She needed time, he told himself. She had every right to be angry, but he had acquiesced, hadn't he? She was coming with him to Egypt, after all. And so he would wait for her return, doing his silent penance, but for how much longer he could not say, for his patience was wearing thin.

There was a small consolation to be had in this rift, one that Nick was a little ashamed to admit. Now he was free to formulate his plans without feeling guilty for spending the time away from her. If his work in Egypt was to succeed, he needed to give himself totally to the work, without distraction, and in this respect, Kate was a major distraction.

With a long sigh, he gathered up the portfolio and carried it into the trophy room, returning it to its proper place on the bookshelf. Though he had been in this room hundreds of times, he always found himself admiring anew the professor's treasures, which now belonged to him. How much greater the pleasure would be, though, if Nick could have discovered them himself.

His eyes suddenly rested on an alabaster piece

beside a pair of unguent jars. It was a lotus cup, like the one—

Incensed, he snatched it up and strode into the front hall, where he found Kate arranging her flowers in a vase. Loosened tendrils of golden hair framed her face, which was flushed pink from the sun.

"Are we to be forever at crossed purposes?" he said. "I'm not accustomed to having my orders disobeyed."

Her eyes flashed. "Orders?" she repeated, raising one brow.

He waved the goblet before her, as though he might smash it to the floor. When Kate was certain he would not, she replied, unpleasantly "If I am to be treated as a child, then you might not act so surprised when I behave as one."

"Keep the goblet if it pleases you," Nick said with a shrug of his shoulders and set it on the table beside the vase. "Only do not expect to discuss with me from whence it came. As far as I am concerned, the man does not exist."

His insouciance clearly annoyed her. "I should be hard put to discuss anything with you, sir!" she shot back.

A smile curved into Nick's lips. As he watched sparks shoot from the depths of her eyes, and her bosom rise and fall with the exhilaration of battle, he realized that he liked this hellcat far more than the bland, feminine creature in the garden. In one swift move, he hooked her waist with his long arm and drew her into an embrace, his lips crushing hers. He was drunk with passion and when she did not resist, he pulled her full against him, his free hand caress-

95

ing her thigh through her skirts. He would have swept her upstairs and taken what was rightfully his, but in that instant Kate regained her senses. Her eyes were wide, and pressing her palms against his chest, she pushed herself out of his grasp and ran to the staircase, putting the balustrade between them.

His hard laugh cut the air. He stepped back and rested against the doorjamb. "So sure of your charms, my dear?" he asked in a cold voice, and then turned and strode back into the study. At the frenzied padding of her footsteps above, and the shuddering slam of her bedroom door, Nick's eyes closed and his brow creased in pain. Damn! He could tell that she had wanted him as badly as he wanted her, yet she had pushed him away with fear in her eyes. What was she so afraid of?

———————

After Kate had swung the door shut, she pressed her full weight against it, as though the devil himself were at her heels. A sob caught at the back of her throat as she slumped to the floor, her head buried in her arms.

She had brought all of this on herself, she thought; she was behaving like a child. She missed him so, all their pleasant conversations and their lovemaking at night. If only she could have been more understanding instead of giving vent to her anger, they might not now be leading separate lives under the same roof, and he mightn't have come to hate her so much. It was too late to take back all that had been said, and pride stood between them as much as angry words.

Kate pulled herself up off the floor, wondering if she would ever be rid of the ache in her heart. Without warning, Nick suddenly swung the door open.

"I'm not going to let you run away from me again," he said, standing firm in the doorway.

She met his determined stare and found herself unable to look away. "I'm a tolerant man," he told her, "I am, but—"

Kate could sense his frustration as he lowered his head, trying to form his thoughts into words. "Listen to me, Kate," he said, regarding her earnestly. "No, don't speak, just listen. Before you came into my life, nothing could touch me. Now here you are, damn you, able to cut me to the quick with no more than a glance, and do you know why? It's because I care for you, perhaps too much for my own good. You do believe me, don't you?"

"I—I suppose I do. I just don't know, Nick. We seem to say such hateful things to one another."

"They say that love and hate are closely connected, too close for any sort of consistency or continuous comfort. I only wish you could trust me enough to share your thoughts, but I see in your eyes that you don't. You've shut me out. Why, Kate?"

Confronted with her husband's honesty, Kate felt quite suddenly ashamed. Had she expected too much and given too little?

"I've stood on my own for a long time," she tried to explain. "Even though my father loved me very much, I learned early on exactly where I fit into his life. I couldn't really rely on him because sooner or later he'd be off on another expedition. Sometimes he'd be away for years. I missed him terribly, but I

97

learned to get by. Now you've swept into my life, promising to be the same type of man. How can I trust you?"

Nick came to her, resting his hands on her shoulders. "Sometimes you must believe what your heart tells you," he said as he lowered his lips onto hers.

CHAPTER VII

*B*y mid-July, when the Society expedition was about to depart, Kate was certain that she was carrying Nick's child. She prudently chose to keep the news to herself, for if Nick were to discover her condition, he would put a swift end to all her travel plans.

It was just before noon when the carriage deposited the two couples on the pier. They were immediately caught up in the confusion. The pier was a tangle of vehicles, passengers and those bidding farewell to the travellers. Nick put a reassuring arm around Kate and ushered her toward the gangway, glancing back to be make sure that Eric and Daphne had not been overwhelmed by the crowd. Trunks and valises were piled high on the deck. As the group boarded, Mr. Thayer waved from the rail. He would be travelling with them, as would Ahmad, who had arrived early to see to their luggage.

Kate was hardly able to contain her excitement, but managed to so as not to distract Nick from his last-minute preparations. They had been getting along quite well lately, but she had begun to feel a little weak, no doubt due to the child growing within her. She was happy to be carrying Nick's child, and so happy to be going to Egypt at last, that she vowed she would be the kind of wife he wanted, no matter how difficult it was for her.

After checking their accommodations, Kate and Nick went into the saloon, where most of the other travellers had gathered. Its size was impressive, some sixty feet, filled to capacity with tables and comfortable chairs. Several deeply unholstered settées had been placed against the wall lined with windows, the draperies drawn so that the guests could enjoy the view.

Kate and Nick spied their little group at one of the tables. As they walked over, Kate noticed that each of them was holding a glass of champagne.

"Ah, our gallant leader," Eric said. raising his glass as Kate and Nick approached, "and his lovely wife."

Nick's heavy brow raised slightly. "Champagne? What an auspicious beginning for our little expedition."

Mr. Thayer pressed two glasses into Nick's hands and promptly filled them. Nick handed one to Kate.

"We shall toast to the success of our expedition, of course," Eric began. "But first I think we should toast the good fortune of my friend, Nick Hammonton, who has this past week been offered a professorship at our own Creighton University. To Professor Hammonton."

He raised up his glass and the others followed suit. Kate's hands were shaking. This was the first she'd heard of such an appointment, and she hoped that her surprise was not too apparent. She tried to catch Nick's eye, but he persisted in staring into his glass, smiling at all the attention he was receiving.

"Congratulations to you," Mr. Thayer offered, "though I can't say this was entirely unexpected. Professor Wrightwood had been grooming you to fill his shoes."

Kate felt suddenly ill, though whether it was due to her condition or to what she had just heard she could not say.

"I hope I can achieve what he expected of me," Nick said.

"You must be proud of your husband," Daphne said to Kate. "Society director and now a professor as well."

The question drew Kate out of her thoughts. "Oh . . . yes, I suppose I must be."

It was an odd reply at best. Setting down her glass, Kate said to the group, "If you will excuse me, I think I'd like to go and lie down for a while. All of the excitement has left me feeling somewhat out-of-sorts."

"If I can be of help—" Eric began, but Kate cut him off.

"Thank you, no, Doctor. A few hours' rest will be just the tonic, I think."

He offered her a generous smile and turned his attention to Nick. "My friend, you must instruct your wife to use my Christian name, as we are all but family. If she persists in calling me Doctor, then I shall feel obliged to call you Professor, and heaven knows that this ship carries ballast enough without having to transport our surfeit of titles. Do I make my case, Professor Hammonton?"

"Yes," Nick replied, amused, "and in your indomitably eloquent style, Doctor Latham."

Nick turned to see if Kate had shared in their little amusement, only to find her gone.

———

Without a backward glance, Kate pushed through the doors and went out on deck. There was a great clanging of machinery and rumble of engines, and then the hissing of steam as the call came to cast off. Many passengers lined the rail, waving a last goodbye to those on shore. She walked blindly past them to the taffrail and stood there alone, watching the black water lap at the hull of the ship.

She ought to have been proud of her husband, Kate reflected, the way any good wife would. Yet resentment welled deep within her, despite all of her good intentions.

———

It was ten days' run from New York to the Azore Islands, where the ship stopped for respite, and yet another seven to Marseilles. Throughout that time, Kate was not spared a day from morning, as well as sea sickness. After the first several days, Nick lost all patience and pronounced that she must doubtless be the worst sailor ever to have crossed the seas. He offered her no words of comfort, which Kate found inexcusable, even though she admitted he might have been different if he had known she was carrying a child.

Throughout the trip she ate only tea and toast, which she consumed in the early afternoon after she had recovered sufficiently. These afternoons she spent with Daphne, in the lee of the paddlebox, were pleasant enough when passed in idle conversation, but when Daphne insisted upon introducing her to patience work of counted cross-stitches, Kate pricked her fingers enough times so as to leave more blood on the cloth than floss. Having proved herself a failure at more genteel pursuits, Kate sought out the gentlemen in the saloon, where they gathered each evening to discuss the work to be done at Thebes, but her arrival always seemed to silence all important discussions.

Kate thus spent many hours in her own company, examining her sketches of the Isis mask and consulting her father's reference books to help her decipher the hieroglyphs. By the time the ship reached Marseilles, Kate had ascertained, through a tedious process of trial and error, that the woman was a priestess in the temple of Isis.

Kate was pleased with her accomplishment, but it was tempered by the fact that she had decided not to share it with Nick.

On the evening the ship dropped anchor in Marseilles, Nick finally spoke to Kate of his plans as he began to dress for dinner. She had just begun packing away her sketchpad and books.

"What's that you're reading?" He asked in a more felicitious tone than he had been using of late.

"Only one of my father's books," she replied carefully and thrust it into her trunk, quickly closing the lid. "I've botched the sampler Daphne started me on and as I am not welcome at your gentlemen's discussions in the saloon, I needed something to pass the time."

With his back to her, Nick unbuttoned his shirt and tossed it over the chair. "We have been neglecting you, haven't we?"

Kate was startled at the sudden warmth in his manner.

"I'm sorry, Kate," he said, while he continued to dress. "There are so many details to work out before we reach Luxor. Eric and Mr. Thayer will be in charge of some fifty men each, and while they have the best intentions, both have only a minimum of experience. I must be sure that they understand what is expected of them."

"Of course," she said softly. "I gave you my word that I'd not be a bother, but I fear I've failed miserably."

He came over to her and patted her hand. "You can't be blamed for seasickness. I've been positively churlish, I know. This whole expedition has begun to seem like an enormous wager in which all that I have—all that I want—hangs in the balance. I'm not by nature a gambling man, Kate."

"I feel certain that luck is on our side. You'll see. When we reach Egypt things won't seem as desperate as they do now."

He smiled at her assurances. She considered how handsome he looked in his white tie and waistcoat.

"I have to go to Paris," he said all at once, "to see Henri Berteau. He's a colleague of mine who has been handling our arrangements with Mariette and the khedive. The others will stay here in Marseille while I'm away."

He paused a moment and studied her face. "I was hoping you'd come to Paris with me, Kate. I've sent word to Berteau, and he's invited us to stay at his house in the city. We've never had a proper honeymoon, and I thought you might like to see the International Exposition. Mariette himself set up the Egyptian exhibit. It's been made to look like a temple, and I understand that they've put Queen Aahhotep's jewelry on display. Of course, if you would rather remain here with the others, I will understand."

"Oh Nick! I would love to see Paris," Kate exclaimed.

"Good," Nick said. "We shall leave in the morning."

———

It was five hundred miles by rail to Paris, and it was, by and large, a silent journey, for both Nick and Kate feared that any wrong word might abruptly end their uneasy truce. Nick plodded through a French newspaper, pretending to comprehend all that he read, yet only translating the half of it, while Kate looked out of the window, admiring the perfection that was the the French countryside.

The train drew into Paris as the sun disappeared over the horizon. Monsieur Berteau was waiting for them at the station, and the three climbed into his barouche while Berteau's man packed their trunks. As they sped along the boulevards they took in the sights of Paris after dark. People out for an evening's pleasure sat at small tables in outdoor cafés, sipping wine and coffee. Gaslight illuminated rows of shops and sidewalks.

"This is your first visit to our city, Madame Hammonton?" Monsieur Berteau asked in his heavily accented English.

"Yes," Kate told him.

"Then we shall show you Paris at her best. The city is truly international now. People from all over the world have come to see the Exposition. For this the emperor has commanded that we all, how do you say it, put on our best faces."

He smiled at her. Henri Berteau was a short man with dark features, a moustache à l'impérial and eyes that seemed to miss nothing. Nick had told her that he was a dealer in antiquities but did not elaborate, which left her to speculate as to the nature of his "dealings." Kate lowered her eyes, wondering if all Frenchman had so bold a gaze.

Monsieur Berteau's home on the Boulevard St. Germain was a venerable edifice. The appointments were of heavy, dark wood and leather, the hangings of rich velvet. The place reminded Kate of a library, even down to its musty odor, the type acquired only by books and houses that have aged sufficiently.

Nick and Kate were supplied with adjoining rooms and left to dress for dinner. Kate was surprised to find her room decidedly feminine, the furniture painted white with gilt and the carpets, counterpane and draperies in patterns of the palest green. The room was a breath of fresh air in an otherwise somber house. She was surprised as well to discover that Monsieur Berteau had put at her disposal the services of Marie, a ladies' maid. Although Kate was not accustomed to such attention, and would normally have found such a presence intrusive, she quickly realized that she liked Marie, regarding her as quite sensible. Marie told her that no lady in Paris would think of being without her maid. Why, who would dress her hair? Who would lace her stays and see to her gown?

Marie took stock of Kate's simple apparel and appearance. Kate knew that by Parisian standards, her appearance left much to be desired. Against her better judgment, she decided to accept the hospitality of the house and Marie's ministrations.

Kate had just settled into a hot bath when there was a short knock on the door, and Nick, in his evening clothes, swept in. A smile twisted beneath his moustache when he saw Kate reclining in the tub. His eyes lingered over her. Kate met his gaze and did not move to cover herself.

"Was there something you wanted?" she asked.

Nick gave a throaty chuckle. "Not that can be discussed at present."

On the opposite side of the room, Marie went about the business of unpacking Kate's trunk, seemingly oblivious to their exchange.

Nick cleared his throat and thrusting his hands into the pockets of his trousers, began again. "Henri has informed me that we shall be dining out this evening. There is to be a reception at the Hôtel de Ville, hosted by the Sorbonne for scholars visiting the Exposition."

Kate sighed. She had hoped for some time alone with him, but said instead, "We have arrived at an opportune time for you, then."

"Yes, indeed. Henri tells me that Professor Klein from the University of Berlin is in town. He's doing some very vital work on transcription of papyri texts."

Kate smiled at his enthusiasm.

"So hurry and dress," he said.

From across the room the clucking of Marie's tongue drew their attention. She had laid out Kate's blue watered silk dress on the bed and was looking at it disparagingly, arms folded over her chest.

"Something troubles you, Marie?" Kate wondered, raising herself up.

"*Excusez-moi, s'il vous plaît, madame.* This will not do."

Nick turned his attention to the maid. "Are you trying to tell us that you do not approve of my wife's wardrobe, Marie?"

The girl blanched under Nick's scrutiny and bobbed a curtesy. "*Pardon, monsieur, mille fois pardon,* but in Paris the ladies are like so many colorful butterflies, each more exquisite than the next."

"And you feel that madame could benefit from the experience of a French dressmaker?"

Marie nodded vigorously, the lace cap atop her dark curls threatening to come loose from its perch. "*Certainement.* Here we have the greatest courtiers."

"I'll not argue that," Nick said. "We shall certainly see to it that my wife is fitted out in proper form, but for tonight this gown will have to do."

"Of course it shall do," Kate chimed in.

She stood up and Nick brought her a towel and wrapped her in it. There was a pleasant warmth where his fingers touched her damp skin, and Kate drew a sharp breath in response.

"While we lead a comfortable enough life," she told him, when she had found her voice again, "we haven't the funds to be wasted on such overpriced fripperies. I assure you, I shall not miss them in the least."

"All the young ladies come home with a Paris gown, it's the thing to do, and you may feel differently before the evening is out. I hear that these Parisian affairs are full of pageantry," Nick told her.

"Well, I've no taste for it, I can tell you that."

Kate dropped her towel and slipped her chemise over her head, then sat down at the vanity table to brush out her hair. "All in all, it's just a lot of simpering misses with empty heads, parading themselves in their jewelry and laces before a lot of wealthy, idle gentlemen who, on the whole, have not a whit to say worth hearing. It's not for me, thank you."

Nick came to stand behind her and kissed the top of her head. "What a cynical view of things you have, Kate. I worry you may be too practical."

Just then Marie cleared her throat to draw their attention. The girl held before her an evening gown she had taken from the wardrobe. It was of rose satin with a veiling of point lace. "*Madame, monsieur voilà!* Is it not beautiful? It belongs to Monsieur Berteau's sister and was left behind. She would not think of wearing it again."

Kate had to admit that it was a pretty piece of work. "I couldn't—" she protested.

"Just a few stitches here and there," Marie said. "I have my needle here."

Nick moved to the door. "I shall leave you then. Henri and I will be in the study. He has some new acquisitions he's anxious to show me."

He stepped back into his own room, and shutting the door behind him, leaned back against it, wiping away the film of perspiration from his forehead. The sight of Kate lounging in her bath had pushed his self-control to the limit. Damnation! He should have dismissed the maid and taken her right there. He could not say that she would have denied him. Her eyes told him that she was willing. What perversity in his character made him keep her at a distance?

He went to the writing table, and poured himself an ample glass of brandy from a decanter. His maps were spread out on the table, and he let his eyes be drawn to the sinuous blue line that ran the length of Egypt. Here was his mistress, the Nile, and if he were not faithful to her, she might not deign to give up her secrets to him. He then had one more glass of brandy to soothe his nerves before going downstairs to see what new treasure Henri had stolen for himself.

CHAPTER VIII

Kate tried especially hard not to be pleased with Marie's efforts, but in barely two hours' time the maid had altered the gown to Kate's figure, helped her into it and dressed her hair. The effects were startling. Kate had always thought herself plain, at best, but this Parisian maid had wrought a miracle. There, staring back from the cheval glass, was elegance personified. Her hair shone like burnished gold in the gaslight. It had been worked in dozens of tiny plaits, each weaved intricately in place at the back of her head. At first Kate had protested that the corsage of the gown was too low, but Marie had remained adamant; indeed, it had the effect of softening her shoulders and accentuating the graceful arch of her neck, as well as pearls that rested in the hollow of her throat. Marie handed her a lace fan and said, "*Voilà, madame. C'est tout.*"

Kate thanked her profusely and ran downstairs to show Nick. She tried to remind herself that one should not get carried away with mere physical appearance, but all to no avail. When she slid the study doors open, both men were dumbfounded. Nick was particularly struck by the change. Was this truly his Kate? She looked like a gemstone that had been cut and polished to dazzling brilliance. Berteau did not hesitate and rushed forward to take up Kate's gloved hand to kiss it.

"Ah, madame, tomorrow all Paris will be talking of *la belle américaine,* but only I am so honored as to have you as my guest."

Nick squared his jaw, and the lines in his brow creased deeper as he watched Berteau fuss over Kate. He did not like the way the Frenchman's eyes assessed every feature of her anatomy. Berteau was a dealer in antiquities, but a collector as well, one who felt compelled to possess everything that caught his eye. Nick wondered if that compulsion extended to women as well. At least Kate had the good sense not to have her head turned by such foolishness.

But a blush stained Kate's cheeks at the man's compliment, and she thanked him for his kindness. Nick's dark features took on an unpleasant scowl.

Berteau was not anxious to release her hand, but Kate withdrew it gently and retreated to the foyer, where Marie helped her into her wrap.

As the two men moved to follow her, Berteau said to Nick, under his breath, "Ah, *mon ami, ce petite chatte est très jolie* . . . delicious creature. If she were not your wife—"

"You're right on one score, Henri. She is a cat, and she'd have her claws in your throat before you'd realized it," Nick replied. His voice was cold, but he was smiling.

"*Mais non, certainement pas*," Berteau disagreed, "for I should certainly fare as well as you and you bear no scars of battle."

Nick moved to capture his wife's arm before his colleague could best him again. "None that you can see," he said over his shoulder.

———————

In the ballroom of the Hôtel de Ville that evening, Kate's senses were particularly acute, as she took in all the color and spectacle of the event. The heat felt stifling to her, even though all the windows had been thrown open. The animated conversations of the thousand guests seemed discordant and harsh on her ear, and the combined scents of the floral decorations and the many different perfumes the women wore hung in the air with a cloying sweetness that left her dizzy.

Nick kept a firm grasp on her arm while Berteau made the round of introductions, as if he thought she might run off. She was, in fact, gratefuul for his attention, as she could rest against his shoulder until her lightheadedness passed.

Dinner was superb, providing the haute cuisine expected of French chefs. And the evening did not prove to be the shallow affair that Kate had anticipated, at least for the men. She heard the most engaging snippets of conversation between the scholars, and scientists and writers in attendance. But she was not encouraged to take part in these conversations, but was viewed as a beautiful ornament, to grace her husband's arm. While Nick's comments were given the utmost consideration, and his wit and eloquence praised, any point she wished to make was looked upon with all the regard one might show a precocious child. By evening's end, she felt as though she had received enough verbal pats on the head to shorten her height by two inches at least.

During the latter part of the evening, Nick's meeting with Professor Klein was arranged, and he and Henri Berteau adjourned to one of the anterooms provided by the establishment. The gentlemen had insisted that Kate would be bored by their discussions and would brook no argument, leaving her on a divan in one corner of the ballroom.

With no company but the potted plant that arched gracefully beside her, Kate found her anger fermenting. She snapped her wrist to open her fan and waved it at a furious pace. Boredom, indeed! Was she meant to be entertained here alone in the corner, watching the crowd? So absorbed was she in these thoughts that she did not notice the gentleman who had sat down beside her until he spoke.

"Pardon me. You are Mrs. Hammonton, are you not?"

Kate turned to him. He was an elderly English gentleman, with broad shoulders and possessed of strong features. He was bald but for a bit of silver over each ear. She smiled politely and nodded, then turned her attention back to the dance floor.

"I understand that your husband recently received an appointment, a directorship—" the man continued.

"Yes," Kate replied, her voice weary. "He is directing the operation of an American foundation, the Society for the Preservation of Antiquities and will shortly conduct an expedition to Egypt."

The man nodded slowly. "He has done well," he said almost to himself.

There was a contracted pause and while Kate again looked out over the dance floor, she could sense the man studying her. "You will accompany your husband to Egypt?" he asked.

"Yes. I am very much interested in Egyptology."

Kate expected yet another pat on the head, but instead the man took on a thoughtful expression. "Ah, yes," he said. "Your father was Elias Wrightwood, wasn't he?"

Kate regarded him with surprise. "Why yes, but how could you know?"

"I, too, have an interest in Egyptology," he explained. "I've been involved in a few expeditions, purely as an amateur, of course. My contributions were, for the most part, monetary, but I have heard of your father."

Kate focused her full attention on him. He seemed an avuncular sort of gentleman, and there was something vaguely familiar about him. She realized then that he had not introduced himself. "Is it possible that we have met before, sir?" she asked, hoping to prompt him into an introduction.

"Hardly likely," he replied looking just a trifle flustered.

He stood up then and cleared his throat. "Mrs. Hammonton, I wonder if you would do an old man a great honor by allowing him to dance with the most lovely lady here this evening."

The color rose in Kate's face and her head

dropped shyly. "Thank you," she said, deciding that she liked this man even if she did not know his name.

She offered her hand, and he led her onto the floor as the orchestra struck up a waltz. He was an accomplished dancer, not hindered in the least by his age. Had Kate closed her eyes for a moment, she would have believed that she was dancing with her husband.

There was little chance for conversation while they danced, but Kate was aware that he was looking closely at her and smiling contentedly. When the dance was over, he led her back to her corner, still without offering his name, and disappeared into the crowd.

———————

It was late before Nick's meeting was concluded, but the festivities showed no signs of abating. Kate did not dance again, though she was asked a number of times. Nick finally came to retrieve her.

"Henri still has some business to attend to," Nick explained, "but he's told me to take the barouche and send the driver back for him."

He did not speak again until they were seated in the carriage and he breathed a heavy sigh. "This was a torturous evening!"

"What?" Kate exclaimed. "You've had your meeting with Professor Klein, and I daresay you've made a favorable impression on the intelligentsia of Paris, if not the world. What more can you ask?"

"You can't expect a man to be unaffected when every Frenchman in the room is leering at his wife."

Kate's eyes sought out of the tips of her shoes.

"Surely not. I found each of the ladies there more elegant than the last, exquisitely garbed and polished of manner. If not for Marie's ministrations, I should have been no more than a poor relation by comparison."

Nick caught her chin in his hand and turned her face up to his. His expression was serious. "You underestimate yourself, Kate. True refinement cannot be bought with a few yards of lace, nor true beauty obscured by the lack of it. Tonight was your triumph. Berteau was right. Tomorrow all Paris will be talking of *la belle américaine*.

His hand slid onto her bare shoulder and caressed it. Kate tried to deny the warmth that coursed through her body at his touch. It made her weak and muddled her thinking. "I was not truly listened to the whole of the evening," she told him, fighting against the pleasant feeling that threatened to splinter her thoughts into disjointed gibberish. "I might have been a china doll on your arm, Nick. Am I expected to be pleased that these people were captivated by what they saw rather than who I am?"

"Alas, Kate, the world, on the whole, appreciates clever women considerably less than beautiful ones. I am, indeed, a fortunate man to have a wife who is both."

Nick was nothing if not a diplomatic man, and his plain assessment of things quelled her ire. She could not help but wonder, though, if this was just another of his pretty remarks.

Suddenly he reached for her, his lips brushing over hers, his eyes looking deeply into hers. Kate's breath was caught in her throat, the sound vibrating in the still night air. There was no denying that he made her weak. It was frightening to lose so much of herself to him, yet she gave over completely. They met in an urgent embrace and clung to one another until the need for breath drew them apart.

When at last they reached Berteau's house, Kate rushed up to her room. Marie took her wrap and began to unplait her hair, asking her about the evening's events. Soon Nick's tall frame appeared in the doorway.

"You may go now, Marie," he said. "Mrs. Hammonton will not be needing you again this evening."

"Oui, monsieur," she replied, with a wry smile only Kate could see.

Nick shut the door behind her. He tossed his jacket on the chair while Kate removed her gloves and laid them on the bureau. Nick came up from behind and breathed a hot kiss against the nape of her neck as he began to unhook her gown. His long fingers were a bit clumsy but persistent, and before long Kate had sloughed off the gown and her crinolines as well.

"You've no need of a fancy French maid so long as I'm on hand," Nick said and Kate laughed.

"No doubt your fingers are numb from the effort."

He waggled them over her shoulder so she could see them in the mirror. "Nimble as ever," he insisted.

As he went to work on her lacing, a chill came over her as she thought he might now notice the physical changes in her body. Perhaps she should tell him now, she thought, but she wished to savor these moments and not risk being packed off to New York in the morning.

Kate slipped off her shoes, and perching one foot at a time on the chair, unrolled her silk stockings, ever aware of his eyes upon her.

Free of her stays and with only a thin chemise to hide her charms, Kate held her breath and turned to face Nick. She was not aware of the fetching picture she presented, and apparently he did not notice the as-yet subtle changes in her.

"You were lovely this evening in your borrowed finery, Kate. I think I shall buy you a trunkful of French gowns."

Kate went over to him and began undressing him. She reached up to unknot the white lawn tie.

"While I'll admit that I was mesmerized by that fancy woman in the mirror at first, she grew quite tiresome by evening's end," she told him.

She unfastened his waistcoat and removed the studs from his shirt, one at a time.

"Whatever do you mean?" Nick asked, wondering why Kate felt the need to separate herself from the elegantly dressed woman she had just been.

"She was so 'lovely,' if I may borrow your word, that everyone's eyes were on her and no one heard a word she had to say."

Kate loosened his watch and chain from his waistcoat pocket. She carried them, and his shirt studs, to the bureau, depositing them in a neat pile.

When she turned back to him, Nick was slipping off his shirt and laughing at her slightly unbalanced logic.

"I'll wager, though, Mrs. Hammonton, that while I was closeted with Henri and Professor Klein, *la belle américaine* did not lack for dancing partners."

"Oh, she had offers enough, but I kept her from making a spectacle of herself. I, for one, was exhausted."

"And so you—er, excuse me, she—did not dance all evening?"

"There was one elderly gentleman that, for courtesy's sake, I—she—could not refuse."

Nick turned a skeptical eye on her. "One elderly gentleman, eh?"

He caught her with one long arm and pulled her full against him. "I've changed my mind," he told her. "No trunkful of French gowns for you. I don't think I want *la belle américaine* intruding on our lives."

Now it was Kate's turn to laugh. It was a melodic sound, light and full of joy, for Nick had chosen her over the woman in the borrowed French gown.

CHAPTER IX

Kate awoke the next morning to a sharp rap at her door and was surprised to find herself still in the cradle of Nick's arm. She eased herself up slowly so as not to awaken him, and pulled the bedclothes to her breast, just as the maid swept in.

"*C'est Marie, madame,*" the girl called.

She was struggling with an enormous rococo vase filled with elegant white iris, vivid red poppies and golden spikes of lupine.

"These came for you this morning, madame," Marie said, as she set the arrangement on a table by the windows. When she turned around and saw Nick asleep, she flushed.

"*Pardon, madame.* I did not know that monsieur—you will please ring if you require anything."

She turned to leave but Kate called out. "Marie, was there no card with the flowers?"

"No, madame," she said as she ran out.

Kate looked down at her husband, assuming the flowers were from him. She leaned down to kiss him and he slowly awoke. After a few moments he sat up and took stock of the bouquet.

"Flowers from an admirer of *la belle américaine*?"

Kate could not say that she was pleased with his tone of voice.

"I thought we'd exorcized her from the house last night," came her reply. "There was no card, but it occurred to me that perhaps my thoughtful husband—"

"If I'd known it was your wish, I'd have seen to it that you had a roomful. Alas, I cannot claim the credit for sending these."

Kate frowned.

"Don't tax yourself, my dear," Nick told her with a smile. "These Frenchmen are effusive by nature." Then he added, "So I shall have to keep my eye on you."

But something in Nick's tone led Kate to believe that this had not been said entirely in jest. If it would have mattered, she'd have thrown the entire bouquet, every leaf and petal, out of the window. But she still would not have known who had sent them.

———

Kate and Nick visited the Exposition all day, but they might have stayed an entire week and still not have seen everything. Within the elliptical structure that had been erected on the Champs de Mars were more than fifty thousand exhibitors from all over the world, displaying the latest achievements in industry and science, and in fashion and the arts.

Kate and Nick marvelled at the exhibits, which included an enormous model of a Siamese elephant, relief maps of the work being done on the Suez Canal and a machine that produced felt hats at an unbelievable rate. They danced a few waltzes conducted by Johann Strauss himself and dined in a restaurant styled after a Spanish café.

But they were most interested in the Egyptian pavilion, which purported to reconstruct certain aspects of life in the ancient civilization. Nick told Kate that the exhibit contained some of the finest pieces from the antiquities collection at Bulak. The pieces were so impressive that the pair was now more anxious than ever to quit Paris and be on to Egypt.

While they strolled between the "Turkish Mosque" and the "Palace of the Pasha of Egypt," an elderly gentleman crossed their path. Kate recognized him immediately: He was the man she had danced with at the Hôtel de Ville, but before she could say anything, Nick's grip on her arm tightened and he abruptly changed direction. Kate saw the wistful expression on the man's face as Nick propelled her away. She might have asked for an explanation immediately, and had fully intended to do so, until she saw the murderous glint in Nick's eye. The question died on her lips.

Kate passed an uneasy night. It was pleasant enough to enjoy her husband's embrace once again, but since the encounter with the man at the Exposition, Nick had turned sullen. She wished now that she had asked the man's identity when she had had the opportunity. As she thought on it further, she realized that this man had known quite a bit about Nick and herself, more than an ordinary stranger. Who was he, and why had the sight of him so upset Nick?

The following morning Kate arose to find him poring over his maps and making notes. She was thankful that they had only one day left in Paris. Nick needed to be at his work in Egypt, the sooner the better.

After lunch, Nick and Monsieur Berteau went off to visit a colleague who had been digging in the Valley of the Kings last season. Instead of going shopping as Nick had suggested, Kate decided to explore Monsieur Berteau's library. As she might have expected, there were a good many archaeological volumes, but they were in French and she had to struggle with the translation. She went on perusing the shelves until a long Brussels tapestry at the far end of the room caught her eye. It depicted a hunting scene, in reds and golds, nothing at all unusual in that, but the reason for its placement was to conceal a door. Curious, Kate pushed aside the tapestry and tried the knob. To her surprise, it twisted easily, and she pushed the door open.

She stepped into a small anteroom that appeared to be entirely without windows. She could make out only vague shapes in the darkness and so went back into the library, where she found a candlestick and matches on the mantel. With the candle's cheery flame to light her way, she reentered the little room and gasped as the yellow light flickered and danced, illuminating a room full of Egyptian gold.

Professor Wrightwood's trophy room was filled with mere trifles in comparison with this collection of Monsieur Berteau's. The pieces in this room had been selected for their aesthetic rather than scientific value. There was a long glass case of jewelry: a gold collar necklace set with turquoise and carnelian, several golden pendants and diadems and a pectoral in the shape of a shrine, depicting the divine mourners supporting a scarab. There was a pair of gold-handled mirrors and a perfume box inlaid with amethyst, jasper and lapis lazuli. In yet another case, she saw half a dozen golden statues of the gods and several beautiful vessels of electrum.

It was a breathtaking display of treasure, and Kate wondered if the pieces belonged to Monsieur Berteau or if he was just storing them here temporarily, until he could find buyers for them. Kate admired the items for some time until she heard Marie calling her.

"Où êtes-vous, madame?"

"I'm here, Marie ," Kate called back as she went into the library to meet her. The woman did not seem pleased that Kate had discovered the secret room behind the tapestry.

"I was only admiring the treasures," Kate explained. "I hope monsieur won't mind."

"Mon Dieu!" the woman exclaimed. "This door, it should have been locked. It must be locked always. I must have forgotten after my cleaning this morning."

She was clearly distraught and regarded Kate cautiously.

"I'm sorry," Kate said. "I did not mean to trespass, I was curious—"

The woman forced a smile. "Surely monsieur would not mind that you have seen the treasure."

"Treasure?" Kate echoed. "Ah, but I cannot have seen the treasure, for you did not forget to lock the door, n'est-ce pas?

The housekeeper stared at her for a moment, sighing relief when she understood what Kate was implying. She found the key on her chatelaine and locked the door behind the tapestry.

"Merci, madame," she said, and then whispered, "C'est merveilleux, non?"

"Marvelous, indeed," Kate agreed.

"But I am forgetting, madame, there is a gentleman who wishes to see you. I have put him in the salon."

"A gentleman, you say? Thank you," Kate replied.

As she crossed the hall to the salon, her thoughts turned to the flowers that had been delivered this morning. Perhaps the gentleman waiting had sent them? Upon entering the parlor, she was handed another bouquet, this one of white roses.

"I understand that these are your favorites," said the elderly English gentleman.

"Why, yes," Kate replied. "But how could you know?"

"I know a great many things about you, Mrs. Hammonton," he responded, and Kate looked more puzzled than ever.

"I realized when I saw you yesterday at the fair

that I owed you some explanation. Come, let's sit down, and I shall answer all of your questions."

He led her to the sofa, and she settled onto it, with her bouquet in her lap.

"To begin," he said, pacing before her as if to collect his thoughts, "let me introduce myself, which I should have done at the first. I confess I was afraid that you would shut me out and—well, no matter." He turned and sat down beside her.

"I am Peter Hammonton."

"Why, then, you are my husband's relative," Kate said.

"I am his father."

The shock was plainly visible on Kate's face.

"That cannot be. My husband has never mentioned—I understood that all of his family was—"

"I am not surprised that my son has neglected to mention me to you. We have not been on the best terms these many years."

"Why?" she wondered aloud.

He sighed. "That's more of a question than I can answer. I must shoulder much of the blame for this estrangement, I'm afraid."

He stared at the fold of his well-formed hands for a long while, as if carefully weighing his words. Kate studied him. He was quite dignified, with a stern, almost harsh profile and sharp jaw that, as she looked at it, reminded her of Nick's. When he regarded her again, though, his eyes were rheumy.

"I never married again after Nick's mother ran off. He is my only child. I have men in my employ who have kept me informed of my son's activities throughout the years: of his studies, his career, his marriage to you. . . . When I learned that you would

127

be in Paris, well, I knew I could not forgo the opportunity—I need to mend this rift between us. I am no longer a young man with time on my side. Perhaps it is selfish of me to seek out my family now, in my declining years, but this rancor can only be harmful to all of us."

Kate laid a hand over his. "What can I do to help?"

He smiled. "My son has made a good choice in you, child. I knew that the first moment I laid eyes on you. All that I ask is the opportunity to talk with him, to have him hear me out. Whatever he believes me responsible for, he can listen at least. I shall expect no more."

"I will do what I can," Kate promised.

They became better acquainted over tea. It was a pleasant chat, though Kate was very much aware that her father-in-law avoided any further mention of Nick. He was polite and intelligent. She learned that Peter Hammonton was also the Earl of Marleigh. Addressing him as Lord Marleigh seemed too formal, and Kate did not yet feel she could call him 'Father.' She she elected to call him Sir Peter, which suited him well enough.

She also learned more about Sir Peter's passion for archaeology, and Kate wondered if this had somehow influenced Nick's choice of career, despite his negative feelings. Though he had had only a minimum of training, Sir Peter had financed several Egyptian expeditions. Kate was totally engrossed as he recreated the highlights of several experiences. He had unearthed a temple, found a cache of mummies and had attempted to decipher the papyri wound up in the wrappings. His remembrances were so vivid that they carried Kate far away from the Paris salon, and she was hardly aware of the time until she heard the outside doors slam.

Kate cast an apprehensive look at Sir Peter and went out into the foyer. Monsieur Berteau gave her a curt bow and disappeared behind the door of his study, leaving her alone with Nick.

"Did you enjoy your visit?" she asked.

"Immensely," he replied and turned to study her face as if he'd sensed her wariness. "I hope you were not too lonely without us. Did you go shopping with your maid as I suggested?"

"No," she told him.

Her mouth was as dry as dust, and for a moment she feared her voice was gone. "Nick, we have a guest."

She gestured toward the salon, and Nick's eyebrows went up. He swung around to peer into the room and when he saw Sir Peter, he turned back to Kate, his expression dark with rage.

"It's your father," Kate managed to whisper.

Nick's voice was deadly calm. "I know damn well who he is, and I won't have him in this house. I am going upstairs now to dress for dinner, and when I come down I expect to find that man gone, do you understand?"

He did not wait for her reply, but turned on his heel and went up.

Kate felt as though the wind had been knocked out of her. She drew a tremulous breath and went back into the parlor. Sir Peter was already on his feet, preparing to leave. He touched her shoulder gently.

"I've stayed too long, I fear."

"He won't see you," Kate explained, not bearing to meet his eyes.

"I gathered as much," he replied with a sigh. "I'm only sorry to have put you between us, dear Kate. I shan't ask it of you again."

"He must come to his senses someday," said Kate, wishing to give him some hope.

Sir Peter merely smiled. "We will meet again," he assured her. "You are bound for Egypt, and it just so happens that I shall be wintering there myself. My friend Major Kennerly and I have arranged to rent a *dahabiyeh*, that's a sort of Arab houseboat, you know. We're to travel the Nile at our leisure. Surely our paths will cross again."

"We shall hope for more pleasant circumstances."

"Thank you for your kindness, dear daughter-in-law," he said and was gone.

The regret that she had seen in Sir Peter's eyes stayed with her as she rushed upstairs and angrily burst into Nick's room. "How dare you bark orders at me as if I were no more than a serving maid! I am your wife, sir, and as such I believe I am owed at least an explanation in this matter!"

Nick calmly fastened his cuffs and turned to her. "You are right, of course," he said, his reaction startling her. "There was no way for you to have known the situation that exists between . . . that man . . . and me. I should have explained matters."

He offered her a chair and continued to dress as he gave his explanation. Not once in his discourse did he meet her eyes. He paced the floor and concentrated instead on the knot of his tie or a waistcoat button or the placement of his watch chain.

"My mother was a fragile creature. She'd had a sheltered childhood, and when first she met 'him' in New York, it was no wonder that she found him dashing. She was a shy thing, and he, a titled young Englishman who whispered pretty words into her ear. She fell in love with him and without benefit of her father's blessing, married him and went to live in England.

"She lived there for nearly two years and yet his grand estate was never a home to her. The servants were all 'his' people. She was ever an outsider. She was painfully shy, but he was fond of parties and cruelly subjected her to endless rounds of society gatherings. She endured this while he gambled and drank and—"

Nick hesitated momentarily and stared at the toe of his boot. "When she discovered—through a 'well-meaning' acquaintance—that he had kept a mistress throughout their marriage, she packed up her infant son and went home to America. My grandfather forgave her, of course, and took us in. She died only a few years later, and that's the whole of it."

Kate watched the bile rise in him. "That man never so much as inquired as to the well-being of his son all those years, yet now he purports to reconcile our differences!"

"He never tried to see you?" Kate asked.

Nick's eyes met hers briefly and then he looked away, as though he could keep her from probing his thoughts. He moved to the window and studied the scene below.

"Once, when I was nearly ten years old, he came to Creighton. He came upon me like a thief while I was out riding. He must have been ashamed to show his face at my grandfather's door. 'Do you know who I am, boy?' he asked. 'No, sir,' I told him. 'I am your father,' he said to me, as though with those words I might rush into his arms, but I knew him for what he was by then. 'I have no father,' I said to him. 'The man who was my mother's husband was a liar, a gambler and a debaucher and caused the death of my dear mother with his callous treatment.' He slapped my face then, but I held up my head and met his eyes without hesitating. 'How did she die?' he asked then, as though he cared. I stared hard at him. 'She died of a broken heart, sir,' I said, and he dropped his head and crept away. I did not see him again until yesterday at the Exposition."

Kate's jaw slackened. There was something dreadfully twisted in all of this. The feelings that Nick had just voiced as if from his memory could not have been the expressions of a ten-year-old boy, unless that boy had learned them from someone older. She wondered whether Nick had considered this himself.

"I cannot believe that we speak of the same person," Kate insisted. "Lord Marleigh seems a decent, respectable gentleman, with titles and properties. He has nothing to gain by coming here except expressing his affection and regret. And you are his only son and heir. Why should he not seek you out in order to resolve your differences?"

With this remark it must have appeared to Nick that Kate had taken up sides.

"Such differences can never be resolved," he

132

spat, and crossed his long arms over his chest as he regarded her. "So, he's impressed you with his long titles and fancy airs, has he? I am surprised, Kate. I thought you a more sensible type. Would you rather be a countess than an archaeologist, then?"

Though Kate realized full well that he was in pain, striking blindly at her, instinct caused her to strike back.

"Do you imply that I am the only member of this family who is impressed by titles?" she asked. "Can you explain to me why you hovered over my dying father like a vulture until you had snapped up both a directorship and a professorship for yourself? Was I only a pleasant diversion?"

She had gone too far, and as she watched the color drain from his face, she knew that she could not repair the damage. In the heat of argument, the nagging suspicion that had festered in the dark corners of her mind had slipped out so easily, and while she might have regretted it, at least now she would have an answer.

She waited for Nick's reply, but he gave none. And he did not attempt to deny what she had just said. The blank look in his gray eyes was not reassuring. Suddenly, without a word, he turned and left her standing there.

CHAPTER X

*C*airo was truly the land of the Arabian Nights. It lay just off the right bank of the Nile in the shadow of the Mokattam Hills, and was exactly what one might expect an Eastern metropolis to be. Its many domes and minarets, and narrow, mazelike streets combined to produce an exotic effect. Kate was pleased, as she had found Alexandria too European and had longed for a taste of Arab life.

She hesitated to think how they would have fared without Nick. She clung to his arm as he waved away a throng of barefoot street urchins.

"*Imshi!*" Nick said sternly and chastised them in Arabic.

Kate imagined that he was rejecting their offers to be guides or donkey drivers or any number of other things. She had to admit that they were a bit of a nuisance as they looked for coins and called out for baksheesh. She glanced back at Daphne, who was fanning herself anxiously. Doctor Latham caught Kate's eye and grinned at her.

"My sister does not find Cairo as charming as you seem to, Kate," he observed.

"It is fascinating," she replied. "The robes and turbans, the bazaars, the extraordinary wares . . . There is nothing at all to remind one of home. It's a different world entirely. I just saw a string of camels pass through the crowd and yet to these people we seem a far more unusual sight."

"Still, it isn't quite what I'd expected," Mr. Thayer put in.

"You'll feel more at home when we reach Luxor," Nick assured them. "Shaikh Yussif is a good friend of mine and has offered us the use of his house there. It's quite luxurious by Eastern standards."

"Are we putting him out?" Daphne wondered.

Nick laughed. "No need to worry. He's a wealthy merchant. The house in Luxor is only one of many he owns. He's residing at Bulak now and has what you might call a palace on the island. In fact we are invited to dine with him there this evening."

The promise of dinner at a palace brightened Daphne's outlook considerably. She seemed to take a greater interest in the bazaar and particularly in a silversmith hammering at his jewelry. Later, with Nick's assistance, she purchased a delicate openwork bracelet for herself.

Kate was too busy absorbing the scenery to notice Nick haggling with a street vendor until he had turned back to her and pressed something small and round into her palm. It was the first real attention he had given her since that day in Paris when Sir Peter had visited.

When Nick finally released her hand, Kate unfurled her fingers. There, cradled in her palm, was a faience scarab with hieroglyphics on the back. She examined them carefully. "Heart . . . peace . . . peace of heart," she said, stumbling over the inscription.

"Peace of heart is better than anger," Nick read.

———————

Hillaleah Palace, on the island of Bulak, was named for Shaikh Yussif's favorite wife, and was a fairly typical example of the summer palaces built by the wealthy of Cairo. It was a long, low mud-brick building, with a façade that gleamed in the moonlight. The rooms were airy and spacious, with patterned enamel tiles on the floor and walls. The furnishings were sparse by Western standards but no less splendid: carpets and tapestries woven in rich designs; bolsters and cushions decorated with floral patterns, and silver and gold brocade; and oil lamps and vases made of glass in deep reds and blues. The gardens were resplendent with sycamore, jasmine and orange trees, and shallow pools filled with clusters of water lilies.

The shaikh had gone to great lengths to see that his guests passed a pleasant evening under his roof, and Kate noted that even Daphne and Mr. Thayer were delighted with this view of Arab life.

There were about two dozen in attendance: other travellers like themselves, consuls residing in Cairo and male members of the shaikh's family. No Arab women were present. Nick told her it was the custom here to keep the women secluded. Kate was about to question him further, but her heart leapt to her throat when she caught sight of Sir Peter, who made his way fairly quickly into the garden. Fortunately, Nick had been involved in conversation and had not noticed his father. Kate tried to concentrate on the exotic meal.

A large central dinner tray contained lamb, fowl and vegetables served over rice. One scooped it up with rounds of bread, using the hands. All of this was followed by "mish-mish," a delicious concoction of stewed apricots, raisins and nuts.

It was all so unfamiliar to Kate, and yet Nick appeared completely at east, renewing old acquaint- ances and chatting easily in Arabic. Kate listened, though she understood nary a word, and nodded and smiled when the conversation seemed to include her. Eric, though not nearly so fluent as Nick, was busy translating what he could for his sister and Mr. Thayer, so Kate was not missed when she went out into the garden.

Beyond the garden walls, the Nile looked black, and a blue haze of moonlight covered the scene. The breeze was cool, stirring the perfumed air, heady mix of roses and jasmine. By the far side of the reflecting pool, Kate came upon Sir Peter and his companion. They were seated on a low stone bench, and both gentlemen rose at her approach.

"Ah, my dear, I don't believe you've met Major Kennerly. Josiah, may I present my daughter-in-law, Mrs. Katherine Hammonton."

"A pleasure, Mrs. Hammonton," the major said, with a slight bow. He was a sturdy little man with a bristly white beard and a stern military air.

"Pleased to meet you, Major Kennerly," Kate replied. "I understand that you have rented a house-boat—a *dahabiyeh*, is it?—and are travelling the river."

"Yes, 'tis the best way to travel . . . on the river."

"I believe that Nick has made arrangements for us to go up to Luxor by steamer," Kate said. "He's anxious to begin his work. I don't imagine our trip will be as leisurely as yours."

"Perhaps we'll do a little digging ourselves when we reach Thebes," Sir Peter put in, "not on any grand scale, you understand, but just to occupy the time. We've experience on our side, at least. Major Kennerly spent more than twenty years in this part of the world in Her Majesty's Service. Quite an adventurer he was, in his youth."

"Far be it from me to interrupt while you're singing my praises," Major Kennerly said, "but I would like to pay my respects to our cousul, Mr. Wilkinson. We are old friends. If you will excuse me—"

When the major was gone, Kate and Sir Peter settled on the bench. Kate snapped open her fan, hoping to relieve the flush of color that she felt rising in her face. She was uncomfortable, not quite sure where she should begin. "I was hoping to get the chance to talk with you again," she said at last.

"You've spoken with Nick about me," he surmised.

"He's told me the whole of it, or at least what he believes to have been so."

Sir Peter met her eyes expectantly. "And you? What do you believe, Kate?"

"I cannot say . . . yet."

She went on to relate all of what Nick had told

138

her, trying as best she could to spare his feelings, but when she had finished, she looked up to see that his brow was furrowed and his eyes mirrored the shimmering light of the reflecting pool. Kate snapped her fan shut and clung to it. Sir Peter touched her arm.

"Do not expect me to decry this story as an utter falsehood," he told her quite honestly. "I was a selfish young man, my dear Kate, and prideful and vain. As I look back, I made a great many foolish decisions, but I have paid for them over and over again throughout the years."

"I know in my heart that there is more to this than either Nick or I have been told," she said to him. "Please, Sir Peter, for my husband's sake, I must know the truth."

Sir Peter uttered a long sigh that seemed to take him back all those years. "Did you know Nick's grandfather?" he asked.

"Only as an acquaintance of my father's."

"Jacob Mallory was a hard man," he began, "who'd made his own way in the world and despised anyone whose fortunes didn't come of his own labor. His wife died young, and he raised his daughter as a companion for himself, never imagining that one day she might marry and leave him. Of course, when Lucy and I told him of our plans, he was furious. He called her an ungrateful wretch and said that she'd not see a penny of his money, nor did he ever wish to set eyes on her again.

"I consoled her, and she seemed to accept the fact that she'd burned her bridges. We were married, and I took her home to England, hoping that in time Mallory wold reconcile himself to the marriage. He never did.

"As I look back on it, I can see that Lucy never forgave herself—or me—for invoking her father's wrath. He had trained her well. So full of guilt was she that, despite my efforts, she became withdrawn and morose. She would not face her social obligations and soon she became so obsessed that we had no life at all together. I'll not deny that I kept a mistress in London. I see that you are shocked, but it is not a thing unheard of for a young man such as I was. She was more of a confidante than a mistress, really, and I had known her for many years. When Lucy learned of her existence, though, she could at last justify running home to her father. I awoke one morning to find her gone, but when she left me, and I shall swear to this, Kate, there was no child."

Kate looked up in astonishment, thinking at first that she hadn't heard him correctly. "Then Nick was born in his grandfather's house?" she deduced.

Sir Peter inclined his head.

"Perhaps I made the wrong choice, perhaps I should have gone after Lucy and convinced her that her place was at my side, but I was angry and my pride had been wounded. There was a scandal, but it died away as scandals will, and I went on alone. I did not learn of my son's existence for nearly ten years, and then only by accident.

"An acquaintance in London who had done business with Mallory Glassworks mentioned Jacob Mallory's grandson to me, and when I inquired as to his age, I knew that he was my son."

"How could she have been so cruel as to keep your child a secret from you?" Kate said. The words had barely tumbled out before she realized that she was now terribly guilty of the same crime. She would tell Nick soon, she told herself. She did not want Nick to suffer as his father had.

Sir Peter breathed a heavy sigh. "I've no doubt that once under Mallory's influence again, Lucy could be made to believe whatever he wished, to do whatever he thought best.

"I sent a man to investigate, and when I discovered that Lucy was dead and that Mallory was raising my son, I was furious. I went to New York, fully intending to claim my son as was my right, but Mallory would not even allow me across his threshold. I resorted to subterfuge in order to see the boy and learned, to my anguish, that Mallory had already poisoned his mind against me."

As if she felt Sir Peter's frustration, Kate began tapping her fan against her knee. "Couldn't you have taken him away then, made him see the truth?" she said, her voice ending on a shrill note.

He shook his head. "By taking him away from the only family he had ever known, I'd have risked earning his hatred for certain. I'd have been, in his eyes, that same evil person that his grandfather had warned him against. I've come to accept that this estrangement from my son is my punishment for not having gone after Lucy when first she left me."

Kate took up his hands. "Nonsense. Come with me now, and we shall tell Nick together all that you have just told me."

"No" Sir Peter said flatly. "I forbid it."

A crease marred Kate's brow. "I don't understand."

"Why should Nick listen to me now?" he asked. "My version of things villifies his grandfather, who is not alive to defend himself. More importantly, Kate, I will not have your marriage with my son jeopardized on my account."

He cupped her face in his hands and kissed her brow. "You've become very dear to me, child. Now you must do as I ask."

"I shall," she agreed, if only to please him.

———

Nick stepped into the garden for a moment's peace. The warm night air was redolent of jasmine and brought Kate immediately into his thoughts. It was her scent, and it evoked some very pleasant memories. A smile crooked on his lips. Where had she gone off to? There were memories to be made yet tonight.

He spied figures on the bench near the pool. The scene that met his eyes was a touching, paternal one, and it did not truly affect him until he had discerned the persons involved. Was this truly Kate conversing with his father, as easily as old friends? How could he trust his eyes when Lord Peter Hammonton, Earl of Marleigh, rose and kissed Kate's brow in parting?

He stepped into the shadows as his father passed by and then approached his wife, surprised at the depth of emotion mirrored on her young face. He cared too much for her, that was his curse, and as he looked on the soft curve of her cheek, he wished he had not witnessed the scene of a few moments ago.

His angry words spouted forth, as if he and she were doomed to be at odds forever. "Does tormenting me hold a perverse pleasure for you?" His voice was hollow. "After all that I have told you of that man, still you encourage his friendship?"

When she did not answer, he thought perhaps

that she'd not heard the remark, but she regarded him for a long moment before dropping her gaze once more. Her silence affected Nick more than any words could have.

———

Nick left the party before anyone else that night, as soon as he learned that the French consul's steamer was heading upriver on the morrow. When Kate and the others returned to their lodgings in Cairo, he was already gone, leaving word that he had to make arrangements for the dig and would go up to Luxor with the Frenchman. Ahmad, an accomplished dragoman, was left to see that the rest of them arrived safely in Luxor on the passenger steamer.

By and large, the trip was uneventful. Kate's thoughts always returned to her husband's conspicuous absence. When they finally reached Shaikh Yussif's house, expecting to be greeted by Nick, they were informed that he had crossed the river with the workmen that morning to set up camp.

Eric declared that it was "damned odd! You'd think that after all this time, a few days more wouldn't matter."

All concurred with this view except Kate, who knew that it was not so much that he was anxious to begin as what he wished to leave behind.

———

The house at Luxor was as comfortable as Nick had promised. Its lattice work proved to be a blessing in the day's heat. There were reed mats on the floor, cushions thrown up against the wall when not in use and low tables of carved wood—the only real furniture. A lovely terrace stood on the upper level of the house, from which one could look out on the Nile and watch boats with curved sails drift by.

From this vantage point, however, Kate set her sights across the river to western Thebes and the Valley of the Kings. She was vexed to have been abandoned here, while all the important activity was taking place there, across the river. After they had arrived, Eric and Mr. Thayer had packed what they needed, whereupon Ahmad had taken them to where Nick had set up camp.

Kate and Daphne had been left in the capable hands of Shaikh Yussif's servants, with the cook's young son, Mustapha, as their guide and translator. The boy had learned a fair amount of English from his father, who had worked on many digs. Mustapha squired the two ladies about Luxor in a proud fashion, pointing out the sights and describing them with all the enthusiasm of a European tour guide.

As the days became routine, Daphne grew content, pleased to occupy herself with domestic matters, but Kate was restless. At first she had been satisfied to roam the forest of columns that were the ruins of the temple of Karnak, to marvel at the carved pictures and hieroglyphs, and to toy with a translation here and there. She had even sketched the scene from several different perspectives, but the real challenge, she decided, was in discovering ruins and she wanted badly to be a part of it.

But it did not appear that her aspirations would be realized. There had been no word from Nick since he had left her in Cairo. He'd been entrenched at the dig for more than three weeks, and might easily have come to see her during that time, the distance to Luxor being not so great. Yet he had not.

In order to put aside unpleasant thoughts, Kate studied anew the notes she had made on the Isis mask. Sitting in the shade of the terrace, she read the inscription over and over again in her mind, convinced that her father had intended it to be the focus of his next expedition. Exactly what she would do with this information, she did not know. But she did know that if this inactivity continued, she would surely go mad.

CHAPTER XI

"*S*alaam aleikum."

The salutation echoed through the hall and wrested Kate from her torpor. She left the cool darkness of her room to join Daphne in the entry hall, where Eric stood, in a triumphant pose, with Panama hat and green spectacles.

"Have you news for us?" Daphne asked, before Kate could catch her breath.

"Naught for posterity, dear sister," came his reply, "but still we plod on, sifting through the sands. Our Mr. Thayer has decided, I think, that his preference is for the business side of this endeavor. He complains of the unfriendly climate and provides some levity for the camp with that parasol he carries to shield himself from the sun."

146

"Eric," chided Daphne, "that's not at all charitable. Samuel is a cultured man."

Daphne went on, ignoring him, but Kate noticed a blush staining her cheeks. It was not from the heat. "He cannot be blamed if he longs for the comforts of home. Why I, myself, have had a time of it adjusting to all these foreign ways. I shall have a deeper appreciation for modern society upon my return, I can tell you. And you must agree that the heat is merciless. You could bake bread outdoors on a paving stone."

Eric grinned. "Enough, enough. While we chatter on, Kate patiently awaits word of her husband. Mrs. Hammonton, I can tell you that Nick positively thrives on desert air. He is tanned as brown as the fellaheen, for he insists on personally supervising every basket of sand that is moved, or at least it seems that way to me. You know Nick."

Eric paused and drew off his spectacles, his expression showing concern as he studied Kate.

"How are you faring in the heat? Have you been ill?"

"No," she said quickly, sensing that he was aware of some change in her. "It's only that I've been resting. I shall go splash some water on my face and pinch the color into my cheeks, and then you'll find me more presentable."

She turned to go, and he called after her. "One moment, lest I forget the purpose of my visit. Nick has asked me to retrieve a packet of maps for him. They were your father's maps, he said, and specifically, he needs those detailing the northern sector of the valley. He was certain you'd know the ones."

Kate nodded. "Was there anything else?"

"No, only the maps."

In her room, Kate threw open the lid of Nick's trunk and rummaged through the contents for the leather pouch that contained her father's maps.

So Nick had sent no word for her, not even a hastily written note to tell her how the work was progressing. She could tell, though, without the aid of any note, that Nick was having no luck. If his own charts were not helpful enough and he needed her father's maps, then he was looking for inspiration.

She had the packet in hand and was about to deliver it when she decided that she would persuade Eric to take her for a visit to the site. Thus decided, she found herself with renewed vigor. She plaited her hair into a neat coil and put on a white linen dress, decorated with embroidered pink roses, and a wide-brimmed hat of English straw. She then draped a lace shawl over one arm to help disguise her newly rounded form.

It was, perhaps, a wasted effort. Kate's condition was not yet apparent to anyone. She promised herself to tell Nick as soon as they resolved their differences, even if it meant being sent back home.

Eric gave her no argument about her desire to visit the site and they set off for the ride across the river. When they arrived, Eric helped Kate disembark and lead her to the *arabiya*, or light carriage, that awaited them. He helped her up and took the reins in hand.

"If it isn't too much trouble, Eric, might we drive by the site that my father excavated when you were here last? He told me so much about it that I should like to see it for myself."

"The village ruins? There's not much to see really."

Kate Hammonton presented a fetching picture as she stared up expectantly at him, the faintest blush staining her cheeks. He found it hard to take his eyes away from her. Clearing his throat, he loosened his cravat. Even with the green spectacles he wore, Eric had to shade his eyes with his hand as he checked the position of the sun.

"I suppose we have time, though," he told her.

They left the small village of Qurna and headed southward. Kate's eyes seemed to examine every feature of the harsh landscape. Away from the river, there was only desolation, sand and sharp-faced rocks burnished by the lengthening rays of the sun. When they reached the desired spot, Eric pulled up on the reins.

"Not much to see," he reiterated as he helped her out of the carriage. "Most of our excavation extended east of this point," he explained, waving his hand across the area. "Of course, the sands have covered it all again. There were remains of several dwellings and a sculptor's studio, as I recall. We could have spent years on this site alone. As it was, we barely scratched the surface. Others mightn't have thought it worth the effort, but your father came out of it with some interesting, if not particularly valuable, pieces."

"Value is a subjective word," Kate said in a cryptic way and began to wander over what appeared now to be no more than random scatterings of rubble.

Eric followed at a distance, watching as she prodded the ground with her shoe to unearth a stray brick and then walked along the remnants of a foundation, pacing off its length. She studied the landscape as if attempting to memorize all its salient features.

Then she whirled around all at once, startling him. "How far are we from the Isis temple?"? she asked.

"Half a mile, perhaps."

Her brow creased as she took this in, nodding solemnly.

"I'd like to get a look at it," she said. She must have seen how her words startled him, for she modified the statement. "Dear Eric, I know I'm being a dreadful bother to you, but I'm afraid that without you as my guide, I shall see no more of Egypt than the Luxor house. Nick spends all of his time at the site. He's not about to give up working so that I might have a tour. So you see, I've captured you."

"I thought that young Mustapha was to show you the ruins," Eric said.

"He's taken us to Karnak, and while it was magnificent, I can't be satisfied with the usual tourist spots. You knew my father; this land was his life. While other children were being put to sleep with fairy tales, my father filled my head with stories of ancient Egyptians. Who knows what we might learn from what they've left behind? The temples and monuments and tombs . . . How can I come to this land and not wish to see every remnant of their civilization?"

Eric was speechless. He could not refuse such an eloquent request, and besides, he thought, was it not a more pleasant prospect to be spending the afternoon with a vivacious young lady, rather than dozens of dusty workmen?

At the temple, Kate moved amid the ruins as if absorbed in thought and even stopped once or twice to copy the hieroglyphics from a battered column or crumbling wall. It was the calculated way in which her eyes took in the surroundings, though, that most surprised Eric.

"Do you know, Kate," he said, "that your husband has that same look in his eye when he's scouting a site?"

She merely smiled and again jotted in her notebook. She wandered amid the stones with wraithlike grace, and Eric found again that he could not take his eyes off of her. He saw now why Nick had been so entranced.

She was no more than five yards away when he suddenly saw her sway, reaching out to the temple wall for support. Her legs crumpled beneath her and she slipped to the ground in a froth of linen skirts.

———

Kate was confused when she awoke and found Eric bent over her, pressing a damp handkerchief to her forehead. The last thing she remembered was admiring a bas relief on the temple wall. "What happened?" she asked.

"You fainted," he replied, "and gave me quite a start."

She raised herself up on one elbow.

"Rest a moment," Eric cautioned. "If you rise too quickly, it's liable to happen again."

"At least I've the good fortune to have a doctor on hand."

He offered her some water from his canteen. "You must be sure to drink enough water; it's vital in this climate. And I'll also advise you to abandon your corsets while we're in Egypt. They'll only further impair your breathing. At this point, fashion must give way to good sense."

Kate studied her hands because she could not meet Eric's eyes. Her weakness embarrassed her. It had been most foolish to have underestimated the strength of the desert sun. Eric helped her to her feet, and she leaned on him. "In the past few days," she said, "I've found myself wondering if it mightn't be more comfortable to adopt the Arab style of dress."

Her companion smiled.

"You're not shocked by my suggestion, then?" Kate asked.

He helped her up into the *arabiya*. "You'd not be the first to try it," he told her. "Now we'd best get on to the camp before we lose the light."

They drove on in silence for a long while before Eric spoke again. "When is the child expected?" he asked, all at once.

Kate was speechless.

"Please don't think me indelicate. I am, after all, a doctor as well as a friend, and am concerned for your health. If you are with child, then we must take special care of you."

Kate met his eyes. "I've not told Nick," she said, hesitantly. "I was afraid, at first, that he'd not let me come to Egypt, and now, well, he has concerns enough without having to worry about me as well."

"You'll have to tell him eventually."

"Not now," she protested, "not yet. The time isn't right. You must promise me that you'll not say a word to Nick about this. I will tell him myself . . . soon."

Eric reluctantly agreed. "I've no right to interfere," he explained, "but you must promise me, Kate, that you will take better care of yourself, and you must allow me to examine you. If I determine that our surroundings pose any danger to you or the baby, I shall see to it that Nick has you on the next steamer bound for New York."

Kate assented, though she could not help but think that Eric was being overly cautious. Women were having babies every day in Egypt, for heaven's sake. But considering how she had just fainted made her glad of his concern.

Twilight had settled in by the time they reached the camp. The mountains seemed all the more immense in the waning light. There was little activity. The sound of pipes in the distance and the glow of the campfires were the only signs of life. Nick must have heard them approach, for just then he poked his head out of his tent. Eric whistled to him. "Look what I've brought you, my friend," he said.

"Where have you been?" Nick called. "I thought you'd deserted us or gotten lost. I was about to come after you myself."

"After me or your maps?" Eric retorted.

Nick's advance stopped suddenly when he saw Kate. He certainly was not ready for a confrontation now. Damn! Why did he have to bring her here? He wondered whether they could gauge from his reaction the amount of his displeasure.

Eric stepped down and reached for Kate's hand. She smiled at him, and Nick felt a twinge of jealousy.

153

"You might have consulted me," he snapped. "This camp hasn't the conveniences that a lady requires, and we haven't the time—"

"I wouldn't think of interfering with your work," Kate shot back.

Before either man knew what had happened, Kate had taken up the reins of the *arabiya* and, turning the rig around, started back the way she had come, at a reckless speed. Nick uttered a curse and mounted the horse tethered behind his tent. He slapped the stallion hard on the flank and galloped off after his wife with the wind whistling in his ears.

It did not take him long to catch her. He edged his mount alongside her and yelled her name, but she pretended not to hear. Nor would she look at him. Darkness would soon be upon them, and Nick knew that if she continued at this breakneck pace, she was liable to upset the rig. He thus cut sharply in front of her, causing her to pull up on the reins sharply.

Her tears had started with Nick's first words at the camp. Now they streamed unchecked down her face, but she would not let Nick see her at such a disadvantage. As he dismounted, she stepped from the rig and began to run, haphazardly, across the hilly ground. As the sand there was hard baked and spotted with patches of coarse grass, it was luck alone that kept her from turning an ankle.

She was not aware of Nick until his hand caught her shoulder and he turned her toward him. She stumbled backwards and threw out her arms to break the fall. Though the ground was hard, she was not hurt. Nick knelt over her and pressed her back flat

154

against the sand. His face was edged in shadow, but she could see the angry glint in his eye. "That was foolish, Kate!" he said. "You might have been killed."

"Leave me alone," she replied, her voice uneven.

He glared at her, but then all at once his expression softened, and Kate knew that he had seen the tears.

"You're crying."

"I've sand in my eyes," she protested.

She hated herself for the weakness in her that had let them spill over.

"Why did you do this?" he asked gently.

When she spoke again, her voice was cold. "You've made it more than clear that you don't want me here. I was merely saving you the trouble of driving me back. Now if you'll let me up, I'll be on my way."

Nick did not move to release her. He lowered his body over hers and stroked her hair, then nuzzled the column of her throat. "Not want you? What a ridiculous notion! I can't sleep for want of you, can't think for want of you."

His mouth captured hers, while his fingers followed the familiar path along her jawline, caressing the soft skin at the back of her neck, then slipped lower. Kate tried to fight off the lightheadedness. She did not want to respond to him when there was so much anger between them, but her resistance waned under his touch.

"Stay with me tonight, Kate! I'll make you as comfortable as I can and see you back to Luxor myself tomorrow."

She could not deny him. She did not want to.

Nick's tent was long and rectangular in the Arab style, not at all like the small military tent shared by Doctor Latham and Mr. Thayer. When Nick lit the lantern that hung from the centerpole, Kate saw that the furnishings, if they might be called that, were eclectic. Turkish carpets covered the sandy floor. In one corner was a mattress of sorts, upon which half a dozen large brocaded pillows had been tossed. A piece of lumber propped between two crates served as a desk, and Nick's charts and notebooks lay open upon it. Behind that stood a campstool, and on another crate, a basin for washing.

"Not so primitive," Kate commented. "I see now why Eric found it amusing that I was considering adopting Arab fashions. All this time my husband has been living out here like a shaikh."

"I hope you approve. Living like the natives is the best way to adapt to desert life."

Ahmad brought them a delicious meal, which ended with a liquorice-flavored water called *ark-assous*. They spoke of Nick's work, and he promised to give her a tour of the site the following morning.

"Please be patient with me, Kate," he said at one point. "I know I've been difficult, but everyone is counting on the success of this venture. It is all in my hands."

Kate rose and peered out at the clear night sky. "My father always believed that you'd be a great archaeologist one day, and you shall be. I've never doubted it. You mustn't either."

Nick came up behind her and touched her shoulder. "Alas, it is the duty of a wife to shore up her husband's confidence when it falters," he said.

He felt her tense beneath his hand. "Take me at my word, Nick. I've little inclination to fabricate compliments only to bolster your ego, duty or no."

He considered her words. Perhaps he had belittled her opinion, certainly she thought so. "Thank you then," he replied carefully, "for your faith in me."

Kneading her shoulders, he pressed his lips against the smooth nape of her neck and toyed with her hairpins, removing them one by one. "Say goodnight to the stars," he whispered against her ear and untied the tent flap that served as a door. He shrugged off his shirt, displaying skin that had been tanned copper by the desert sun. He drew her up to him, his mouth capturing hers. They communicated so much better this way, Nick decided, with no possibility of being misunderstood.

Kate responded by edging her body nearer to his lean hardness. Her hands anxiously travelled the length of his back, and for a while she forgot the gulf that stood between them. He needed her and that was all that mattered.

Nick concentrated on the long row of pearl buttons down her dress, and when he had unfastened each of them, she slipped it off, and the cotton shift she wore beneath it as well. She was bathed in shadows, the golden highlights of her hair illuminated by the lantern's light.

He reached for her, and his hands slid over her silken skin, relishing each soft curve. If those curves seemed more rounded than he remembered, he attributed it to the fact that he had not touched her in weeks, and his memories paled beside reality. As their lips blended again, he lifted her easily into his arms and carried her to the far corner of the tent, tossing her lightly onto the heap of pillows that lay there. He struggled with his boots and shed his trousers, and when he came to her, she reached for him anxiously. He settled into her embrace, his body molding itself to hers, and then he filled her, a low moan escaping her parted lips. They moved together, breathlessly striving toward fulfillment, and when at last it came to them, they lay silent in one another's arms, wishing to maintain this intimacy they now shared. As he fell off to sleep, Nick considered keeping her in this tent instead of sending her back to Luxor tomorrow. If she lay beside him each night, perhaps she mightn't invade his dreams.

———

Kate awoke the following morning to the songs of the Arab workmen. They had begun their tasks early, with the sunrise.

Nick had not attempted to wake her, but left Ahmad outside the tent to tend to her when she awoke. He brought her a breakfast of bread and dates with thick coffee. As she ate, Kate decided that, in light of the peace between them, it would be an ideal time to tell Nick of his impending fatherhood. She rehearsed a bit, searching for the right words, but was confident that, after the tenderness he had shown her the night before, he would not send her away. After she had finished breakfast, she went out of the tent in search of her husband.

The blaze of the morning sun was overpowering. Even though her eyes were shielded by the ample brim of her straw hat, the light reflected off the rocks practically blinded her. She kept blinking, trying to adjust to the light.

"You wish to see the work?" Ahmad said, as he came up to her before she had taken more than a dozen steps.

"Of course," she answered, and fell into step beside him. He led her over a rise to the site where workers were laboring to clear a ravine. The area where the digging was taking place was a cloud of dust.

"A good morning to you, Mrs. Hammonton," Mr. Thayer called as he approached, carrying his parasol. "And how are you and Miss Latham faring in your house by the river? Well, I hope."

"Yes, thank you," Kate replied.

"How fortunate for you to have come to visit on such an auspicious day."

"What has happened?"

With the knowledge that something was afoot, Kate realized that the workers were moving about in a purposeful way.

"Good morning, Kate," Eric said, joining them. "How are you taking the heat?"

"I'm fine, thank you," she replied, anxious to brush aside the subject of her health. "Eric, has Nick found something?"

"A doorway lintel, he thinks. The workmen came upon it just after they began digging, there in the crevice of the cliffface and that area of fallen rocks."

With Eric and Mr. Thayer at her heels, Kate made her way to the spot and clambered down, unaided, into the ravine. When Nick saw her, he took her arm and kissed her lightly on the cheek. "Come, look what we've found," he said.

He led her to the place that had just been dug out and ran his hand along a rectangular piece of stone.

"It's a doorway," he said. "The entrance is not sealed, but that damage might have happened in the rockslide."

"Oh, Nick, this is exciting!" Kate exclaimed.

"We've a lot of work to do before we can clear the entrance. All of this debris must be moved and that section shored up so there'll be no further danger of falling rocks."

"How long will that take?" Kate wondered.

"Several days, perhaps a week," he replied. "I'm sorry, but I won't be able to take you back to Luxor today. There's too much to be done here."

"Then I'll stay. I won't be a bother, and I might help in some way. I could make sketches of the site. How can I go back to Luxor and sit on my hands when all of the excitement is here?"

"We've discussed all this before," he warned. "I'll have someone take you to the ferry, and I'll come for you myself when there's something to show you out here besides desert and rock."

His tone told her that he would argue the point no further. A sharp rejoinder died on her lips as weariness washed over her. She turned from him, and Eric caught her elbow, helping her up the slope. When they were again on firm footing, he pressed the back of his hand against her cheek. "I don't like your color," he told her. "Nick is right. You can't stay. The heat in this valley would be too much of a strain. If you'd like, Mr. Thayer or I can take you down to the ferry."

"I need Thayer here to make notes for the Society," Nick shouted from below, and both Kate and Eric were surprised that he had overheard Eric's comments, "but if you're so damned concerned, take her yourself!"

At this, Kate strode away from the site without so much as a backward glance. When she reached the top of the rise, Ahmad was waiting for her.

"It is good that you have come," he told her. "Now perhaps Hammonton-*effendi* will take his rest. He works shoulder-to-shoulder with the fellaheen, Missus Kate. None may say that he asks what he himself would not do, but the men begin to say that he is driven by demons."

"Perhaps they are right," Kate replied. "I am afraid, Ahmad, that my husband will not rest until he has his success."

She left him there, with his wide brown eyes full of compassion, and made her way back to the camp, where Eric caught up to her.

"You haven't told him, have you?"

"Just take me back to Luxor, Eric," she said, miserable.

"He's preoccupied. The work fills all of his time and thoughts, especially now when he's on the verge of a discovery."

"I'm done with making excuses for him. He's obsessed, and I, more than anyone, ought to understand. Sending me back to town is appropriate, I suppose, and no less than I deserve."

Eric looked bewildered as he helped Kate into the *arabiya*. She searched his eyes as if deciding whether to confide in him, and the explanation tumbled from her lips. "I've my own obsession, you know. Ever since I was a child, I've wanted to come to Egypt and be a part of a dig. I wanted it so badly, in fact, that when Nick proposed to me, my first consideration was that, as his wife, I could be a part of his work and accompany him on his expeditions. You think me awful now, don't you?"

Eric stared hard at the leather straps in his hands, remembering Nick's initial consideration of the professor's proposal. "People marry for many reasons," he said, after a while.

"I suppose that's so."

"I do believe, though, that I've not met two people more suited to each other than you and Nick," he said honestly.

"Perhaps we're too much alike to be good for one another," she replied.

As the carriage moved on, the two of them stayed silent, lost in their own thoughts. When they neared the riverbank, Kate said suddenly, "I fear I've spoken out of turn. You have been too kind."

Eric smiled at her. "I don't wish to see my two friends unhappy," he said, "and while I cannot condone Nick's high-handed behavior, I think you know, as well as I, the pressure he is under."

Kate nodded, and her eyes were bright with tears. "Regardless of my motives at the start, I want you to know that I love Nick. That's what makes all of this so unbearable."

Both of them pretended not to notice the tears that trailed down Kate's pale cheeks, and it seemed to Eric that she was more surprised by her revelation than he.

CHAPTER XII

*U*pon her return to the Luxor house, Kate sought relief from the afternoon's heat in the shade of the terrace. She found Daphne there, sitting with her head bent over a piece of embrodiery, her fingers still and her breathing slow and even.

"Good afternoon, Daphne" Kate said, as she gently nudged her.

"Oh!" Daphne cried, immediately resuming her sewing as though she'd been at it all the while. "So you've come back. You caught me napping, I'm afraid. It's the heat. Is Eric with you?"

"No," Kate replied, sitting down beside her. "He took me as far as the ferry and then headed back to the camp. There's some excitement out there. They've found what looks to be the entrance to a tomb."

"Good news at last. I was beginning to think

we'd travelled all this way only to be disappointed."

"It's a tedious process, but they'll have their hands full now."

"How are they getting on out there? Eric seemed a trifle thinner, and I fear poor Mr. Thayer is not at all suited to this climate."

"They are faring well enough, even your Mr. Thayer. He will be working closely with Nick now, as it is his job to report all of their finds to the Society members."

Daphne blushed. "*My* Mr. Thayer? Why, hardly that."

She focused her attention on the low table beside her and poured Kate a glass of mint tea. Kate thanked her, but did not stray from the subject at hand.

"I have noticed that you and Mr. Thayer have developed a rather special friendship, and he did inquire about you when I was at the camp."

Daphne fanned herself with her hand, flustered. "About me? How very kind of him?"

"I am pleased to see the two of you getting on so well. It lessens my guilt somewhat. I know that one of the reasons Nick asked you along on this trip was to keep me company, but as it turns out, I have been preoccupied most of the time."

Daphne reached for Kate's hand. "I have complained about the inconveniences, I know, but this adventure has been a godsend for me. My life had become so orderly, with no hope of change. Now, who knows?" There was a gleam in her dark eyes that Kate found intriguing. Here was a woman with pleasant expectations for the future.

Kate rose and went to lean against one of the

pillars that supported the terrace roof, staring out at the boats on the Nile, their curved sails filling with the sweet, river breeze.

"I'm carrying Nick's child," she told Daphne, all at once.

She did not seen entirely surprised, and her mouth turned up at the corners. "I must say that I expected as much. No one could suffer so many bouts of seasickness as you did all in one crossing."

Kate managed a thin smile. She was thinking of Nick and his angry words this morning when Eric had shown more concern for her than for the work. Did he think everyone was as single-minded as he? Once Kate had believed that the work drew them together, now it seemed to always stand between them.

"Well, my best wishes to both of you," Daphne said, hugging her.

"Good afternoon!" someone called out.

Kate turned at the sound of footsteps striking the tiled floor. "Why . . . Stephen Perry . . . whatever are you doing here in Luxor? Daphne, you remember Stephen."

"I'm sorry if I've startled you, ladies," he apologized. "Your servant let me in, and I said I'd find my own way."

He looked thinner than Kate remembered. He'd shaved his beard but was sporting a stubble, and his face was mottled from the heat.

"Would you care for a glass of mint tea, Mr. Perry?" Daphne inquired.

"I'd much prefer a brandy, if you have some," he said, removing his hat to mop his brow. He took the chair beside Kate.

"Not at all good for you in this heat," Daphne replied, "but I think Eric left a bottle here in the cupboard."

Ever the correct hostess, Daphne poured a finger of brandy into a tall glass and said that she must check on the dinner preparations.

"Will you stay for dinner, Mr. Perry?" she asked as she took her leave.

"Thank you, no, Miss Latham. I've only come to pay my respects. I'm on my way upriver to the Third Cataract."

"How exciting!" Kate said when Daphne was gone. "Do you plan to excavate?"

"One never knows. You're looking exceptionally well, Kate. You must find the desert climate agreeable."

She nodded. "One grows accustomed to it, though I'll admit it seems unbearable at times."

"How is your husband?" he asked, although Kate could tell by his tone he was only being polite.

"Nick positively thrives on the heat and the sand."

Kate was uncomfortable under the scrutiny of his eyes, cold as green ice. She shivered despite the heat.

"You are happy with your new life, then?" he asked.

"Why, yes . . . of course."

Kate fidgeted in her chair, hoping that his eyes could not read her thoughts.

"Truthfully, I was surprised to find you here in Luxor. I thought you would be at the excavation site with your partner."

Kate was well aware that these were her own

words come back to haunt her. Anxious to put a halt to his probing, she changed the subject. "I've only just returned from there, actually. Nick has come upon something very promising in the valley. I'm sure he'd be pleased to see you if you went out. Perhaps you could even lend a hand," she suggested.

He finished off his brandy and put down the glass.

"I haven't the time."

"No time for pharaoh's gold?"

He glared at her, angered by what Kate could only see as harmless words.

"I'm not a man who likes to share, Kate . . . Not women, nor glory, nor even pharaoh's gold. Let Nick and others like him waste their lives digging in the desert sands; I can come by plenty of pharaoh's treasure . . . for a price."

Kate was outraged by this remark. "How could you even imply such a thing, Stephen? Trafficking in stolen antiquities is illegal and immoral. I don't believe you're capable of that."

He pulled himself out of the chair and crossed the terrace to gaze upon the Nile.

"Then you don't know me very well. We can't all be as lucky as your father was, nor have the foresight of your husband. Now there's a man who knew how to go about getting what he wanted. Just look what Nick Hammonton has achieved in the past year: professor of Ancient Studies at Creighton University, director of the prestigious Society for the Preservation of Antiquities . . . And now, here he is in Egypt on the threshold of a great archaeological discovery, and all this was achieved solely because he had the foresight to accept the deal your father offered him."

Kate followed him, leaning against the rail. She was full of trepidation, almost afraid to hear any more. "Deal?"

Stephen found the brandy and poured himself another glass. "'Marry my daughter and all that I have is yours,'" he said with a smug grin.

Kate felt as though she'd suddenly had the wind knocked out of her. "I don't believe it. You're only being spiteful because—"

"The rumor was all over the university, Kate. Ask any of your friends here. They can tell you. Ask Nick."

She turned from him and looked deep inside herself for strength. There was a long moment of silence before she turned back around and spoke. "Is that the reason you came here today? To spew your venom? I suppose that the rumors of the deal precipitated your ever-so-convincing proposal of marriage?" she guessed.

"I warned you about my character, you'll remember. I can't abide not having what I want. Don't be disheartened, dear Kate. You are a beautiful and fascinating woman but, I must admit, too much of a damned bluestocking for my taste."

Kate suspected that more than a little of his speech had been fabricated to hide whatever feelings he might have had for her, but she would never know for certain.

"And more of an archaeologist than you'll ever be," she shot back. "Little wonder my father chose Nick as his heir apparent; he, at least, has the spirit to succeed!"

Nick pencilled figures in his ledgerbook. At the rate the digging was going, it owuld be another week before he knew for certain what he'd found. Out of the corner of his eye, he saw Eric come in but pretended not to notice. He hadn't forgotten this morning's scene, and he wasn't pleased with the change that had come over his friend, who was suddenly fussing over his wife.

"I took Kate as far as the ferry," Eric told him.

"This method of excavation is damnably slow," Nick said in reply, knowing full well that it was the only approach to take given the terrain. "If only I had fifty more men—"

Eric thrust his hands in his pockets, looking like an errant schoolboy. "She said she'd be fine, that I should start back in case you needed me. She'd like us to think she's strong, you know, but this climate's taking its toll on her."

Nick did not seem to be listening. "I hope there'll be timber enough for the shoring. The opening is in such a precarious spot. I'd hate to clear it out, only to have it fill up again."

Eric moved to stand right in front of Nick. "I think you ought to go and see Kate," he said.

This was absurd. What had gotten into Eric? He'd never been the serious sort. Nick slammed the ledger shut and set off a flurry of maps and papers. "What? Now? In the middle of things? I can't leave now, that's for certain. When we've opened the tomb, I'll bring her out here to see it. She'll like that."

"She needs you *now*, Nick."

Nick's patience had worn thin. How could Eric presume to know what Kate needed? "Needs me? She's grown bored with Luxor and 'needs' entertain-

169

ment, you mean. Is that why you brought her up here yesterday? Well, this isn't some theatre. I warned her she'd soon be bored, and I can't be expected to provide entertainment. There's serious work to be done here."

Eric shook his head. "Kate was right. You are obsessed, and while she may claim to understand, I cannot be so charitable. You have a wife who loves you and wants to share in your work, and yet you shut her out. It's as if you lack any feeling at all."

"Unlike you, my friend. Where my wife is concerned, you appear to have more feeling than is seemly."

"That's unfair, Nick, and since I put a higher value on our friendship than you seem to, I'm going to leave now and forget what you've implied. But mind what I say: Keep relegating Kate to second place in your life, and she'll come to resent it. One day you'll come for her, riding the crest of your success, and she'll be gone." With that, Eric turned and left.

Nick sat there for a long while after Eric left. He could not help but feel that there was much in Eric's warning that had been left unsaid. Nick could not tolerate this sort of pressure now, now when he was so close . . . If Eric thought he could make him feel guilty about Kate, he was mistaken. There would be plenty of time later to make it up to her; she'd understand. But only when he considered Eric's possible motives did Nick feel a chill creep over him, for it sounded as though Eric had half fallen in love with Kate himself.

170

Kate's room was dark, the lattice closed against the heat of the day. She settled herself into a corner stool, soothed by the shadows. Her eyes were curiously dry. She wondered why she had not realized herself that her father had made some sort of arrangement with Nick. But she could not fault her husband. He had been no more dishonest in his intent than Kate had been in hers at the outset. That she had fallen in love with her partner was the cruelest twist of fate.

It especially grieved her to think that her father had felt the need to ensure her future. But more than anything else, Kate felt betrayed by the two people she had loved the most in her life. It seemed as if they had considered her part the professor's possessions, which Nick had inherited in the bargain.

Well, she would show them—and herself—that she had not wasted all those years of studying! Perhaps she could achieve, at the very least, a footnote in some archaeological tome.

Kate drew a long, uneven breath and pulled herself up off the stool, revitalized. She gathered up her notes and sketches of the Isis mask and retrieved the remainder of her father's maps from Nick's trunk. She knew exactly what she would do, as if in the past weeks some unconscious part of her mind had been formulating a plan. From her own trunk, Kate pulled out an *abbayeh*, a long black robe, and a *yasmak*, a veil, which was worn by Muslim women to shield their faces from public view. Dressed in these, she looked like any other Arab woman, with only her blue eyes to possibly give her away.

Thus disguised, she left the house with her papers tucked under her arm, and walked unnoticed

171

through the town. She went down to the river to Sir Peter's *dahabiyeh*. Though she startled the rais when she spoke to him in English, he took her to the cabin where Sir Peter and Major Kennerly were playing cards.

Sir Peter looked up from his hand at her. "Yes, madam, how may we assist you?"

At this, Kate unwrapped the *yasmak*. Both gentlemen were startled when her blond head was revealed.

"Why, Kate! What's this?" Sir Peter asked.

"Gentlemen," she said, tossing her papers on the tabletop. "I have a proposal for you."

They offered her a chair but she refused, preferring to pace the length of the small cabin as she put her case to them. When she drew from amongst her papers the sketches of the Isis mask, they were intrigued, and when she offered her translation of the hieroglyphs, Sir Peter interrupted her.

"You've more than a casual interest in Egyptology, Kate. Why didn't you tell me?"

"There was no point," she explained, "until now."

Major Kennerly tapped the cards he held on the table and then set them in a neat pile.

"Oughtn't you to be showing this to your husband, Mrs. Hammonton?" he wondered.

Kate stiffened. "The Isis mask is mine, a legacy, if you will, from my father. Nick is preoccupied with his own pursuits and is hardly interested in any contributions from me."

She pulled out one of her father's maps and unfolded it on the table.

"Surely you've heard, Major Kennerly, that my

husband is working a promising site in the Valley of the Kings. My proposal, however, is for a site somewhat farther south. Here," she pointed to a spot on the map, "between the village that my father unearthed and the Temple of Isis."

And what is it that you hope to discover?" Sir Peter asked.

Kate was not certain whether he was truly interested or merely amused by all of this. "Perhaps a burial ground of an ancient village," she replied seriously. "It is highly presumptuous of me, I know, to approach you this way, but you did say that you might be doing some digging, and I want to accomplish something on my own before—"

Sir Peter's brows went up. "Before?"

She met his gaze unflinchingly. "I'm carrying your grandchild, Sir Peter. He'll be born in three months' time, and while I've managed to hide it from Nick thus far, he's bound to discover my condition soon, and then I'll be packed up and sent home. You can be sure that, with a child in tow, he'll not have me on any further expeditions. This is my only opportunity."

Sir Peter was dumbstruck. He slowly got up from his chair and embraced his daughter-in-law. "A grandchild! My dearest Kate, what wonderful news!"

Major Kennerly cleared his throat. "I'll leave you two just now—"

Kate put a hand on his shoulder. "No, Major. You must stay and consider my proposal. I've no assets of my own and so cannot expect to be a partner in this venture. If the two of you will underwrite my scheme, you will realize a full percentage of any profits. I wish only the freedom to pursue my ideas."

Sir Peter bade her sit and then pulled up a chair for himself. The three began seriously studying the maps on the table.

"It does seem a likely spot for a dig," Major Kennerly said at last.

"I'm sure it was my father's intention to continue his work in and around the village he'd excavated," Kate assured him, "and he was especially intrigued by this Isis mask, as he called it."

Nonetheless, Sir Peter's brow was furrowed.

"Are you well enough, though, to be tramping about the desert?"

Kate was touched by his concern. "Doctor Latham has been keeping a close eye on me and has threatened to see to it that Nick has me shipped home posthaste if he senses any trouble."

It was obvious by his expression that Sir Peter was not pleased with this possibility. Having found an amenable relation in Kate, he was doubtless loathe to lose her again. And, of course, there was the impending birth of his grandchild to consider. He had been robbed of a son but, by God, he'd not lose a grandson as well!

"We shall take particular care of you then, my dear," he said promptly. "Josiah and I shall make the arrangements for the dig. You need only worry yourself about the task at hand."

"Thank you. Thank you both," Kate said, and sprang from her chair to kiss them each on the cheek.

———

Within weeks, Lord Marleigh had assembled a team of workmen and had begun to dig in earnest. Kate insisted upon being an anonymous collaborator in

174

the venture. She knew that if Nick were to learn of her ties with his father, he would be furious, and she did not know if she had the fortitude to cross him now. All her energy was focused on the place she had come to call the south camp, where she was directing the digging.

The camp was south in relation to Nick's site, but yet not so very far from Luxor. Each morning, under the pretext of making sketches of local temple sites, Kate would set out with young Mustapha. He had become a conspirator in her ruse, her translator and confidante, and as any young boy would, he saw it as an adventure. Once outside the house, Kate would don her veil and robe that she might proceed unnoticed on her way through the village. She and Mustapha would then take the ferry across the river and travel south to the camp by carriage.

Over the ensuing weeks Kate directed the workmen to dig trial pits near the cliffs, to no avail. But her belief that the general area was correct was more than intuition. She had followed an ancient footpath from the Isis temple high into the Theban hills, winding up at the ruined village that her father had unearthed. There was a connection; It was only a matter of finding the right spot. But there were so many cuts and crevices in the hills, that it might take a long time, perhaps even more than one season, to find a burial site.

While searching for a spot of shade late one afternoon, Kate came upon a hieroglyph scratched into the smooth amber cliff face. It was just a bit of Egyptian graffiti, typical of many such instances she had seen in the temples and on the monuments she had visited thus far. But, on instinct, she decided to have Sir Peter direct the workers deeper into this valley on the morrow.

———————

Nick sat in the shade at the mouth of the tomb, elbows resting on bent knees. He turned to look into the empty passage behind him, the bare walls and unfinished corridor, and then back again, disgusted. He poured a generous amount of whiskey into his tin cup.

The sun had crossed behind the cliffs, bringing a little relief from the intense heat. He took a generous swallow of the whiskey as he noticed Eric heading down.

"Come and have a drink, my friend. I was saving this particular bottle to celebrate. No need to save it any longer."

He held out the bottle to Eric, who shook his head as he sat down.

"Lord Marleigh's digging south of here, have you heard?" Nick said. "Just snapped his aristocratic fingers and got himself some workers, supplies, whatever he required. I'll wager he didn't need two Frenchmen to intercede on his behalf to Ishmael Pasha either. Just snapped his fingers—"

"What's all this about?" Eric asked. "You act as though you'll never get a second chance."

Nick swallowed some more whiskey, but his mouth stayed as dry as dust. "There's not enough time. I was so sure of this spot. All those weeks wasted—"

"There'll be other seasons—"

Nick shook his head. "How many more expeditions do you imagine the Society will fund without some sort of return on their investment?"

"They can't hold you personally responsible," Eric said. Standing up, he shoved his hands into his trouser pockets and began to pace the length of the stone corridor. "You've said yourself that archaeology is a speculative venture at best. Every member of the Society is aware of that."

Setting down the bottle, Nick got to his feet and followed Eric into the shadowy hall. "All the pretty excuses aside, I'm to blame. They'll say that Professor Wrightwood put too much faith in my abilities, that I hadn't the experience for the position. Damn it, Eric, they'll say I married Kate only to get the appointment!"

Eric turned to him, a single brow raised. "And?" There was an uncomfortable pause before he went on. "You can't honestly say that the offer wasn't made."

Nick surveyed his friend. He seemed perturbed, which was so unlike him, almost as if he himself believed what Nick had been saying. If Eric had been any other man, Nick would have struck him down. "Nevertheless, I love my wife," Nick finally said.

"You love your work. Is there room in your life for more than one passion?"

Eric turned and walked out of the tomb. Nick ran after him, his head reeling from the whiskey as the sunlight washed over him. "What are you saying?" Nick shouted after him.

The words echoed through the valley. Eric turned back. "All this time you've pursued fame without a care for the wife you claim to love. I'm tired of being your conscience, Nick. If you enjoy drowning your sorrows and feeling sorry for yourself, that's your choice. I'm going back to Luxor, where I can be of some use. People there need a doctor, more than another amateur archaeologist. I'll leave you to your bottle."

With that, he walked away, leaving Nick to contemplate his words.

"Kate will understand," Nick told himself when Eric was gone. "She will!"

If he thought the words would reassure him, he was mistaken. How could she understand such abject failure, she who was accustomed to her father's triumphs? He sat down with the bottle and poured himself another drink.

———————

It was late in the afternoon when Kate took the ferry back to Luxor. She rested on the hard wooden bench and contemplated the next day's work. Mustapha sat cross-legged at her feet. At first, she was not aware of the man who had come to sit nearby.

When she looked up, she recognized Henri Berteau at once. She could not say that she was pleased to see him. She had found his manner too familiar for her liking, his eyes always seeming to assess her as if she were just another objet d'art. Even though her costume would make it difficult for him to identify her, she still averted her gaze from him and turned to look out on the water. She was finally relieved when they reached the opposite shore, so that she and Mustapha could return to the Luxor house.

She stopped in an alleyway to divest herself of

her disguise and sent Mustapha on ahead. As she unwrapped her veil, she wondered why Henri Berteau was here. She'd had no idea that he was to be in Egypt this season; he'd certainly never mentioned such plans in her presence and Nick hadn't thought to tell her if he had known.

She had just tossed the veil over her arm when she looked to see him standing before her.

"Ah, *la belle américaine*. So it was you, Mrs. Hammonton. I was certain that I could not have mistaken your eyes. And what's this disguise? Have you come back from a tryst with a lover?"

He leered unashamedly. Kate was appalled by his manner and could feel the color drain from her face but would not allow him the satisfaction of seeing that he had shocked her. She ignored his remark and pulled off her robe. The linen gown beneath did little to hide her now-rounded figure. Berteau was clearly surprised.

"*Pardon, madame*. I see the monsieur has laid his claim. I should have expected no less. How goes his work?"

"Well enough," Kate said, wishing he would move aside so that she could be on her way.

"He's made a discovery, I hear."

"He's found an entrance of some sort, but for the rest we shall have to wait and see."

"Does it appear promising?" he asked. "Has he reached any chambers? Are there paintings on the walls, any clues at all?"

Kate was sorely tired, and Berteau was clearly annoying her. "I can't say. I've not been to the site myself in weeks."

Now suddenly Berteau's interest had shifted. "I

thought, madame, that you had only just come from there. What else is there to interest you across the river?"

She was at a loss for words. He waited as she anxiously sought a response. "I was visiting . . . a relative. He is wintering in Egypt."

"A relative?" Berteau echoed.

Kate knew that he would not let it go at that, and so she took the offensive. "And you, monsieur? What brings you to Luxor?"

"Business, as usual. You see, Madame Hammonton, I have neither the talent nor the inclination for discovery, and so I must wait for men such as your husband to succeed and make an offer for the treasures they unearth."

"I am afraid that where my husband is concerned, you shall be disappointed," Kate told him. "Whatever antiquities he may discover, apart from those appropriated by the Egyptian government, belong to the Society for the Preservation of Antiquities."

His laugh was not a pleasant one, falling harsh on her ear. It had been intended to make her feel naive. "Ah, but they are so very far away. Who is to know if a piece of jewelry or a funerary statue were to 'disappear' from the catalogue of items? It is not unheard of, madame, I assure you. Agreements can be made."

Kate did not want to listen. The atmosphere in the narrow alleyway was becoming oppressive. On either side, the mud-brick walls gave off the heat they had accumulated throughout that day. Kate's dress clung to her skin, dampened by perspiration, and she felt suddenly lightheaded. She looked past

180

Berteau, hoping that Mustapha would come back to see what had detained her. Instead she saw Eric Latham, to her great relief.

"Eric?" she called out, waving as he turned round.

He came to her, eyeing Berteau suspiciously.

"Kate, I was coming to see you."

"I'll walk with you then," she replied. "I'm just on my way home myself."

"Oh, Eric," she said, as if she had almost forgotten the little man. "This is Monsieur Berteau, whose hospitality Nick and I enjoyed while we were in Paris. Monsieur, this is Doctor Eric Latham, who is working with my husband."

"*Docteur*," Berteau said and gave a curt bow. "Perhaps we might meet later at my lodgings for a drink. I'm very much interested in the work you are doing in the valley."

"Perhaps later," Eric said, not missing the beleaguered look on Kate's face. He pushed past the little man and extended his arm out to Kate. "Now, though, I must see Mrs. Hammonton home. I can see that this infernal climate is distressing her. She needs her rest, you understand."

"*Mais oui, certainement,*" Berteau replied.

Kate felt his shrewd eyes on them as Eric escorted her down the crooked street. When they were well out of earshot, Eric remarked, "He's an odd sort, seemed particularly interested in the dig."

"Henri Berteau is a dealer in antiquities," Kate explained, "and as I understand it, totally without scruples. He was grilling me about Nick's work when you arrived. He implied that Nick might sell him some of his finds."

"There are hundreds of his kind in Egypt," Eric told her. "Men with no real interest in archaeology. Money is their main ambition."

"What a horrid little man!" Kate exclaimed.

Eric regarded her earnestly. "You really don't look well, Kate. You've not taken my advice to stay indoors surely. What have you been up to?"

"Why, I've only been sketching the temples. It's not strenuous, and I keep in the shade."

Eric eyed her skeptically. "And why is this costume thrown over your arm?"

Kate would not meet his eyes. She did not relish lying to him.

"I told you I was thinking of adopting this form of dress for comfort. Besides, I like to walk around unnoticed."

"I see, he replied thoughtfully. They finally reached the house, and he pushed open the door and ushered her inside.

Kate was relieved to find it measurably cooler within the house. She leaned back against the tiled wall, listening to an exchange between Daphne and the cook. First a few words of English drifted down the hall, followed by a rapid reply in Arabic; then there was silence. Kate imagined that the two had resorted to sign language to make themselves understood. Though Daphne had not acquired much of an understanding of Arabic during her stay, she was an accomplished 'charades' player, which served her well as she dealt with domestic matters here.

After a few moments, Eric followed Kate into her room so that he might examine her.

"If you've left off interrogating me, doctor," Kate

said, "I should like to know what, besides my health, has brought you back from the camp?"

"Alas, I am by no means as dedicated a man as your husband. I think I can be of more use as a doctor while I'm here," he told her.

"What, to treat the tourists who come through, you mean?"

Eric's expression was serious, his fair head bent as he studied the design of the carpet on the floor. "No, Kate. The villagers, the children especially, are in need of a doctor. If I can gain their trust, I may be of some good use while I'm here."

He took hold of Kate's bare foot, poking and prodding at it. "You must promise to stay off your feet for a good portion of each day," he said. "Do you see the swelling around the ankles here?"

Kate changed the subject. "How's the work on the site coming along?" she asked.

Eric shook his head. "It's over, Kate. We've dug out all there is. It turned out to be a shaft strewn with rubble, that's all . . . an unfinished tomb."

Kate was silent, her thoughts centered on her husband. She could well imagine his disappointment. More than a year of planning, the labor of hundreds of men, leading only to an empty shaft. She feared the effect that this failure would have on him.

"Are you drinking enough water?" Eric asked her. "It's vital to your health in this heat."

"If you listen carefully when I walk, you can hear the sloshing about inside."

He laughed and poked her with his stethoscope.

"Truly, Kate, you must take my suggestions seriously."

"I won't do anything to jeopardize my child," she promised. She paused, then asked "How is Nick taking the setback?"

Eric thought for a moment "He was calm at first. He went over the interior walls again and again, certain that he was missing something, that the appearance was a trick to fool tomb robbers. And then a few weeks ago, we got word that Lord Marleigh was digging south of the valley. Nick was infuriated. Why this news should matter to him at all is beyond my comprehension."

Kate eased herself into an upright position, seeming to smooth the wrinkles in her clothes.

"And he's been drinking," Eric added. "I've never seen him this way."

He regretted the words before they'd left his mouth. She kneaded her brow as if it would soothe her pain, then met him with eyes that were like luminous pools of blue beside the translucent pallor of her skin.

"I shouldn't say anything, perhaps," Kate began, "but you are Nick's friend. I can't see the harm in your knowing. Lord Marleigh is Peter Hammonton, Nick's father."

Eric was astounded. He had taken for granted that he knew all there was to know about Nick's life.

"He is the husband that Nick's mother ran away from all those years ago," she said. "Nick hates him and feels he abandoned him. The news about the dig must have been doubly humiliating for him: to have failed on his own and then to have the father he hates come along to quite possibly show him up."

"I'm glad I know now," Eric replied. "I was beginning to wonder if the failure had unbalanced him."

He took hold of Kate's hands and helped her to her feet. Her look was plaintive, and Eric had to resist the urge to hold her in his arms and whisper comforting words.

"What should I do?" she asked.

"I think you ought to talk to Nick," he said, clearing his throat.

"You will take me to him in the morning, won't you, Eric? I've so many things to explain."

Eric nodded. "He may not admit it, but he needs you with him now. The news of his impending fatherhood may be just the tonic."

Kate put her arms around him and drew him as close as she could. "You've been so kind," she said. "How can I thank you?"

His hands slid over her slight shoulders, allowing them to wander to the soft nape of her neck. Resentment of Nick welled in him. How little he appreciated this woman! He remembered then something that Nick had said, that he had more feeling for Kate than was seemly. Yes, it was true, Eric finally admitted to himself, and it mattered little that she was his best friend's wife. He might have told Kate of his feelings, offered to care for her and the child, and let Nick rot in the desert. But he knew that despite how she had been treated, Kate was in love with Nick, and nothing Eric could do would ever change that.

Nick stood on the threshold of the Luxor house, wondering how he should apologize to Kate. He'd treated her badly these past months, as he had been totally obsessed with the now-failed expedition. It seemed that he was destined to be a disappointment to the Society, to his wife and to himself. All that he could do now was to try to patch things up with Kate. She was a level-headed woman. If he was suitably contrite, she'd listen and surely she'd understand.

The house was dark and cool. He rested against the door to gather his strength, for he was still feeling the effects of the whiskey. He heard Daphne trying to converse with the cook, and decided to make his way down the hall to Kate's room, but he suddenly stopped short at the doorway. In the shadows beyond, he saw his wife locked in an embrace with a fair-headed man. Even though his back was turned, Nick recognized him as his best friend.

He felt the painful twist of his heart in his breast, and was frozen on the spot, unable to believe what he saw. They were unaware of his presence. As he stared at their damning silhouette, his jaw clenched tightly and anger rose like bile in him.

"I see that the two of you have become better acquainted in my absence."

At the sound of Nick's voice, Kate looked up over Eric's shoulder, her face washed of color, but she would not release her hold on him.

"You see that I come empty-handed," Nick said. "I had hoped to bring my faithful wife some small trinket from the tomb we'd been excavating, but as you have no doubt heard, it was a wasted effort. I've led one hundred men on a merry chase without so much as a pottery shard to show for their pains!"

"Nick, you don't understand," Eric insisted, and when he turned to face his friend, Kate hid herself behind him.

"Oh, don't I?" Nick shot back. "I wondered why you'd given up the dig to stay in Luxor. It was not so noble a cause as doctoring, was it?"

"You're a fool, Nick," Kate said to him, her voice cold and clam, "to strike out at those who love you most."

The words hit him hard, he as quickly turned on his heel and stormed out of the house.

Kate watched him leave, her anger ebbing away. She felt empty inside.

"Go after him, Kate," Eric implored. "Try to explain what all this is about."

Kate shook her head, weary. "No. I won't go running after him. If he has so little faith in me, what good are my words?"

Chapter XIII

*T*he workmen sank several trial pits in the valley floor without success. The last one reached a depth of ten feet before they came upon the sloping shaft in a crevice of rock. Kate was not as surprised as the others. For some time now she had considered the possibility of such a discovery, and while in Egypt had compiled the evidence.

The workmen worked tirelessly, and Kate almost felt guilty about it as she rested on a long outcropping of rock that served as a natural bench. Sir Peter and Major Kennerly moved excitedly among the men, supervising their efforts and taking turns rushing up to inform Kate of the progress. The air was charged with anticipation.

Suddenly Sir Peter made his way up and

shouted, "You've done it, my dear! It is definitely a burial site!"

Kate managed a weak smile that hardly mirrored the thrill that coursed through her. This was the moment she had longed for, but her swollen body betrayed her, sapping more of her precious strength. She took Sir Peter's hand and leaned on the wall to steady herself.

"Take me down, please," she said a little weakly.

When they reached the work area, the men were clearing away the rubble from a plastered doorway that was obstructing the passage.

"Is it sealed?" Sir Peter called as they approached.

Major Kennerly examined the plaster as the rubble was cleared away, while Kate copied down the hieroglyphic seals stamped on it.

"Here in this corner," the major said. "It's an opening, I'm afraid."

Heavy silence hung in the air as they realized that their discovery was a plundered tomb.

It seemed like forever before the wall was breached and the hole made large enough for a comfortable entry. They lit lanterns to help guide them through the dark passages within. Sir Peter went in first and then helped Kate through the hole. The major cautiously brought up the rear, while a dozen workmen stared through the hole.

The three trod downward carefully; the passage sloped at an angle, which made balance difficult. Kate kept a firm hold on her father-in-law's arm. There was little relief from the broiling heat within the tomb.

They had advanced no more than twenty feet

when a stone that had been kicked up by Kate's shoe skittered across the floor and fell silent. Seconds later, it struck rock somewhere below. Sir Peter stopped short and held out the lantern. Just beyond them, the passage dropped off into a pit that must have been forty feet deep.

"Good heavens!" Kate exclaimed.

"A feature to discourage tomb robbers," Sir Peter said, his voice echoing through the corridor. "Not entirely successful, however, he added pointing out a coil of rope that lay below, in the bottom of the pit. "Others have been here before us."

"The burial cannot be intact, then," Kate said, disappointedly.

"Perhaps something of value remains," the major put in, though none of them believed it.

Kate's attention was focused across the chasm to a hall beyond, its walls barely lit by the uneven lamplight. Even so, she could see the murals upon them. Elegant figures with graceful hands were engaged in the ancient rituals. The painted hieroglyphs were a blur from this distance, but the colors in the drawings—reds and yellows and blues—were particularly vivid, as if they'd been applied only recently.

"We must get across!" she said.

"It will take time," Sir Peter told her. "A walkway must be built across this pit. It cannot be done all in one day."

Kate nodded her head in agreement and did her best to contain her eagerness. So much of this work involved patience, and lately her patience had worn thin.

Sir Peter laid a hand on her arm. "You're tired, Kate, and you don't look well. It might not seem so, but the work will be hard for us now. Perhaps you ought to send for Nick to help."

Kate was angry, thinking that Sir Peter might be using her to get to Nick. "I assure you I'm well enough to finish the task I started," she snapped. "If you think me incapable—"

"Not at all, my dear," he replied in soothing tones. "You've gotten us this far, haven't you? I worry about you, though, taking on all of this with only a pair of foolish old men to aid you. If you promise me you'll go back to Luxor and let Doctor Latham have a look at you, I shall set the workmen at their task immediately. They will have bridged the pit by the time you return in the morning, and we can get on with our work."

Kate was feeling lightheaded and short tempered. She regretted the sharp words she had dealt Sir Peter, and thus readily agreed to his suggestion. A night's rest would help, she told herself. By the time she had reached the Luxor house, though, her face was washed of color and her mouth was dry. Dauphne caught sight of her.

"You look awful," she said. "Lie down at once and I'll send Mustapha to fetch Eric. He's tending one of the villagers."

Kate did not argue. She splashed some tepid water on her face and lay down on the bed, hoping that some of her strength would be restored on the morrow. There was so much work to be done.

The Nile shimmered gold in the evening sun. Luxor was a welcome sight to a man who'd spent weeks sifting the Theban sands. Nick chose not to dwell on the dozens of trial pits he'd excavated without luck. Mr. Thayer had become more temperamental lately, especially after Eric had left. Eric's enthusiasm and lightheartedness had, on many occasions, raised their spirits and spurred them on. He had provided the perfect contrast to Nick's serious, almost obsessive dedication.

Nick had had nothing but time these past weeks to reconsider the scene he'd come upon in Kate's room. Surely he'd misread what he had seen. Eric was his friend; he would never betray him in such a way, and Kate—

How he'd missed her! He'd not made much of their marriage thus far. He could not have blamed her if she had turned from him, but no, he would not believe it, no matter what he thought he'd seen.

As Nick crossed the threshold of the Luxor house, he was nearly run down by Mustapha on an errand.

"Pardon, Hammonton-*effendi*. I bring message for the missus, most important message."

The boy drew a folded sheet of paper from his shirt.

"For my wife?" Nick asked. "You may give it to me then. I will see that she receives it at once."

Mustapha put the note into Nick's hand and disappeared into the house. As Nick handled the note, it unfolded, and he recognized the handwriting as Eric's. Good sense gave over to jealousy, and without hesitation, he read what was penned on the paper.

Dearest Kate,

I will come to you when I can get away. Wait for
me in your bed. You have filled my thoughts
since I saw you last. I looked for you yesterday in
the temple, but you were not about. I should like
to see those sketches you are making. I hope you
are not keeping secrets from your friend who
cares for you.

                                    Eric

Nick was stunned with disbelief. Blind anger
infused him, and he stormed into Kate's room to
confront her.

He found himself in the shadows, the lattice
closed against the slant of the evening sun. Kate lay
on the bed beneath the great drape of mosquito netting, her back to him, golden hair splayed across the
pillow.

"Eric?" she called when she heard his footsteps.

"No," Nick replied, distaste in his voice. "I'm
afraid he'll be detained a while yet."

"Nick?" she asked, not attempting to rise nor
turn her head.

"Yes, the cuckolded husband come home at last.
Shall I read you the note I intercepted?" he asked.
"He wants you to wait in bed for him. Will he be
surprised to find me here when he comes? Disappointed, I expect."

"What are you going on about?" Kate asked, tired
and confused.

"My wife and my dearest friend, I suppose loyalty is too much to ask."

He raised up his hand and crushed the note in

his fist. At length Kate moved to rise, and with her back to him still, she went to the vanity table.

"You've had more loyalty than you deserve," she told him.

Sitting down, she put her head in her hands and after a while, she looked up to meet his eyes. "You hide yourself away in the desert for months at a time, and the rest of us be damned! Professor Hammonton must have his success, no matter the cost. Now when you deign to honor us with a visit, it is only to deliver accusations."

"This room is shut up like a tomb!" he said as he went to throw open the lattice. As the evening's light spilled into the dark corners of the room, he turned on her again. "And you might at least have the decency to give me your attention when I'm talking to you."

She rose in such a slow, deliberate manner that it served to further annoy him. "Let me assure you, my dear husband, I have shared my bed with no one in your absence," she said.

His expression was unforgiving. "I don't need your lies, Kate!" he growled.

When she turned to him and he saw her pregnant state, he stared in disbelief and his jaw hung open.

"Dear God! How could you keep such a thing—Why didn't you tell me?"

He stepped toward her, but she moved a step back in response.

"At first, I thought it would make it too easy for you to send me home. You never wanted me here, and you've made it more than clear that I've gotten in your way."

"You can't believe that," Nick said.

"Don't play me for a fool, Nick. I know you struck a bargain with my father. How did it go exactly? 'Take care of poor little Kate, my boy, and all that I have is yours'?"

"I won't lie and tell you that such an offer was never made. What can I say to make you understand?"

Kate picked up her black robe from where it lay and tossed it over her arm. "You've said quite enough for now," she turned and walked past him. Standing in the doorway, she turned back again. "Don't worry yourself about poor little Kate. My reasons for agreeing to this marriage were no less mercinary than yours. I've sold myself for a passage to Egypt. What a sad pair we are," she said as she left him.

She stopped in the hall, dropping back against the wall as her brow ceased in pain. She took a deep breath to regain her composure and went out of the house.

———

Nick was stunned enough by the turn of events to let her go. It was a few minutes more before he decided to go after her, but by then she had left the house.

He walked the narrow streets in the twilight, contemplating his impending fatherhood. He would never have guessed the secret that Kate had been harboring, and it underscored just how great the distance was between them.

He was sure that he would meet her around the very next corner; she had had time enough to walk off her anger. But he did not meet her. The darkness settled in, and his anxiety increased.

He went to the house where Eric was tending a sick boy, hoping to find Kate and to apologize to his friend. But Kate was not there, and Eric was grim.

"Daphne sent word that Kate was not well. She oughtn't to be out wandering."

"It's my fault," Nick admitted. "What I said to her . . . and to you was unforgivable. What can I do Eric? Where could she have gone?"

"Back to the house, no doubt," Eric assured him, "after she'd calmed down. I've finished here. Let's go back; I'm sure we'll find her resting in her bed."

When they got back to the house, Kate was still not there.

———

Across the river only a few miles away, Kate rested as best she could on the cot in Sir Peter's tent. She was exhausted and anxious about tomorrow. And when she tried to sleep, she found her thoughts turning to Nick and their latest confrontation. Tears pricked the corners of her eyes. Any day the child would come, and Kate did not even know whether Nick was pleased at the prospect.

What had become of their deep friendship? She finally had to admit that their ambitions had pulled them apart. Instead of forging a bond between them, their common interest had sent them off in different directions and eroded the foundations of their marriage. She knew that there was an answer to their dilemma. They would need to work together, but she could not say that Nick would be agreeable, and pride would not let her make the first move.

With the dawn, the workmen began again, but it was well into the afternoon before they had nailed the last boards of the walkway that bridged the pit. Kate was finally able to cross over and study the murals.

She knew at once that the woman to whom this tomb belonged was the same as that of the Isis mask. The wall paintings told much of the story. She had been a priestess in the temple of Isis and the most beloved daughter of the pharaoh. Kate found herself mesmerized by the painted scenes: of Maat, the goddess of truth, as she weighed the heart of the priestess against a feather; of the blue-skinned god of the underworld, Osiris, to whom the priestess made offerings; and of Isis herself, leading the priestess into the presence of Khepri, the beetle-headed god of resurrection. . . .

Kate followed Sir Peter and Major Kennerly as they traversed the hall in silent anticipation, but disappointment came upon them at once as they entered the first chamber and stared upon the carnage there. Unguent jars and chests had been emptied of their contents and smashed, as the thieves had searched for valuables. The scene was much the same in a small adjacent antechamber. All that was left was a jumble of splintered wood, shredded linen and pottery shards. The two men shook their heads as Kate mused on what they might have found had they been the first to enter the tomb.

Dispirited, they ventured on, finally descending a staircase cut into the rock floor and finding themselves in a small pillared room, the burial chamber itself. Sir Peter lifted his lantern high, its yellow light illuminating the painted stars on the ceiling and the hieroglyphic text on the surrounding walls. This room was also in shambles, but the far wall and a portion of the ceiling had collapsed into the center of the room. Kate drew an astonished breath as the lantern shone on the rose-colored stone of a sarcophagus, with its lid still intact, buried in the rubble.

"What could have caused such a thing?" Major Kennerly asked.

"Perhaps a fault in the rock," Sir Peter replied. Kicking at the pile of rubble, his foot dislodged what appeared to be a human bone. "Look here."

He set the lanter aside and bent down to investigate. There were more bones and shreds of cloth. "I've seen burial sites where robbers dug their own shaft to access the tomb. Perhaps that's what this poor unfortunate fellow was up to when everything collapsed."

Kate was excited. "Then the thieves who ransacked the other chambers mightn't have had the time to dig out the sarcophagus."

Sir Peter nodded. "The wall will have to be braced," he said, considering practical matters, "before anything can be moved."

"Yes, yes," the major agreed. "We shall have them begin at once."

"How long?" Kate asked, unable to contain her impatience.

"Tomorrow, my dear," Sir Peter replied, patting her shoulder. "For now, let's see if we can find anything worthwhile amidst the desecration of the other chambers."

To Kate's surprise, they did find several artifacts intact: a wooden unguent spoon whose handle was in the shape of a duck, a mirror of polished brass, several strings of faience beads and a pair of ushabtis with delicate faces that had been masterfully carved.

By evening, the workmen had shored up the wall of the burial chamber. In the morning they would begin the tedious task of removing the rubble from around the sarcophagus. Sir Peter installed two guards at the entrance of the tomb, and the rest of the party retired for the evening.

CHAPTER XIV

Sir Peter came into the tent that he had given over to Kate, and found her at the desk he'd assembled from packing crates and boards. She wore a serious countenance as she made notes in her book, and he watched her in silence for a time. His affection for her had grown these past months, and the pallor in her lovely face distressed him.

"I'm going down to Luxor for supplies," he told her. "I shall be back in the morning."

He hesitated before continuing. "Kate, are you certain you won't accompany me? Nick must be terribly worried about you."

Kate stopped writing but did not look up from the page. "As worried as he might be if he lost any of his possessions."

"How can you say such a thing?"

"I'm sorry if it upsets you," she went on, "but it is the truth. You should know, Sir Peter, that ours is not an idyllic marriage. Your son considers me, at best, a distraction for his work."

Having begun in this vein, Kate went on as if there were pleasure for her in being reminded of her pain. "You should know, Sir Peter, that your son only married me because my father made it most profitable for him to do so. I had hoped that, in time, he might have developed a fondness—well, no matter, the situation has grown intolerable."

"Kate, what are you saying?"

"I've given a lot of thought of late to this child and the life it will have. I've had the same sort of life myself. It was fraught with loneliness: a life spent in anticipation of my father's return from one expedition or another, and of trying to capture his attention when he was at home and occupied with his research. Is this the best that I can offer my child?"

Sir Peter looked stricken. "No!" he said, a hysterical strain in his voice. "I won't see it all happen again!"

He turned and was gone, leaving Kate confused and feeling guilty for having agitated him.

Her eyes were tired of straining to see the page in the dim light, so she closed her notebook and blew out the lantern, settling herself onto the cot. But she did not sleep. She was ashamed of that perversity in her nature that made her strike out at Sir Peter when her quarrel was with Nick.

The stillness of the Theban night was broken suddenly by a sharp crack resounding in the hills. Another followed in rapid succession, and Kate was certain that the sounds had come from the excavation site. She poked her head out of the tent, but it seemed that no one else in the camp had been disturbed by the noise. Had she only imagined it?

She could not put it out of her mind, however. She lit the lantern, picked up her *abbayeh* and went out to investigate. She moved like a cat across the landscape, seeking the mouth of the tomb by the light of her lantern and the pale moon overhead.

"Hello?" she called to the guards.

There was no reply.

Before she could take another step, she saw them. Laying together in a heap. Both guards were dead, a spreading circle of crimson staining their white robes, glazed eyes staring heavenward.

There was movement from within the tomb, and without giving thought to the danger, Kate went in. There, a handful of tattered Arabs were picking through the debris in search of valuables. When one them used his rifle butt to splinter the lid of an already damaged chest, Kate cried out despite herself.

"Stop this! You don't know what you're destroying! How dare you break in here!"

At the outbust, a swarm of men came out of the burial chamber and Kate suddenly realized the danger she was in.

Her heart was pounding furiously. She considered taking flight, but she could never outrun all of them. Perhaps if she screamed with all her might— And then she heard the familiar voice.

"Madame Hammonton, you should be asleep in your bed. It is not healthy to wander the desert at night."

"Monsieur Berteau! I cannot believe this! How can one who appreciates the value of these artifacts allow such ... such carnage? Is this how you acquired all of the treasures in your hidden room?"

"Alas, madame, I have not the energy for trial and error. This is so much easier, you see."

"You're no better than a grave robber."

"*Mais non*, I am a connoisseur. Come see what marvelous treasures I have found."

Reluctantly, Kate followed him into the burial chamber, which was now brightly lit by many lanterns. Berteau's men had dug out the sarcophagus and removed its heavy lid, and the painted lid of the inner coffin as well. The Frenchman bade her come closer, and when she did, he pushed aside a crumbling linen shroud to reveal an exquisitely formed death mask of silver set with lapis. The resemblance to the trial piece her father had given her was remarkable. It was the same woman, the same high cheekbones, full mouth and eyes that slanted seductively.

"*C'est magnifique, non?*"

Kate's heart sank. It *was* magnificent. It was priceless, in fact, but it should have been her discovery. She stood by, helpless, as Berteau stripped the mummy of the jewelry hidden within its wrappings: a golden diadem, amulets, rings and necklaces set with turquoise, carnelian and lapis lazuli. When he and his thieves had finished, they gathered up the treasures and prepared to leave.

"I do not wish to harm you, madame, but I must have time to make my escape. So I shall leave you here. You understand that I must have my men destroy the bridge over this pit so that you do not return

203

to your camp and set the hounds at our heels. They will come and find you in the morning, and all will be well. *Au revoir*, madame."

With this, he left her. His men hacked at the walkway with axe and spade until the planks gave way and tumbled down into the abyss below. With only the light of the lantern to cheer her, she sat down in the hall to wait for the morning, contemplating the figures and hieroglyphics painted on the wall across from her.

Soon she was haunted by a vision of the exquisite mask that Berteau had stolen. How pleased Sir Peter would have been with such a treasure. But then an undeniable ache started across her back. She tried to forget about it and closed her eyes, hoping that she might fall asleep despite the uncomfortable conditions. But she could not sleep.

Though she tried to deny it, the persistent ache that Kate was feeling at very regular intervals now could only mean one thing.

"Not now," she whispered, "not here."

———————

Nick leaned his hands on the low terrace wall and looked across the river to the hills of western Thebes, silver in the moonlight.

"Damn! Where is she? We've searched the entire village."

Eric stood beside him. "We shall have to face the possibility that she may have left Luxor. She could well have taken the train up to Cairo and be heading home. She is headstrong."

"Headstrong, yes, but not foolish. You told me that the baby is due any time now. I can't believe that she would risk travelling. Besides, she took none of her things."

"There is one other possibility," Eric said and paused until he had his friend's attention. "She might have gone to your father."

Nick was tired and upset, not ready to accept this possibility. "She wouldn't go to him. She knows how I feel."

Eric laid a hand on Nick's shoulder. "We've been friends for so long, I can't believe that you never told me that your father was alive . . . that the two of you were estranged."

Nick began pacing to expend some of his nervousness. "There was nothing to say about the man. His behavior was reprehensible. What he did to my mother cannot be excused."

"But you don't know the man," Eric protested.

"My grandfather told me all that I need to know."

Eric began again, patiently. "I think," he said, "that all of the kindnesses your grandfather accorded you may have blinded you to the true man. I recall, even if you do not, the arguments between you, how he tried to mold you into something you were not."

The words gave Nick pause. "What are you saying?"

"Jacob Mallory was not a man without motives. Would it not have been in his own interest to have you growing up hating your father? You must remember how badly he wanted you to take over for him. He wouldn't want your father to take you home to England."

Nick was pensive and Eric pressed on. "You could least remain somewhat more neutral," he said, "until you have heard his side of the matter. He is, after all, your father, and your prime concern at this point should be finding Kate."

The last statement sounded very much like an accusation, daring Nick to deny his selfishness, but he was not angry. Eric had given him a new perspective, and he was invigorated. "You're right," he said. "Let's go and find my father."

———

It was chance alone that led them first to the river, where they found Peter Hammonton supervising his men as they loaded supplies onto the *dahabiyeh*. He did not seem as surprised to see them as they might have thought, but his expression was guarded. Nick approached him without hesitation.

"Lord Marleigh," he said. "I am looking for my wife."

"Careful with those sacks," Sir Peter called to the rais. "Omar, tell them to take care."

"As you say, *effendi*," came the reply.

Finally, Sir Peter turned his attention on Nick. "I see. Your wife, is it? And does she wish to be found, do you think?"

Nick could not help but be irritated by the man's superior attitude, but managed to maintain his composure. "She is my wife. She is carrying my child, and I have a right to know where she is."

"No more right than I had when my wife disappeared without a trace," came the retort.

"What do you mean, sir?" Nick asked. Suddenly his anger spilled over. "You allowed my mother to take me into her father's house. You did not even try to stop her or bring her—or me—back."

Sir Peter looked tired. "When Lucy left me, there was no child, nor any hint of one. I did not discover that I had a son for more than ten years, and by then it was too late. I had lost my son to his grandfather."

Nick paused to take in his father's words. Was it possible that he had misjudged his father? That he had been raised on half-truths and deception? He studied the man's face and was almost surprised to find it without guile.

"I cannot believe it!" Nick paused. "But if what you say is true . . . then all these years . . . my grandfather was lying to me?" Nick ventured.

Sir Peter looked at him sadly. "Jacob Mallory was a self-made man. He hated me for my aristocratic titles and inherited fortunes."

"You see, my friend," Eric put in, "how things have gotten horribly twisted?"

Nick felt unsure of himself as he was forced now to question many of the things he had taken for granted all his life. There was an awkward moment of silence before he reached his decision.

"It seems," Nick said at last, a little formally, "that I have grievously wronged you, sir. Please let us end our misunderstandings here and now."

He held out his hand to his father. Sir Peter took it firmly and pulled his son to him. "At last," he said, "at long last."

It was with a great deal of pride that Sir Peter introduced his son to his men, but Nick could not enjoy the moment as much as his father was. He was uneasy about Kate.

"Please, sir," he persisted. "I must see my wife, if you know where she is. There are things between us that need to be said and the sooner the better."

"Of course," Sir Peter replied. "She is at our camp across the river. We shall leave as soon as the supplies have been loaded. She is upset, and last night she said things—well, I'm certain she didn't mean them. Make things right between you," he advised his son. "I can't stand by and watch your young family come apart as mine did."

"It shan't be," Nick assured him, and he was determined to make it so.

———————

At Sir Peter's suggestion, they rested in his cabin as the vessel was loaded with supplies and sails were set for the western shore. Nick found it nearly impossible to sleep, consumed with Kate's accusation about the deal he had made with her father. How could he explain that he would not have assented to the professor's wishes no matter how much he'd wanted the position, if he hadn't fallen in love with her first? Kate was worth more to him than any title, any treasure. She would never take him at his word, yet it was so.

It occurred to him that she might not care what his true feelings were. She had said that she had agreed to marry him only to get a passage to Egypt. The thought twisted his heart, but no, he told himself, it was not so. When he held her, her body could not deny that she loved him.

It was nearly dawn when Nick stepped out onto the deck of the *dahabiyeh*. The stark cliffs of Thebes rose up against the pink sky, where the moon formed a perfect circle. It seemed like hours before the others awakened and the supplies were loaded onto the wagons and the donkeys waiting on the shore, and the caravan started for the campsite.

When they reached the site, Sir Peter went ahead, disappearing into one of the tents. He came out again, looking bewildered.

"What is it?" Nick asked.

"She's not there."

"Where could she have gone at such an hour?" Eric wondered.

Nick's heart dropped. Would Kate truly have been so foolish as to try to travel home on her own?

Major Kennerly came out of his own tent, dabbing his face with a towel.

"Good morning, Peter," he said and acknowledged the newcomers with a nod of his head. "Gentlemen."

"Josiah," Sir Peter began, "this is my son, Nicholas Hammonton, and his friend, Doctor Eric Latham. They've come looking for Kate."

"Why, she's asleep in your tent," the major said.

"I've looked. She is not there now."

"Perhaps she's gone ahead to the tomb. She was so anxious, you know."

"Yes," Sir Peter agreed, looking relieved, "you're probably right."

Sir Peter and Major Kennerly led the way along the rock cliffs to the entrance of the tomb.

"You have been successful, then?" Nick asked his father as they followed the precarious path.

"Yes, we have found a tomb. The wall murals are very well preserved, as you shall soon see, but the burial was not intact."

"It was kind of you to allow Kate to observe your work," Nick said.

Sir Peter and Major Kennerly exchanged a long look.

"Yes," Sir Peter replied, ". . . kind."

"Congratulations, sir," Eric offered. "Such a find is, indeed, a great accomplishment."

"I am not to be congratulated," Sir Peter admitted. "While I am the primary financial backer of this venture, I cannot take the credit."

"Major Kennerly?" Eric assumed.

"Not I," the major responded quickly. "I haven't the head for these scientific pursuits."

"Who then?" Nick asked, curious now.

"It is our own dear Kate who directed this expedition," Sir Peter replied, laughing at their surprise. "She came to us with the proposal some months ago, when she tired of sitting in the Luxor house away from all the excitement."

"No wonder she's been exhausted," Eric said. "She told me that she'd only been sketching temples."

"I should have guessed," Nick began. "It seems, gentlemen, that I know less of my wife's activities these past months than all of you. I am well aware that I am to blame for this situation. Whilst I busied myself trying to build my reputation and justify my position, it seems that my wife was able to succeed where I failed."

"I hope that you are not bitter," Sir Peter told his son.

"Not bitter, only ashamed that I did not believe in Kate's abilities. We should have been working together all along but for my damned, sinful pride."

Sir Peter laid a hand on Nick's shoulder. "It is not too late to repair the damage," he said. "Kate

210

loves you, I'm sure that she does, but she's at least as stubborn as you are. She needs to rest now. She's pushed herself too far. Perhaps if you told her what you've just told us and offered to help—"

"I shall," Nick said, "but will she accept help from me?"

"This is an important find," Sir Peter explained. "We will need all of the trained help we can muster."

"You've told us that the tomb was plundered, sir," Eric put in. "Was not everything of importance removed from the tomb?"

Sir Peter smiled a sly smile. "Ah, gentlemen, I shall tell you our great secret. We have found a stone sarcophagus, half buried in the rubble of fallen rock; an undisturbed sarcophagus."

"It shan't be a wasted season after all," Eric said.

Their lightheartedness left them all at once when they reached the entrance of the tomb to find the two guards lying dead.

"My God!" Sir Peter exclaimed as he knelt beside one of them. "What happened?"

Suddenly there came from within the bowels of the tomb a wail that brought to Nick's mind the so-called pharaoh's curse that was so popular among the uninitiated, but he dismissed it at once as nonsense. Three-thousand-year-old spectres could not have put bullet holes into those two guards. And then he remembered that his wife was very likely inside the tomb. "Kate!" he shouted.

He did not wait for the lanterns to be lit, but rushed into the darkened corridor at a reckless pace.

It was fortunate that the yellow circle of light from Kate's lantern illuminated the pit, else Nick would have rushed headlong into it. He halted at the edge, staring down on the remains of the ruined walkway as the others joined him.

"What's this?" Major Kennerly said. "Someone's smashed up our bridge."

As Sir Peter held up his lantern, Nick's eyes followed the light across the pit to the opposite side where Kate lay curled on the floor of the hall. Recalling the bloody scene outside, panic seized him. "Kate!" he cried out, anxiously seeking a way across.

"Are you hurt, Kate?" Eric called.

"It's the baby," she said and then gasped for breath. "Please, please hurry!"

Nick had found a coil of rope amongst the supplies and directed the three men to hold it while he lowered himself into the pit. Much of the broken walkway lay at the bottom, but there was a section and several crosspieces that he judged would suffice. Using them as a makeshift ladder, he clambered up until he was within ten feet of the top. It was not enough. Eric threw him another length of rope, which he used to lash yet another broken section of the bridge to the last. He climbed again, putting his weight close to the wall to steady the precarious ladder, and at last he was able to pull himself over the top.

He rushed to Kate beside her, afraid to touch her. "Kate, what happened?"

She looked up at him, her face washed of color. Perspiration beaded her brow. "They killed the guards. Everything is gone; all that we'd worked for. There was a death mask, so beautiful, like nothing I'd ever seen before. . . . and jewelry, too. All gone . . ."

"Who?" Nick asked. "Did you recognize any of the thieves?"

212

Her breathing was labored, her eyes fiercely bright. "Berteau!"

Nick was stunned. "Henri Berteau? In Egypt? But he never mentioned that he'd be here this season—"

An awful realization crept over Nick. Berteau had been using him. He'd helped to make arrangements with the government for the dig, and all the while he was scheming. Nick had been too trusting, and now Kate had suffered because of it.

"I'm sorry," he told her, stroking her hair, "so sorry."

He tried to lift her into his arms, but she gathered her remaining strength to pull away from him.

"Sorry?" she said contemptuously. "Don't touch me! Don't ever touch me again! Henri Berteau was your friend; you must have known what he was about. You're to blame for all of this!"

Nick winced as though she'd struck him. How could she believe such a thing?

With the advent of another pain, Kate doubled up and groaned.

"Eric!" Nick shouted.

He was already on his way across, using the same precarious method Nick had used. Before too long, he came to kneel beside Kate.

"How long have you been here?" he asked as he checked her.

"Hours," she replied when the pains had abated. "Five, maybe six."

Eric untied the handkerchief from around his neck and used it to mop her brow.

"Carry her into the antechamber," he told Nick.

"We cannot possibly get her across that pit. She will have to deliver here."

In the meantime, Sir Peter and Major Kennerly went to rouse the men that they might begin to reconstruct the bridge. Nick carried the necessary blankets and canteens of water to Eric, then busied himself in helping rebuild the walkway. He could not forget Kate's accusations. Though he would not have believed Berteau guilty of such treachery, he had heard rumors of how the man acquired his treasures. He should have guessed that greed fueled Berteau's interest in archaeology. Perhaps he *had* guessed, but he had needed Berteau to pave the way for the expedition. It hadn't mattered then what kind of man Berteau was. Nick vented his anger as he hammered nails into the wooden planks. The man would pay; he'd see to it!

Nick ceased his assault on the planking when his father approached. "Kate will be fine," Sir Peter assured him. "She is young and strong, and your friend is a competent doctor I daresay. We must think about sending a party of men after this Berteau fellow. Perhaps we can still catch him."

"Not now. My place is with Kate. Leave Berteau to me. I promise you this, sir. If anything happens to Kate or the child, I shall kill him myself, bury this accursed tomb in the sands and never set foot on Egyptian soil again!"

CHAPTER XV

The lusty cry of an infant halted the work in the tomb, and a cheer went up from the workers.

"*Allamdulilah!*"

Sir Peter and Major Kennerly both came to shake Nick's hand and offer their congratulations. Nick was relieved yet sad, for it seemed that this time Kate would not forgive him.

Eric appeared, bearing a small squirming bundle.

"My friend," he said, "meet your new daughter, Lucy."

Nick reached out to gently touch the small head, the soft down of dark hair. She was perfect. His child . . . his and Kate's, and Kate had chosen to name her after his mother.

"Is Kate . . .?"

"She's fine," Eric assured him. "You may see her if you like."

"I can't, not now. You're certain she'll be all right?"

"Quite certain."

Eric handed Lucy to Nick, who cradled her cautiously. Sir Peter drew close, his eyes rheumy. Nick suddenly felt ashamed for having deprived him of his family for so long.

"She's given us back our Lucy," Sir Peter said.

Nick kissed his daughter's brow and handed her back to his friend. "Take care of them for me, Eric. I must go after Berteau. Kate's right. I'm to blame for what he's done."

"She didn't mean that," Eric insisted.

"It's true nonetheless. I needed Berteau, and so I chose to ignore his reputation. I could have guessed what he was capable of."

Rage motivated him now, burning away the sadness that would have paralyzed him. Berteau would pay, dearly! "I shall recover what was stolen from you, sir," he told his father.

"We shall go together," Sir Peter replied. "This is my fight as well."

"What shall I tell Kate?" Eric wondered.

Nick thought about it. "Tell her—"

His features softened for a moment, but then he shook his head and his grim expression returned.

"Tell her I've gone to reclaim her treasure," he said.

———

Kate closed her eyes. All throughout the pain of her labor, she had focused on the figures of the priestess

216

and Osiris, animated in the flicker of the lamplight. Had she only imagined the malevolent looks they sent her as if her presence disturbed the sanctity of the tomb?

She tried formulating what she would say to Nick. She certainly hadn't meant to blame him for what Berteau had done. The words had just spilled out carelessly and she had been immediately sorry. When she now heard footsteps approaching, she opened her eyes to see Eric, cradling Lucy in his arms. Kate was disappointed, as she had been expecting her husband. "Where is Nick?"

He gently handed Lucy back to her.

"Gone . . ." he replied. "He and his father have gone after Berteau."

Kate felt her heart thud in her breast. There'd be no chance for apology now. Her rash words would be added up like so many bricks in the wall that stood between them.

"Together?" Kate echoed. "Nick and Sir Peter?"

"Yes," Eric told her. "He finally decided to listen to reason. I think he's discovered that his father is not the ogre he'd been made to believe."

"That's good news, at least," Kate replied. "Have the men repaired the walkway yet?"

"Very nearly. Don't worry. We'll have you and Lucy out of here and installed in the Luxor house in no time at all."

"No!" Kate protested. "I'll not be going back to Luxor just yet; there's too much to be done here."

Eric was irritated, pacing the small space of the antechamber before he came and knelt beside her.

"You need to rest. We have plenty of help here.

They've sent for Mr. Thayer, and then there's Major Kennerly and I to supervise the workers."

"I won't be pushed out now," she told him. "The baby and I will be quite comfortable in Sir Peter's tent while he's away. I've notes to take and, of course, sketches to make of the murals, and an inventory to prepare of all salvagable artifacts. . . ."

Eric shook his head, seeing that it was futile to argue with her. "I'll send for Daphne then, to help with little Lucy."

"You needn't bother. Daphne mightn't take to camp life so well."

"You told me yourself the accommodations were quite comfortable, and besides, if she's not allowed to help you with the baby, she'll be very hurt."

There was a long silence while Kate looked down at the newborn baby in her arms and marvelled at her features. Eric was about to leave when Kate suddenly called to him.

"Eric? Did Nick see the child?"

"Yes," he said. "He held her and kissed her brow, as happy as any proud new father."

She seemed pleased at this. "But did he have no message for me?"

"He did say—"

"Yes?"

"Well, he said, 'Tell Kate I've gone to reclaim her treasure.'"

Her brow furrowed. This was not at all what she'd hoped to hear. They were bitter words, even coming second-hand as they had. This was no simple quarrel. She'd wounded him so deeply with her accusations, that Nick would not be so quick to forgive this time.

Sir Peter began to wonder about his son's mental state. When they left the camp in pursuit of Berteau, the half dozen men in their party had all been anxious to retrieve the stolen artifacts. Now, after two days, Nick was leading them still westward into the desert.

None of them were prepared for such a journey; they had only the minimum of supplies and enough water for only a few more days. The landscape was desolate, the heat nigh unbearable. Nick had lost none of his fervor, though. He seemed obsessed as he drove his stallion on, as if he knew exactly where Berteau was headed. Surely enough, on the third day, when the sun was at its zenith, just as the men had begun to grumble amongst themselves and Sir Peter considered abandoning their effort, the fringe of date palms appeared on the horizon.

"An oasis!" Sir Peter called out to his son. "How could you know?"

"I tried to make good use of the seasons I spent in Egypt," Nick said, "listening and learning as much as I could. This oasis is under the dominion of Hassan, a Bedouin shaikh. It is a safe haven for enemies of the pasha and all manner of criminal."

Sir Peter's enthusiasm evaporated. "You have led us into the lion's den," he said.

"We are as safe here as any other man. Hassan will not abide bloodshed within the walls of his 'city of thieves.' If we do find Berteau here, we shall have to wait until he leaves the city to confront him, else we risk our own necks at the hands of Hassan's men."

"Is this then the honor among thieves that is so much spoken of?" Sir Peter wondered.

"A practical system," Nick told him as they led their mounts along the hard-baked path that was the main thoroughfare, past mud-brick houses interspersed with date palms and olive trees.

The shaikh's dwelling was impressive, surrounded by a high white wall that protected lush gardens. The shaikh extended the hospitality of his home. The men were shown to an airy banquet hall and given refreshment, while Sir Peter and Nick were ushered into a cool room to have an audience with the shaikh.

A girl carried in a tray of sliced melon, apricots and dates, and another tray of honeyed cakes. She also offered sweet dark tea before vanishing silently as Shaikh Hassan appeared in the arched doorway.

"Gentlemen," he said in a deep voice that was devoid of emotion.

He was not tall, but his bearing was impressive. Sir Peter guessed him to be about five and forty years, for he was still virile, though his long moustache was threaded with gray. He studied them with shrewd dark eyes as he approached the low table and bade them sit.

"Thank you for your kindness in receiving us," Sir Peter told him as he settled onto a cushion.

The shaikh acknowledged this with a nod. "It is a pleasure to offer you the hospitality of my home, Lord Marleigh, is it?"

"Yes, thank you, and this is my son, Professor Hammonton."

Sir Peter noticed the long scar that rang along the shaikh's cheekbone and ended at the base of his nose. Here was a dangerous man, he thought, and wondered anew at his son's wisdom in bringing them here.

"Tell me, Lord Marleigh, are you here as an emissary of your government?" the shaikh asked, startling Sir Peter.

"Good heavens no," he replied. "I am on holiday and have been assisting my son and his wife. They are archaeologists."

The shaikh crooked a brow. "And are you here to dig for pharaoh's gold?" he asked Nick.

"We have finished digging for the season," Nick told him. "We have come in search of a . . . colleague of mine—a Frenchman, Berteau is his name. I wonder if you have seen him?"

"I receive many strangers here, most have no name," came the reply. "This is a place for lost souls, gentlemen: those men with a price on their heads, those fleeing the pasha's work gangs and the sting of the kourbash, those forced to become thieves to feed their families. . . . All find safety here."

The shaikh's words hung in the air for a long while as Nick and his father concentrated on the refreshment, neither knowing how to reply.

"I wonder, professor," Shaikh Hassan said at last, "why you have ridden three days across the desert to find this 'colleague' of yours."

"It is an urgent matter; one I am most anxious to resolve," Nick responded.

"Then certainly you may make inquiries among my people. May your search be fruitful and may Allah reunite you with your friend. My house is at your disposal."

Nick and his father enjoyed the shaikh's bounteous hospitality while they searched for Berteau or any knowledge of him. It took two days and the crossing of many palms with silver before they learned what Nick suspected the shaikh could have told them the first day. Berteau had arrived in the city several days earlier, had paid off his pack of henchmen and then left, heading for Cairo. He would have reached his destination by now and finding him would be like finding, as Nick so aptly put it, "a needle in a haystack."

CHAPTER XVI

Kate's eye caught her reflection in a pane of glass in the Cairo hotel, and she paused to assess what she saw. Would Nick be pleased, she wondered? She had taken great care in dressing this morning, choosing a cool white linen dress, edged in eyelet and lavender ribbons. While Lucy slept in her basket, Kate had painstakingly plaited her own hair, then looped up all the plaits under a wide-brimmed straw hat. All of this primping was by way of apology to Nick for her hateful behavior and those awful accusations. She'd spent the entire last month regretting her sharp tongue.

Through a letter sent by Sir Peter, she had learned that they'd chased the Frenchman into the desert, lost him and then picked up his trail once more in Cairo. They'd appealed to every authority for help: the consulates of their respective countries, those working for Auguste Mariette in the Antiquities Service, local officials, even representatives of the khedive himself. Nick had stirred things up so much, in fact, that one could not walk down a street in Cairo without hearing talk of the fugitive Frenchman. But all of this was not done as a last act of desperation, Sir Peter pointed out. Nick knew that Berteau could be hiding anywhere in the city, but with many people aware of the situation, it would be difficult for him to leave Cairo unnoticed, and to leave the country would be all but impossible.

In the meantime, Kate and the remainder of the party had finished the work at the tomb site and had come down to Cairo. They were to meet Nick and Sir Peter at the hotel, and soon they would all travel home, if Nick could be shaken loose from his purpose.

It wasn't practical to continue to hunt for Berteau. After all, Kate reasoned, it was more than likely that the khedive would claim the most spectacular pieces of jewelry and, of course, the death mask for himself. Under the most ideal circumstances, the artifacts would be turned over to Mariette's Antiquities Service. A less palpable alternative would be for Ishmael Pasha to give away the treasures as gifts to his European cronies. The archaeologists would then receive token artifacts, those items considered of little intrinsic value. Whatever happened, Kate thought, the thrill of discovery and the knowledge gained from it had meant more to her than any tangible treasure could have. She hoped Nick would agree.

"Kate?" Daphne called, rousing her from her thoughts. "Would you like me to take Lucy upstairs for her nap so you might have your lunch?"

Kate smiled at her. "Thank you, no. Look how peaceful she is here on my arm. I'll manage. Besides, you've barely touched your own meal."

"I'm preoccupied, I suppose, thinking about going home," Daphne said. "I'll admit that I was overwhelmed at first by this drastically different way of life, but it's all been so exciting—I fear things at home will seem rather dull by comparison."

"Not at all," Kate assured her. "After all, you've wedding plans to make now." Kate had not been very surprised when, several nights ago at dinner, Mr. Thayer and Daphne had announced their plans to marry.

Daphne blushed and studied the tablecloth. "Yes, I suppose that's true. Things will never be the same as they were."

Eric suddenly sat down and joined them. "Where've you been hiding?" Daphne asked.

"At the railway depot with Mr. Thayer, seeing to the baggage. It's no small chore, I can tell you."

"His Christian name is Samuel," Daphne corrected, "and I wish you'd call him that. After all, he's soon to be family."

Eric grinned. "It'll take some adjustment, but I'll manage . . . for your sake, dear sister. Now I'm famished. Where is that waiter?"

"Have you seen Nick?" Kate interrupted.

"No," he replied. "What was it his note said?"

"To meet him in the hotel dining room at noon, that he has made arrangements for our return home.

But it's a quarter past, Eric, and he's not arrived. You don't suppose he's still bent on catching Berteau, do you? I was certain his father could dissuade him."

"No doubt he has," Eric said. "Give him time, Kate. He'll be here. Sit and enjoy your lunch and, for heaven's sake, let me have mine."

"You're right. I'm sorry."

Before Eric could reply, the maitre'd approached Kate. "Mrs. Hammonton, there is a disagreeable little urchin in the lobby who says he has a message for you from your husband. I told the clerk that he was likely after baksheesh, but he insisted that I relay the message to you on the chance that the little beggar is telling the truth."

"Thank you," Kate told him. "I am, as a matter of fact, waiting word of my husband. I shall go and see the boy at once."

"I'll talk to him," Eric offered.

"No," Kate said, "sit and order your meal. I'll talk to him."

Kate went out into the lobby, cradling Lucy in her arms and wondering what could have kept Nick.

A grubby looking youngster standing in the center of the hotel lobby was evoking the most disdainful glances from the patrons. The desk clerk looked positively mortified, as if the sight of the boy was enough to drive away prospective guests.

"You have a message for me?" Kate asked, addressing the boy.

"You are Missus Hammonton?"

"I am."

He reached into his ragged shirt and pulled out something that glinted in the light. He pressed it into Kate's hand.

"This from Hammonton-*effendi*. He say you come with me."

Kate looked down at her hand. It held a gold necklace, set with carnelian and turquoise. She recognized it at once. It was from the mummy of the priestess. Nick had found Berteau!

"You come with me now," the boy urged.

"I must tell my friends," Kate said to him, but the boy would not wait, bolting out of the door into the street and waving for her to follow.

Kate looked back toward the dining room, clutching the necklace in her fist, and went after him. It was more than she could have hoped for. She could not wait to see Nick again. They could examine the artifacts together, and she would show him her notes from the work of the tomb. Yes, they would celebrate tonight!

Lucy began to squirm in Kate's arms. Kate stopped to throw the blanket lightly over her, shading her from the evil sun, only to find the boy tugging at her skirts.

"Hurry!" he said.

He led her out of the European quarter, past coffeehouses, through the bazaars, along the streets of the leathermakers, goldsmiths and brass founders. There was no time to watch the strolling players perform in the square, nor listen to the street vendors shouting up to the balconies overhead. The boy took her down the narrow potter's street and into a squalid shop at the end of the row.

"My husband asked you to bring me here?" Kate said, and only then did the suspicions creep into her mind.

There was no one in the cramped shop. As Kate

examined the rows of crockery, the boy drew aside a drape that sectioned off the living quarters at the back and motioned for Kate to follow.

She prayed that she would hear her husband's voice or see his familiar frame when she stepped into the darkened back room, but by now she had guessed there was something amiss. It was too late to turn and run. She would be hopelessly lost in the maze of winding streets, and she could never outrun a pursuer while carrying her child. She drew a long breath and followed the boy through the drape. The ring of triumphant laughter caused her to start, and as her eyes adjusted to the half light, she vaguely made out the features of the face she'd hoped not to see.

"Berteau!"

"*Bonjour, madame*, and with a child now, how wonderful for you."

"What do you want with me, monsieur?" she asked.

"We shall not mince words. That is how it is said, is it not?"

Kate looked on him coldly, but he continued.

"Your husband has been hanging on my leg like an angry cur, and try as I might, I cannot shake him loose."

"And you think kidnapping me will put him off?" she guessed.

"If he cares at all for his family and wishes to see them safely returned to him, then he will look aside while I make my escape."

"I cannot believe that you would harm us—"

He stared her down, his dark eyes narrowing. "Then you underestimate me, madame. Desperate situations call for desperate measures."

228

Nick strode through the hotel lobby, pulling at his freshly shaven chin and straightening his cravat. He was finally returning to a normal life with his family and friends. It had been madness to think he could find Berteau in this squalid city, teeming with thousands of impoverished souls. The Frenchman could be anywhere, under any bundle of rags, wearing any of a million different disguises.

He spied Eric's fair head in the dining room and went to the table. Mr. Thayer had already joined him and Daphne. When Nick came up to the table, Eric stopped eating and pointed his fork at him accusingly.

"You're late," he said.

Nick took the empty place. "I was seeing to some last minute details. Where's Kate?"

"She hasn't been back since she received your message," Eric told him.

"Perhaps she's taken the baby up to her room," Daphne suggested.

"Message?" Nick echoed. "I sent no message today."

Professor Hammonton?" the maitre'd said, coming to the table and pressing an envelope in Nick's hand. "This was left at the front desk for you, sir. It is marked urgent, and so the clerk thought—"

"Thank you," Nick replied, examining the envelope before he broke the seal and pulled out a folded piece of paper.

When he unfolded the note, a lock of blond hair fell from it onto the table. Daphne caught her breath, and Nick's face paled as he read the message.

"What is it?" Eric asked.

"It's Berteau," Nick explained, his expression grim. "He has Kate and Lucy. He says that I must forget about the artifacts and quit hunting him or else he'll—"

His voice cracked as he crushed the note.

"Heartless bastard!" he said through clenched teeth, banging his fist on the table.

"What can we do now?" Eric asked.

"We must do nothing," Mr. Thayer interjected. "No doubt all this Berteau fellow wants is to get out of the country with his ill-gotten goods. Once he's out, I'm quite certain he'll free Mrs. Hammonton and the child."

Daphne took her fiancé's hand. "I hope you're right, Samuel."

"Of course, I'm right, my dear. You mustn't distress yourself. Perhaps you should rest for a while."

"Well, I won't truly rest until Kate gets back. But it is particularly stifling today. Perhaps I will go upstairs."

"I'll take you up," Samuel offered.

When the two had left, Eric said to Nick, "Well? Do we take the train to Alexandria? If he's headed out of the country—"

"Berteau won't try to leave the country yet," Nick said. "I'm not the only one looking for him, and he knows it. What he needs now is a safe place to hide until everyone's forgotten about the Frenchman and his stolen treasure."

Chapter XVII

Heat rose in shimmering waves off the endless sea of sand. Shutting her eyes, Kate tried to recall Creighton in the winter, when the river was frozen over with ice and the north wind howled down the valley, drifting snow up to the window ledges. The exercise gave her but a moment's relief. The vision evaporated when the camel's gait jostled Lucy in her reed basket and she awoke, wailing. Kate drew her out of the basket, speaking to her in soothing tones.

The camel was a filthy foul-tempered beast, but Kate had come to appreciate it nonetheless, for it had carried her and Lucy these past three days without complaint, and spared them from making the journey on foot. She had learned that it made little difference to her captor how she travelled. Berteau and a handful of men had made their escape from Cairo by night, and in disguise. Kate and Lucy had been unceremoniously rolled up in a carpet and carried to the dock, then tossed into the hold of a cargo boat. They'd travelled for days on the river before Kate saw Berteau again. He finally appeared, to present her with an *abbayeh* and *yasmak*. He suggested that she keep herself heavily veiled, as they were headed for a haven for outlaws, men who would be all too curious about the charms of a fair-headed maid.

Kate looked up at the horizon, then blinked to assure herself that she was not witnessing a mirage. There in the distance was the green fringe of date palms. When at long last they passed over the crest of the dune, a thriving settlement came into view, full of lush foliage and mud-brick houses. Kate almost laughed aloud when she saw the barefoot children who came to greet them, all chattering and running around the ungainly camels, but she thought better of it and drew her veil across her face, as Berteau scattered them with a stern warning.

At the far end of the village was a long low building, surrounded by exotic perfumed gardens and a high wall. Kate deduced that this must be the residence of some important official, and it was here that Berteau halted the caravan.

Kate refused his help in dismounting. When the camel had been brought to a kneeling position, she jumped down on her own, nearly turning an ankle. She tended to Lucy and tried to ignore Berteau as he spoke to her in a low voice.

"I will tell them that you are my woman," he began.

""How dare you!" she said, bristling. "Why not tell them the truth? That you have stolen me away

232

from my husband and dragged me halfway across the desert as your hostage. Perhaps I shall tell them myself."

Berteau only laughed. "It would do you no good to speak out against me to anyone here. They call this place the city of thieves and it is aptly named, I do assure you."

He grabbed her arm roughly. "Remember, madame, that you have no protector here but me. This is the home of Shaikh Hassan, a most important man. We shall, neither one of us, offend him, comprenez-vous? I will tell him that you belong to me, and you will be given the hospitality of his harem. Cross me, madame, and you and the child will suffer for it. I promise you that."

Kate shuddered at the threat. She had begun to believe Berteau capable of any evil, and instinct made her take Lucy out of her basket and hold her close. For now she would acquiesce. She had no other choice.

Hassan met Berteau with a cordial air, and while they conversed in Arabic, a young girl named Zeyneb took Kate to the women's quarters, in a separate wing of the house.

Zeyneb was a lovely creature: fine boned with clear amber skin and a full red mouth. She wore a caftan of muted stripes, tied with a woven belt, and embroidered slippers. The silver bracelets on her wrists and ankles jangled as she walked. She led Kate to a small room off a long corridor and bade her enter.

"We are a small household," she said in impeccable English as she opened the tall latticework doors that led into a courtyard and gardens, "but not unaccustomed to guests. I hope that you and your child will be comfortable here."

"Yes, thank you," Kate replied.

The room was not spacious, but Kate welcomed the privacy after so many days in Berteau's company. A divan, strewn with colorful cushions and draped in netting, had been placed against the far wall. Opposite this stood a chest and a long mirror, edged in gilt.

Kate laid Lucy on the bed and unwound her blanket. The child stretched in response, kicking and waving her arms. Kate threw off the *abbayeh* and *yasmak*, and saw Zeyneb's brow arch in surprise at the sight of her blond hair. Kate's linen dress was in deplorable condition, the hem ragged and torn, the bodice stained with perspiration, and the folds of her skirt streaked with dust.

"I shall fetch some clean garments," she said, "and then I will tend to the child while you bathe."

"You are very kind," Kate told her.

When the girl returned, Kate had shed her dress and was standing in her chemise. She was reluctant, though, when Zeyneb told her that she could bathe in the shallow pool in the courtyard.

"Outside?" Kate said.

Zeyneb laughed, with a sound soft on the ear, like tinkling bells. "It is the garden of the harem. There are high walls all around. You will not be spied upon."

Thus assured, Kate slipped out of her chemise and padded barefoot across the patterned tiles of the courtyard. She eased herself into the pool, languishing in the water as the center fountain splashed droplets on her.

Zeyneb came out with a soft blanket for drying, a tray of perfumed oils and a balm for Kate's lips, which were becoming painfully cracked. The girl disappeared into the house and came out again, carrying Lucy.

"Are there other women living here?" Kate asked.

"There is Lateefeh, who is the sister of Hassan's mother, and Fatimeh, her daughter, and the wives of Hassan: Selima, Leila and me."

Now it was Kate's turn to be surprised. At first she had taken Zeyneb to be a servant, then she thought she might be a daughter of the household, but she hadn't imagined that this young girl was a wife of Shaikh Hassan.

"Do the others speak English as well?" Kate asked.

"No," Zeyneb replied. "I learn because it pleases my husband, but he vows that he has no patience for the others."

Kate splashed water over her shoulders, and it trickled down her back. Zeyneb knelt beside the pool and began to bathe Lucy, who was nestled atop a bed of soft blankets.

"Hassan is a good husband," she said, "and Allah has smiled upon our union. Soon I shall give him a son."

"How wonderful," Kate replied, though she thought it too early to make assumptions about the child's gender.

"It pleases me that you husband has brought you to visit with us. There are no other children here. Selima's sons have grown into men, and Leila's daughter was married last spring."

Kate started to protest that Berteau was indeed not her husband, but thought better of it, in light of his warning.

"What is your child called?" Zeyneb asked.

"We call her Lucy, after my husband's mother."

"Lu-cy?" The girl rolled the name over her tongue and jangled her bracelets to capture the child's attention.

Kate rinsed her hair, then wrung the water out of it and stepped from the pool. The sun that had been her enemy these past days seemed gentler now, its waves of warmth caressing her body. Her skin tingled as the droplets of water evaporated. She then poured a little of the scented oil into her hand and smoothed it down one arm. Her palm traced circles across her skin, where the warm oil left a sheen. Kate then went back to her room and put on a fresh *abbayeh* of black silk.

As she was brushing out her hair, Kate caught her breath when she saw Berteau behind her in the gilt mirror. How long had he been watching?

"*Très jolie*," he said. "Much improved if I may say, though I shall always remember you best at the Hôtel de Ville."

He reached out to lay a hand on her shoulder and Kate shuddered at his touch. She did not move or speak.

"Perhaps you will forget this husband of yours and come with me to Paris, *non*? I would dress you in silks, buy you gloves and bonnets and parasols by the trunkful. We could share this treasure of mine. With the jewelry of the priestess, you would be the envy of the empress herself."

236

His hands, damp with perspiration, encircled Kate's throat in a light touch, and she did not breathe. "You would like that, *non?*"

She could feel his breath on the back of her neck and it made her flesh crawl.

"Never!" she spat and pulled away. "Nick will come for me, he will, you'll see, and you shall be sorry you ever laid eyes on us."

Berteau shrugged his shoulders and a smile twisted on the thick lips beneath his moustache. "You forget, madame, that I know this husband of yours. If he comes at all, it will be for the treasure, not for you."

He turned and walked out of the room, the sound of his boot heels on the tiles marking each step as his cruel laughter filled the air.

CHAPTER XVIII

Kate waited patiently. Weeks passed, and still Nick did not come. Berteau's cruel words took on more truth with each day that went by. Nick had hunted Berteau ceaselessly when in pursuit of the treasures, but where was he now? Kate told herself that he was only being cautious, that he feared Berteau's threats against his family, but with the passage of time, she only felt forgotten.

She knew that it was left to her to escape, but to attempt a three-day trek across the desert on her own with Lucy would be foolhardy. So she put aside these thoughts for the present and settled into the routine of the household, helping the women to prepare and serve the meals as best she could, and caring for Lucy.

She was thankful for Zeyneb. The older women

of the harem seemed to keep Kate at a distance, and though her knowledge of Arabic was not thorough enough to confirm it, Kate was certain that they often spoke ill of her. Zeyneb had told her that they pitied her because she could not cook, she had given her husband a girl-child, no son of whom he could be proud, and she had no gold except the one ring on her finger. As Zeyneb explained, an Arab woman's jewelry was security for her old age. It was hers alone and could not be taken away, even by her husband.

Kate had laughed to herself when Zeyneb told her all this. The women must have thought her a useless creature, indeed. She could never explain to them her hopes and aspirations, so different from their own; her quest for knowledge, her passion for archaeology.

Zeyneb proved to be a good friend. She tutored Kate in Arabic, though it seemed a hopeless task. She taught her to make loaves of round, flat bread, and to cook rice. She spoke to Kate of the shaikh, of whom she was very proud, and of events in the village. Kate learned that it was as much a refuge for dissidents as thieves and murderers. Many of the people had settled here to escape the pasha's work gangs, who were digging the canal for de Lesseps and the French, and many had opposed the rule of the Turks and Ishmael Pasha, who was their puppet. Kate wondered in what other ways Berteau had twisted the truth to his own advantage, and she also wondered if she dare confide in Zeyneb.

———

The rays of the afternoon sun shone through the lattice, making patterns of light and shade on the carpet. While Lucy slept, Kate rested on the divan, stirring the air with a reed fan. Suddenly, Zeyneb opened the lattice and motioned Kate outside. They walked to the far side of the garden behind a stand of gnarled trees, where there was a chink in the high wall.

"Come and look," Zeyneb told her. "There will be guests for dinner tonight. I watched them ride in."

Kate peered through the wide crack and saw a band of riders approaching on the town road.

"But how do you know they will come here?" Kate asked.

The girl looked offended. "All visitors come to pay their respects to my husband," she said, as if to remind Kate how important a man Hassan was.

"Of course," Kate replied.

They took turns watching the newcomers until they had passed in front of the garden wall. There were perhaps a dozen Arabs on camel and horseback, led by a tall man on a gray stallion. The ends of his black turban were wound around his face to keep out the dust and sand.

"Do you see him?" Zeyneb asked. "The leader. He is fearful to look upon. I wonder who he is."

Kate could only stare as he dismounted, throwing back the ends of the turban over his shoulder. She shivered as she looked upon the stern visage, the dark beard and the patch that covered one eye. He wore a pistol and a sheathed dagger in his sash, and strode toward Hassan's gate without hesitation. He then turned to shout directions in Arabic to his companions. This was no dissident, Kate decided, no runaway from a work gang.

As the women cooked dinner, they tried to guess

who he was, making him out to be all manner of criminal and earning the displeasure of Lateefeh, who was supervising the work. At last, they got their answer from the boy who was carrying the lamb in from the outside.

Zeyneb interrogated him thoroughly and relayed the information to Kate.

"His men call him Shaheen, which means the Falcon. They say he is known for his bravery, that once he stole into the palace of the pasha himself and made off with a jewel case."

"Audacious fellow," Kate replied to this, "but what is there for a jewel thief in the desert?"

"Safety," Zeyneb replied.

━━━━━━

The evening meal was served in the large reception hall to accommodate the shaikh's many houseguests. As always, Kate and the women of the harem laid out the feast ahead of time, carrying in the huge round trays of rice, meat, broth and bread, and bowls of vegetables, only to withdraw before the men arrived for their meal.

Kate did not approve of this separation of the sexes. Her weeks in the harem had given her plenty of time to consider it. Under the guise of protecting the women, a man could lock up his wives with no fear that they might catch another man's eye or find another man who caught theirs. But these assurances and measures of protection had their price, for they preclude any social interaction between men and women, and Kate thought this sad, indeed.

But when she compared this society to the Western world, Kate could not honestly say that the latter was much more enlightened. She remembered all too clearly the way she had been patronized by the scholars at the Hôtel de Ville. And closer to home, she remembered how her own father and husband had tried to protect her, even deciding her future for her.

Still, they were the most enlightened men she knew, perhaps encouraging her more than their upbringing would allow. Yes, she had had more freedom than most women, but why should that be so? Why shouldn't all women have as much freedom as they could manage? Now, as the sound of men's laughter and music wafted through the halls of the harem, Kate became quite irritated.

"Are you content to sit there sewing?" she asked Zeyneb, "while your husband entertains his guests, and to wait for your supper like the mongrel who gets the kitchen scraps?"

Zeyneb looked up from her needlework as if Kate had suddenly gone mad, and then shrugged her slight shoulders. "It is the way of things," she answered calmly. "When the men have retired, we shall fetch the trays and see how well our meal was received."

"I want to go see," Kate insisted. "Aren't you at all curious? Perhaps the travellers have news from Cairo. And what about this Shaheen? I'll wager he has a story to tell."

"Hassan will tell me all that I need to know," Zeyneb replied, as if by rote, and once more she looked up from her sewing, but this time there was a glimmer of girlish excitement in her eyes. "Selima says that they have sent for the *ghawazis* . . . the dancing girls."

Kate knew she had piqued the young girl's curiosity and thus formulated her plan aloud. "Lucy is asleep. If we can get away without the others seeing us, we can put on our *abbayehs* and go into the central courtyard. The darkness will hide us and we can watch without being seen."

And so the pair of conspirators crept into the courtyard, lingering in the night air like two shadows, to catch a glimpse of the festivities.

Inside, the musicians played earthenware drums called *taraboukehs* and reed flutes. Kate was mesmerized by the *ghawazis*, so different from the women of the harem. They wore wide-legged trousers in the Turkish fashion, gathered at the ankle, and low-cut bodices of colored gauze. Their slippers had pointed toes, and their chains of coins around their necks jangled with each sinuous motion of the dance. Each of them had finger cymbals called *crotales*.

"It's very late," Kate heard Zeyneb whisper. "Let us go back before we are missed."

"No, wait . . . look!"

Kate pointed to Shaheen, seated in a place of honor beside the shaikh. He had on a clean headscarf, or *kaffiyeh*, and his dark beard was neatly trimmed, revealing the sharp bronzed planes of his face. His clean white caftan, called a *gellabeya*, was belted with a striped sash. In its folds he carried his dagger. Kate decided that it was the patch over his eye that gave him such a frightening air. Without it, he might even have been handsome.

Zeyneb was anxious to retreat. They got ready to depart, but just then Shaheen decided to step out into the courtyard to take some air. Kate and Zeyneb stood on either side of the archway, not daring to breathe as he passed them. He paused less than two feet from where they stood and with a sigh, looked up at the crescent moon.

"Perhaps you would like to dance for us, too," he said to them in Arabic, without turning around.

Zeyneb, clutching her *abbayeh* tightly around her, ran and disappeared across the courtyard. Kate, however, stood her ground as he turned to face her.

"Why do you not run away like your sister?" he said.

"I am not a frightened hare who fears the falcon," she said to him in his own tongue, hoping she had said the phrase correctly.

Laughter rumbled deep in his chest.

"You have a quick tongue, little sister. You have seen what you came to see. Now be off with you. It is not safe here."

He drew near and toughed her lightly on the shoulder to prod her. Though she could not explain it, his very touch sent a wave of pleasure through her. The air around him was redolent of sandalwood and smoke, and she found it a heady combination. But still she would not give up her ground.

"Go now," he warned. "I am as dangerous as the rest, perhaps more so."

What curiosity was it that held her there as his hands reached to release her veil? She drew a ragged breath and looked up to him. As he regarded her, he appeared disconcerted.

"Nazrani?" he said. It was the Arab word for Christian.

The word restored her senses, and without allowing herself a second thought, she fled.

Zeyneb was waiting when Kate returned to the harem.

"You must tell no one that he spoke to us," she cautioned.

Kate assured her that she would not, and after they had retrieved the dinner trays and were having their own meal, Zeyneb's curiosity got the better of her.

"What else did he say to you?"

"We were alone for only a moment," Kate insisted, and Zeyneb's sidelong glance seemed to say that even this was too much.

"He told me to go in, that it was not safe," she continued, "and I told him that I did not fear the falcon."

Zeyneb's jaw dropped. "No! Truly?"

The two had drawn the interest of the older women, so they turned their attention to their meal and ate the rest of it in silence.

"You must take care," Zeyneb whispered, after they had finished, "lest you incur your husband's wrath."

Kate forgot for a moment that Zeyneb meant Berteau. Her confusion must have been mirrored in her expression, for Zeyneb reached over and patted her hand. "Do not worry. I should never tell your husband of this. It is our secret."

Kate thanked her and wondered how much longer she must keep up this charade.

Sleep eluded Kate that night, and when at last she had drifted off, she was soon awakened by Lucy's cries. As nothing else would soothe the child, Kate carried her into the garden and rocked her, humming a lullaby from her own childhood. She looked up at the stars and thought of Nick, wishing she could be with him now.

Lucy finally settled into a deep sleep. After Kate had returned her to bed, she went out again into the courtyard and sat beside the pool. She wondered how much longer Berteau would wait before attempting to flee the country. And whether he would leave Kate and Lucy here for Nick to find, or drag them back across the desert as his insurance.

As she contemplated her seemingly hopeless situation, tears began to fall. She fluttered her fingers in the pool to distort her reflection.

Suddenly she heard a voice say in heavily accented English, "In the night, her beauty is revealed."

Kate looked up, startled. She feared it might be Berteau, but it was not. It was Shaheen, perched atop the wall, an elbow resting on one bent knee.

"What do you want?" she asked, feeling strangely naked without her *abbayeh*. "Leave at once, else I shall cry out and awaken the household."

"You've naught to fear from me, lady. Tell me, how did the great Hassan find himself an English wife?"

"American," she corrected.

He jumped down from his perch and came nearer.

"He is, indeed, a fortunate man to possess such a jewel. But why do you weep, my lady? Is it because Hassan craves the company of another tonight, she who may bring him a son?"

The lies were twisted around her like ivy. Zeyneb thought that Berteau was her husband. Shaheen thought she was one of Hassan's wives. She could refute neither.

"Please leave me," Kate begged him.

He was very close now. Kate stared hard at her toes.

"If I had one such as you for a wife—"

He paused for such a long while that Kate looked up to make certain that he had not disappeared into the jasmine-scented air like some phantasm. It was her undoing, for she met his intense stare as his hands reached out and caught hers.

"There would be no need of others," he said at last. "I should keep you ever beside me."

"You . . . are kind," she stammered, wondering why it was suddenly so hard to breathe, and then he drew her into the circle of his arms. She could feel his dagger as he pulled her close and captured her mouth with his own. She did not resist, even though he was a dangerous man . . . and even though she was a married woman. But she needed his strength, God help her; her own reservoir was dry.

He cradled her head in his hands and kissed her tear-stained face, stroking her unbound hair. Kate could scarcely believe that this man's touch could be so soothing. She wished she could read the expression on his face but the darkness prevented it.

Drawing a tremulous breath, she slipped from his embrace. There could be no more of this, she thought.

"You risk death by your presence here," she told him, which was probably not far from the truth. If

Hassan's men were to discover Shaheen here in the harem, they would certainly not stop to make polite inquiries. Kate shuddered.

"You fear for my safety, lady? This thief, who has made his way in and out of the palace of the pasha on the wind?"

"That's a good story for children, but by this action you have betrayed Hassan's hospitality."

He grabbed her wrist roughly.

"Do not take me for a fool. I knew full well the risks, but I had to see your eyes once more, and if you have a care for my pitiful life, then it was worth the risk."

He began massaging the burn that his grip had just made on her wrist, and then bent down to press his lips to it. His breath was hot against her skin, and her head reeled.

"Please," Kate whispered, "go now."

"I shall do as you ask," he said, releasing her hand. "Remember this, though. Your tears have won a heart this night. Only utter one word and Shaheen, the thief, shall serve you."

He bowed low with a flourish of his hand and, like a graceful cat, slipped over the wall and was gone.

CHAPTER XIX

The next morning was like all of the other mornings Kate had spent in the harem of Shaikh Hassan. She tended Lucy, bathed her and then put her back into the reed basket so that she might help the women bake the bread for breakfast; yet this morning was also different, from the others for today Shaheen had intruded upon her thoughts. She tried to convince herself that she had dreamt their meeting in the garden, but to no avail. And even though she could not form a clear picture of his face, the memory of his lips on hers was too vivid to erase, even if she'd wished to. Why hadn't Nick come for her? If he had come, she never would have met this desert Falcon . . . and never have known his embrace. . . . .

She did know that she could no longer sit idle,

but must take action of some sort, so she turned her thoughts to finding what Berteau had stolen. Certainly he had brought the treasure here; he was too greedy to have left it behind in Cairo. Kate decided that it must be hidden in his room, but how was she to search for them?

Her opportunity came the following day in the late afternoon, when the oppressive heat had found its way into every corner of the house. While the women were resting, Hassan was taking Berteau and some of the men to examine his latest acquisition, a much-prized Arab mare.

Kate watched them go out to the stable, and then crept along the courtyard, to where the men were quartered. She was very cautious, for she did not know which room off the long hall belonged to the Frenchman. Kate moved silently to the first door, which was ajar, and dared not even breathe as she peered inside. As she had expected all of the rooms to be empty, she stifled a gasp when she saw an elderly Arab sprawled on his cushions, snoring. Somewhat rattled, she pressed on. The next room was uninhabited, and the one across from that had the lattice drawn and was bathed in shadows. She paused here for a moment, though, when she spied a striped sash that she recognized as belonging to Shaheen.

As luck would have it, Berteau's room was the very last one off the central courtyard. Kate recognized it immediately; here were his riding crop and hairbrushes, cravat and shirt studs, the place fairly reeked of his dreaded presence. Her instinct was to run back to the harem, but she began to search the room instead. She first inspected his trunk, then looked beneath the cushions piled on the divan. The rolled carpet leaning against the wall reminded her of how she had been smuggled out of Cairo. Upon closer inspection, she discovered the silver death mask hidden inside.

It was heavier than she had imagined, and the workmanship was indeed exquisite; every detail of the woman's features were wrought in silver and set with rich stones. Reluctantly, Kate rewrapped the treasure, leaving it just as she had found it. She soon came upon the cache of jewelry, wrapped in rags and hidden in an empty clay water jar.

Her purpose fulfilled, Kate left the room by way of the courtyard and carefully shut the lattice behind her. She had walked only a few steps when someone grabbed her arm roughly, turning her around.

"Looking for me, were you?"

She met Berteau's eyes, glittering fiercely.

"What do you mean?" she asked him.

The sound of blood rushing in her head was deafening.

"You were in my room just now, madame. Did you find what you were after?"

"No, I wasn't—"

"Liar!"

Without warning, Berteau struck her with the back of his hand and sent her sprawling. Her jaw throbbed, and she could feel the trickle of warm blood from the corner of her mouth. She flinched as he threatened to strike her again and suddenly saw Shaheen approach, dagger unsheathed. She fairly threw herself at him.

"No!" she cried out. "No, please, Shaheen."

At this, Berteau scrambled off. Shaheen gathered her up in his arms without a word and took her to his room. He settled her gently on the divan and shut the lattice firmly behind him.

"I cannot stay here," Kate protested. "I must go back to the harem."

"Not before I know what goes on here," Shaheen replied.

He took a cloth from the chest in the corner, dipped it into the water jar and came to sit beside her. He dabbed at her lip, then pressed the cool cloth against her bruised jaw.

"Are you hurt badly, Kate?"

She looked up in surprise at his use of her name. "How do you know my name?"

He looked away, concentrating on the patterned rug at his feet.

"I wanted to know everything about you," he explained. "I listen to the talk, and I have learned that you are not a wife of Hassan."

"I never said that I was."

"They say that you are the Frenchman's woman, but that is a lie as well."

"How do you know?"

Leaning over her, he bathed her face with the cloth and smoothed her hair. "If you were his wife, then he would not have run like a jackal when I confronted him. He would have defended his right."

"His right to strike a woman?"

"If you were his wife, it would be his right," he replied impassively.

"And if I were your wife, would you find a need to strike me?"

"If you were my wife . . ."

His voice drifted off as his ministrations became caresses. His lips only barely touched her bruised face, then slid along the taut arch of her neck to the hollow of her throat. A light sigh escaped her as his long bronzed fingers played over her body. She captured his face in her hands and wished he were not bathed in shadow that she might more clearly see his features. Her own fingers slid over the planes of his rugged face and his soft dark beard, as though she were blind and could see only through her touch. There was something familiar about the feel of him, as if somehow they were meant to be together like this. Kate longed to close her eyes, forget all else and lose herself in the sensual dream, but good conscience had not abandoned her entirely. She made him look into her eyes.

"No, Shaheen. I cannot—"

She raised herself up sharply, and he let her go. With her back to the lattice, hidden in the darkness, she continued.

"While I am not Hassan's wife, nor Berteau's, I do have a husband."

"Then where is he, and how did you come to be here, under the Frenchman's protection?"

Kate considered his question for a moment. There was no point in continuing the lies. She felt she could trust him.

"My husband and I are archaeologists, come to explore the ancient tombs of Thebes. Berteau, the Frenchman, stole some valuable artifacts from us,

253

then kidnapped my child and me to make good his escape."

"Where is this husband of yours? Why has he not come to claim what is his?"

Kate found herself defending Nick, without hesitation. "He cannot," she said. "Berteau has threatened to kill us if he does."

"And so he waits on the whims of this French man?" He came to stand beside her. "I do not think that this husband of yours is much of a man."

Kate's eyes flashed. "What would you have him do? If he were lucky enough to guess where Berteau has taken us, would you have him simply ride into this village and demand what is his? Who would believe him?"

"Perhaps the shaikh does not know that a viper is nesting in his bosom."

"Perhaps not, but would you have my husband risk his life and that of his family on such a possibility?"

Shaheen stiffened. The vehemence of Kate's argument spoke more of her devotion to her husband than anything else, and seemed to stick at his pride.

"Forgive me. I have no right—"

Kate laid a hand lightly on his arm. "Thank you for coming to my aid."

His arm hooked her waist, pulling her to him, and his breath was harsh on her ear. "Tell me that he does not love you, that your father chose him for your husband because he was wealthy and could pay a handsome bride-price."

"Our customs are not the same, Shaheen," she said, though it struck her that he was not far from the truth.

Her brow furrowed as a flood of remembrances washed over her: the arguments and recriminations, Nick's steadfast refusal to share his work with her. There never had been trust between them.

Shaheen pressed his lips against her throat. "Tell me that he does not love you, Kate."

He pulled her full against him. His lean frame was taut as a bowstring, and his heart drummed close to hers. Her head dropped, resting for a moment on his broad shoulder, and she sighed lightly as hot tears flooded her eyes. "Yes," she said. "Yes, it's true, but you mustn't think that makes a difference. He is my husband. Please, Shaheen. Do not ask me to betray him."

All at once Shaheen let her go and cleared his throat. "I shall take you away from this place and see you safely back to Cairo, if that is what you wish."

She nodded, wanting to escape Shaheen as well as this place, for he made her feel what she should not.

"Wait for me tonight in the garden of the harem," he instructed.

"I cannot leave without the artifacts," she told him. "Berteau has them in his possession."

"Rolled up in a carpet and hidden in a water jar."

"But how did you know?"

"I have not forsaken my vocation, dearest Kate. What do you think brought me to this desolate place? There was talk all over Cairo of the Frenchman and his stolen treasure."

Kate's eyes widened. So Shaheen had come here for the treasure.

"You needn't fear," he assured her. "I've found a

more precious jewel. Now go back to the harem, and take care to say nothing."

———————

Time passed at a torturously slow pace. Kate's fears multiplied with each advancing hour. Was Shaheen as good as his reputation? Could he and his men whisk Kate, Lucy and the artifacts out from under the watchful eyes of Berteau and Hassan?

She regretted that she could not tell Zeyneb of her plan that she might say goodbye. She had come to depend upon her friendship, and it saddened her that the girl would be left with the older, humorless women of the harem. But things would be better for Zeyneb, she reassured herself, when her baby was born.

When night had fallen, Kate finally settled Lucy in her basket. She paced the small space of her room as she waited for Shaheen. Suddenly she noticed a bundle on her divan. There was a note attached: "Will you dance for me?"

Tied up in the bundle was a costume like the *ghawazis* had worn. It included a bodice of turquoise gauze, full trousers of matching stripes, which gathered at the ankles, soft leather slippers with pointed toes, a sheer veil, and a necklace, belt and headpiece strung with gold coins. Kate smiled and changed into it. The coins jangled softly as she stepped out to look at herself in the reflecting pool.

"You will forgive me, madame."

Kate was startled at the sound of Berteau's voice, his dark eyes raking over her as she faced him.

"What costume is this? I find it most pleasing."

As he approached, Kate flinched. "I do apologize for marring your pretty face, *cherie*, but you must learn not to cross me."

"Leave me alone," she said.

"This is so much more flattering to you than that black shroud."

Kate dared not breathe. Her mind raced as she contemplated his next move.

"Yes, I do like this. You have been more trouble than you are worth, madame, until now. Come here."

Kate was frozen in her place, but when he reached out and grabbed her arm, she tried to wrench free. He pulled her to him.

"Do not scream, else I shall have to hurt you again, and who is here to aid you? Surely your husband in Cairo cannot hear you. He waits on my instructions and I can keep him waiting a long time if it pleases me, if you please me."

She tried to pull away, but his arm was like a steel band across her back. "Hassan has chided me for neglecting my wife, and so I must oblige my host, *n'est-ce-pas*?"

He dragged her into her room and threw her onto the bed. Kate lifted herself up on the cushions and sought a weapon, to no avail. When Berteau stopped to remove his frock coat, Kate nearly laughed, but the evil glint in his eyes silenced her.

"I will enjoy this, yes. Your husband has confounded my plans once too often, and now I will have my revenge. When I am finished and he knows what I have done, the very sight of you will sicken him. So I shall spare you that unhappiness. I will take you to Paris with me."

"I'll see you in hell first. If you touch me, monsieur, best watch your back, learn to sleep with one eye open."

"You'll feel differently after I've had you. I can show you things, madame, things you would never learn from your husband, *monsieur le professeur.*"

Kate's actions were tempered by the fact that Lucy lay sleeping nearby in her basket, and Kate would do nothing that would jeopardize her child's safety. She could not run, but as Berteau threw himself on her, she raked her nails across his face, drawing blood. He only laughed. *"Ce n'est rien, petite chatte."*

His lips crushed hers. He tasted of stale food and garlic, and Kate gagged, wanting to retch. She gasped for breath and then screamed, despite his warning. His hands were brutal, leaving bruises in their wake. Kate sobbed as he fumbled with his trousers.

When she could stand no more, she gathered her strength and with one great shove, pushed him away. He recoiled and struck her so hard that lights flashed in her head. Suddenly she heard the exchange of blows and the lattice being crashed open, and saw Shaheen pummeling the Frenchman.

Shaheen cursed Berteau as he struck him again and again, and would probably have beaten him to death were it not for the fact that he saw Kate collapse onto the floor. He left Berteau lying unconscious and went to her, lifting her up into his arms. He did not speak but pulled her close to him.

Out of the darkness came one of Shaheen's men, who scooped up Lucy in her basket. Together the two men made their way to the far end of the garden, where they lifted Kate and Lucy over the wall.

As Kate regained her senses, she was aware of the party of men on horseback outside the shaik's house. Shaheen mounted his gray stallion and pulled Kate close to him. She threw her arms around his neck, and they galloped off into the night.

CHAPTER XX

They rode on through the night, while Kate pressed close to Shaheen for warmth. Although neither he nor the stallion seemed to tire, Kate had to fight to keep awake.

It was still dark when they reached the camp some of the men had made, and at the sight of the black tents, Kate finally succumbed to exhaustion and fell asleep in the curve of Shaheen's arm.

She later awoke to the sound of his voice. Opening her eyes, she discovered that she was inside his tent and that he was rocking Lucy and speaking to her gently. The baby cooed in response and reached up to grab one of the fingers he was waggling over her.

When he noticed that Kate was awake, he put

Lucy back into her basket and said, "The child will be a beauty, like her mother."

Kate smiled at him. "Again I must thank you for rescuing me. It seems that I owe you a great deal."

He came to sit beside her.

"The time has come to collect on that debt," he said, moving so near that she could feel his breath against her cheek.

"When we reach Cairo," she said, her voice unsteady, "my husband will pay you and your men in gold."

She was very much aware of her scant costume as his gaze fell upon her.

"I don't want your husband's gold," he whispered, winding a lock of her hair around his finger. "I think you know what I want."

He leaned over her and lowered his mouth onto hers. The kiss was warm and demanding, and Kate fought against her senses to keep a clear head. Much as her body ached for the tender caresses she had been missing for so long, she could not give way. Shaheen was aware of her reticence, surely, but would not be dissuaded. "He does not love you, you said as much yourself. Why do you cling to him yet? Stay with me, Kate. I can love you as he cannot. Let me show you."

Shaking, Kate clambered to her feet and backed away.

"No, I cannot. Don't you see? You remind me again and again that my husband does not love me. He married me because of what my father offered him; I was a pleasant distraction, no more. Yet having told you this, still I cannot betray him."

"He is not worthy of you. Stay with me. I am not

261

a poor man, as you might think. I have a house in Cairo and servants. I can make a comfortable home for you and the child."

"Why have you never asked me how I feel? Is that not important to you?"

"I have my answer when I hold you in my arms. If you say that you feel nothing for me, then you are lying to yourself; your body tells me so."

"It is not enough. God help me, sometimes I wish it were. I cannot stay with you, Shaheen, because I love my husband. It doesn't matter that I am an insignificant part of his life, that he shuts me out. I remember a time when it was not so, when we were friends and lovers and I hope—"

"One cannot live forever on hope."

"It is all that I have."

He would have argued, but Kate's expression made him see that it would be useless. His head dropped in defeat and, turning from her, he left the tent.

Shaheen did not speak to her again for the rest of the journey. In the three days that it took to traverse the desert, he did not come to her tent. She was given her own mount, and she and Lucy were tended by a wizened servant. Once or twice Kate caught Shaheen glancing in her direction, but when he saw he had been discovered, he quickly turned away.

She regretted having hurt him, but tried to reassure herself that she had made the right choice. Shaheen did not really love her. He was fascinated because she was so different from the other women he had known.

They travelled the last leg of the journey on the river and as they drew closer to Cairo, Kate felt a mixture of emotions. Although she was anticipating returning home with her family and friends, she had been affected by Shaheen's attentions. She had to admit to the ache in her heart that had begun when she had sent him away. Now she would probably never see him again.

When their craft docked, Shaheen approached her. "I must leave you now," he said, without expression. "I have business that has been too long neglected. My men will see you to the hotel."

"Will you not see my husband and claim your reward?" Kate wondered.

"I told you that I do not want your husband's gold," he said as he stepped onto the gangplank. "Goodbye, Kate."

He turned from her, her heart hammering painfully against her breast as he walked away.

"Shaheen!" she called out.

He turned to her once more, expectant, but she could find no words to tell him how she felt. She realized that she would carry this ache in her heart forever.

"Go with Allah!" she said.

And she watched him until he had disappeared into the crowd.

━━━━━━━

At the hotel, Kate learned that Nick and the others were staying with a friend of Sir Peter's in the European quarter of the city. A carriage was arranged to take her there, and when at last she stood on the doorstep with Lucy in her arms, she found herself trembling.

"Time to meet your father," she told the child,

"and your grandfather. Don't cry now, you'll like them both . . . and we'll be going home soon."

She knocked briskly on the door and was shown into an airy entry hall, where at last she shed her *abbayeh*. She was still wearing the striped thaub Shaheen had given her to wear over the dancer's costume.

"Kate? My Lord, it is you, child?" Sir Peter rushed over, and drew her and Lucy into his arms.

"We feared that you— Are you hurt? The bruises on your face—Doctor Latham, come quickly!"

"I'm fine," Kate assured him.

"Come into the parlor and sit down," he said as he led her to an overstuffed sofa. Eric and Daphne soon appeared, as did Mr. Thayer and Major Kennerly.

"Kate!" Eric shouted. "Thank God! Daphne, tell the maid to fetch my bag."

"It's nothing, Eric," Kate said, but he immediately began examining her bruises as Daphne came to take Lucy from her arms.

"Praise be!" Daphne said. "We've all been so worried."

"Where's Nick?" Kate asked Eric.

"He's gone out. How did this happen?" he asked, poking at the cut on her lip. "Nick's searched half of Egypt for you and the baby. He's only just come back. He hardly said a word; he's been positively distraught."

"He'll be so relieved," Daphne chimed in. "We all are. My heavens, look at how this child has grown already! When that package arrived this morning, I told everyone that you'd be coming home, too, and I was right."

Kate's head was throbbing and she wanted to lie down, but instead asked, "Package?"

"Yes," Sir Peter replied. "Quite a miracle, really. A crate arrived early this morning, addressed to Nick, and in it were all of the artifacts that Berteau had stolen. They're marvelous, Kate, you should be proud."

But Kate was not listening. "Shaheen" was all that she said.

"What's that, dear?" Daphne asked, but Kate did not reply, her thoughts being elsewhere.

So Shaheen had kept his word. He had brought her safely out of the city of thieves, and the treasure of the priestess as well. He hadn't wanted a reward, nor the stolen treasure. "I've found a more precious jewel," he had said.

"Tell us what happened," Sir Peter prompted. "If you can, my dear. However did you escape?"

Kate told them the whole story, of her abduction, of the desert trek, and of the city of thieves . . . and of Shaheen. But she did not mention what had passed between them.

"What an exciting tale!" Daphne said at last. "And that Shaheen does sound like a dashing fellow."

"Nonsense!" Major Kennerly put in. "A thief and a scoundrel. One wonders why he offered his help at all."

"I would expect him to show up at the door sometime soon to claim his reward," Mr. Thayer said.

But Kate knew that he would not.

She looked up then to see Nick's frame filling the doorway, tall and tanned, his white linen suit perfectly tailored and without a crease, despite the heat.

265

He stood very still, and his gray eyes gave away nothing; only the twitch of one corner of his moustache told her that he was affected. Then, all at once, he ran up to her and took her into his arms.

"Kate!" he whispered. "My God! I was so afraid—"

Her tears spilled over and she melted against his chest, too weary for words.

———————

Arrangements were made for the return journey, and the major artifacts were seen safely into the hands of the authorities. Sir Peter suggested that the discovery be considered a joint effort, with all credit going to the Society for the Preservation of Antiquities. Although Kate agreed, Nick felt a little uncomfortable about it, but was grateful nonetheless.

Kate spent much of the time in her room. Eric assured the others that after her recent experiences, she needed a great deal of rest. Even Nick did not cross the threshold of their adjoining rooms.

It was not the happy ending one might have wished for. When they were alone, Kate and Nick seemed to draw apart. He was polite, yet distant, and Kate was skittish at his very touch. They no longer argued, but something stood between them, and though Nick may have been confused, Kate knew very well what it was. She could not look at her husband without hearing Shaheen's words, "He does not love you. I can love you as he cannot. Let me show you."

If she had sent Shaheen away because she loved Nick, why was she miserable still?

Two days before they were to depart, Nick ventured into her room and found her sitting before the window, with the shutters open. She was staring out over the city.

"What happened to you in the desert, Kate? Was it Berteau? Did he—did he touch you?"

Kate's eyes travelled over the flat roofs to the spires of the minarets and the dome of the Ibn al Tulun mosque. She remained silent.

"Please tell me," Nick persisted. "I know that something happened out there, something that changed you. I want to help. I know you haven't forgiven me for causing all of this—"

These words touched her. She hadn't meant to hurt Nick. Why could she not be happy?

"I never meant to accuse you," she told him. "I was hurt. I said things I didn't mean. Nothing happened to me in the desert, Nick. I've told you all there is."

Kate would not let him look into her eyes. She was afraid that he would be able to read what was there, what she had tried not to admit to herself: that she longed for the tall Arab who had swept through her life like a whirlwind.

Nick hesitated, and said gently, "We've been invited to dine this evening with Shaikh Yussif at Hillaleah Palace. "The pasha's representatives will be there to offer his thanks. It will be your night, Kate."

"I don't feel much like celebrating, I'm afraid, and I can do without the thanks of Ishmael Pasha."

Nick began to pace. "Still we must be diplomatic about this—"

"Couldn't you and Sir Peter—"

Nick silenced her with a look. "Despite the story you and my father have concocted for the Society, I

267

had nothing whatsoever to do with this find. It was your work, your abilities . . . We both know that I've failed miserably in my own attempts."

Kate was on her feet, facing him. "That's not true. I only followed my father's ideas. If I had trusted you enough to show you the Isis mask at the first, you'd have made the same assumptions and this discovery would be yours."

She was suddenly uncomfortable under his gaze and turned away. "But I was too selfish. I wanted to prove I was as good an archaeologist as you, yet I had the advantage all along."

"Do you know, Kate, that I was intimidated by your abilities from the first time I saw you with mud smeared on your cheek and your hand full of pottery shards? I wondered then how a mere child could be so absorbed in the work, and I doubted my own dedication.

"Later, when I was afraid that my feelings for you would get in the way of my work, I shut you out, without even thinking about what I might lose. There has been a considerable lack of trust in this marriage of ours, hasn't there? Is it too late for us, Kate?"

Kate sat down and silently stared out of the window, taking in all that he had said.

"I don't know," she answered slowly.

CHAPTER XXI

*H*illaleah Palace was bustling with activity as darkness fell on the island of Bulak. The shaikh had invited a number of diplomats and European travellers for the celebration. The evening could not compare with the fantastic evening the shaikh had provided for them on their last visit. But he had another master to please tonight. The lavish buffet tables, the imported crystal and china, the men in cutaways and women in colorful crinolines were all examples of how anxious Ishmael Pasha was to adopt Western ways. Kate could not look upon any of it without remembering what Shaheen had told her: that this "progress" was achieved at the expense of the fellaheen, who were taxed into poverty, their lands confiscated, and sent to work on the French canal, while Ishmael ordered special trains and commandeered river steamers to transport himself and his friends about the country, borrowing money from the Europeans at an alarming rate. Thus, Kate could enjoy none of the festivities, not even when Nick was presented with several small pieces of jewelry from the tomb of the priestess, in honor of their work.

Nick was his usual eloquent self, mingling easily with the diverse crowd. The others seemed to be enjoying themselves as well: Daphne and Mr. Thayer were dancing, content in each other's company, and Eric had attached himself to a pair of English ladies. Kate wished she had stayed behind with Ahmad and Lucy. Sir Peter seemed to sense her discomfort and remained at her side.

"I wish you were having a better time, my dear," he said.

"I'm sorry. I suppose I'm tired and anxious for us to be on our way home."

"I'm so pleased that Nick has consented to a visit to England next year. There's so much I want to show you both."

"We look forward to it," Kate told him.

"I promise you a restful holiday, not like this season," he said understatedly.

Kate was still haunted by her disturbing memories, only a few words being required to conjure them up again. "If you will excuse me, Sir Peter," she said in a tenuous voice, "I think I'd like to go into the garden for some air."

"Would you like me to escort you?"

"No, please, enjoy the evening. I think I'll rest a bit and then go after Nick. He's managed to lose himself in the crowd."

Kate drew her lace shawl over her and went out. It was chilly in the garden, but she welcomed the opportunity to be alone. She walked in the courtyard, past the reflecting pool, and admired the hedge of jasmine flowers as their perfume enveloped her. This was a land of contrasts, of extremes, she thought, of exotic gardens and desolate wastelands, of opulent wealth and destitution; even the Nile itself was of two natures. Its shallow, placid nature would, when replenished at its source, flow down gloriously, its waters red as blood as they overran the banks. No matter what impression Egypt left one with, Kate reflected, it was certain to be a strong impression. And tomorrow Kate would bid it all goodbye.

Suddenly a firm hand pulled her by the arm into the dark outer recesses of the garden. She would have screamed but for the kiss that silenced her. Her gaze drifted up to the familiar *kaffiyeh*, the patch over one eye.

"Shaheen!" she whispered when she was able to draw breath. "It is dangerous for you here. The pasha's men are everywhere. If they recognize you—"

"You needn't fear for me, dearest one, I am quite safe."

"Why? Why have you come?" she stammered.

"You still don't know?" he asked. "My life is a misery without you."

"But I cannot come away with you, I've already explained—"

"You've told me that your husband is the one you love. If it is true, then why do you turn from him even now?"

"How do you know this?"

He regarded her with a serious air. "Look closely at me, Kate."

She did so, and noticed then that his beard was shorn. Now there was only a dark moustache. As she watched him remove the ominous eyepatch and throw back the *kaffiyeh* her mouth dropped open: It was Nick!

Kate was dumbstruck. How could she have been so blind? She quickly found herself angered by his deception and stepped back. "Why didn't you tell me from the first? You had plenty of opportunity that night in the garden. Was this a test—a test of my fidelity? Did you enjoy setting me against myself? You must have had a good laugh at my expense."

"I meant to tell you that first night," he protested. "I felt certain you'd recognize me, but when you didn't, I couldn't find the words. I don't know why. Perhaps I thought it was a way to begin again, by becoming someone else."

Kate's gaze dropped before him. "I never wanted anyone else."

"That's not what you said in Luxor. Or do you recall? You said that you'd only agreed to our marriage because it meant a passage to Egypt for you."

She turned away, looking out over the shadows of the garden. "What did you expect me to say after I'd learned about your bargain with my father?"

Cautiously, Nick placed a hand on her shoulder. "He made the offer, it's true, but I didn't accept him until after you and I—until we'd become friends. I love you, Kate, you must believe it."

From behind, he wrapped his arms around her, and she did not reject his embrace.

"Once, I thought I was the luckiest woman alive," she mused, "to have a husband who was my friend, whose passions I could share, but then I found that I had to compete with your work for your attention."

"I'll make no excuses for my behavior. I was so desperate to prove myself that I tried to do so at the expense of all else. All I've proven is that I'm a fool. I was so intent on fame that I very nearly lost my wife and child in the bargain. I haven't lost you, have I, Kate?"

"What? Lost me to the Arab, you mean?"

Kate laughed at the idea. "It was a neat little trap you set. On the one hand there was you, and on the other . . . you—a veritable Hobson's choice."

"For a time I feared you might decide to ride off into the desert with Shaheen."

"You tried very hard to convince me to do just that."

"I had to know what you truly felt and to make you admit it to yourself. Despite how I'd hurt you, you still came back to me. I'd been willing to lay Shaheen to rest for good, but in these past few days I learned that you'd fallen in love with him. So I had to resurrect him this once more."

"I liked him very much. He was colorful and proud. And he helped me see so many things. And he seemed so authentic. I didn't realize that my husband had such a talent for theatre," Kate mused.

"It wasn't all fabrication. During my winters here I worked on digs, but in the summer, I lived with the Bedouin in the desert. It was they who gave me the name Shaheen. I learned a great many things from these people."

"And the rest of it?"

"One cannot live with the fellaheen and not see how Turkish rule is destroying them. I'll admit that I did what little I could on their behalf, even if it meant that my actions fell somewhat outside the law."

Kate turned in his arms and lifted her face up to him. "I do love you, Nick . . . both of you."

"I'll never let us be apart again, Kate. We shall work together as we should have from the first, and we'll take Lucy with us. What a team we'll make!"

Kate nestled on his arm, imagining the future he had planned and considering the infinite possibilities . . .

Helen Ashfield

The Regency Jewel Series

Glowing Novels of Passion and Fate

Emerald	____ 90173-9	**$2.95**
Sapphire	____ 90442-8	**$2.95**
Pearl	____ 90471-1	**$2.95**
Garnet	____ 90611-0	**$2.95**
Ruby	____ 90318-9	**$2.95**
Opal	____ 90597-1	**$2.95**
Topaz	____ 90790-7	**$2.95**

14

Enchanting Regency Romances

A LONDON SEASON by Anthea Bell
There's malice, mystery and merriment as two lively ladies set Regency society astir!

_____ 90234-4 $3.95 U.S.

RAMILLIES by Barbara Whitehead
A shy young earl must choose a bride, but his heart is given to two beauties.

_____ 90512-2 $2.95 U.S.

LADYSMEAD by Jane Gillespie
Sophia was almost resigned to a quiet life in the country when love surprised her.

_____ 90490-8 $2.95 U.S.

TEVERTON HALL by Jane Gillespie
She was only the daughter of the rector, yet she'd lost her heart to the heir to Teverton Hall.

_____ 90674-9 $2.95 U.S.

THE MISER OF MAYFAIR by Marion Chesney
The delightful first volume of the new series, A House for the Season, by one of the superstars of the Regency Romance.

_____ 90689-7 $2.95 U.S.

Lose Your Heart to These Captivating Romances

THE CRIMSON FALCON by Sara Hylton
Her mother's ruby falcon necklace leads Rachel to enchanting Vienna, then to Castle Meinhart where the secrets of the past lie hidden and her romantic destiny awaits.

_____ 90513-0 $3.95 U.S.

DESERT SPLENDOR by Sara Hylton
Kathryn St. Clair's dreams are haunted by ancient Egypt and a tragedy of love, jealousy and betrayal. When she falls in love with a man she cannot have, she seems fated to repeat the past. Can she break the threads and find her true heart's desire?

_____ 90136-4 $3.95 U.S.

THE TSAR'S WOMAN by Pamela Hill
She was a peasant girl who was swept into the scandal and intrigues of the court of Peter the Great. No one dreamed of the magnificent future that awaited her.

_____ 90668-4 $3.50 U.S.